I0689390

Götterdämmerung

by

Robert Boyd

Published by Rhomboid Publishing 2015.

rhomboidpublishing@gmx.com

Set in Open Sans

ISBN 978-0-9934279-1-6

For Livia and Thea,

in the hope they enjoy it, one day.

Götterdämmerung:

German, literally, twilight of the gods, from *Götter* (plural of *Gott* god) + *Dämmerung* twilight;

a collapse (as of a society or regime) marked by catastrophic violence and disorder;

from Ragnarök in Scandinavian mythology.

". . . whether we are describing a king, an assassin, a thief, an honest man, a prostitute, a nun, a young girl, or a stall-holder in the market, it is always ourselves that we are describing, for we are obliged to ask ourselves the following question: *'If I was a king, an assassin, a thief, a prostitute, a nun, a young girl, a stall-holder, what would I do, what would I think, how would I behave.'* "

Guy de Maupassant

Chapter 1

DEFRA Headquarters, London

1400 hrs, 12 January

Slumped in his chair, he pretended to ignore her. It was difficult. He'd never seen such an attractive woman. About five feet five he reckoned, long-legged and elegant. Luxurious, medium-length, straight black hair fell forwards, partly obscuring her face and those heart-stopping brown eyes. Her Irish Celtic ancestry, he supposed. He could almost taste the deep-red lipstick on those full, oh so kissable, lips. He stole a sly look at her gentle breathing, moving her tight green sweater...

He remembered how abrupt she could be at times.

Sheila Wilson sat demurely but ill at ease beside him. I hate being the only woman at these meetings, she thought. Is this guy Stewart going to examine me all afternoon? Still, he was quite good looking. I wonder if he is really as cynical as he seems? Well, there will be plenty of time to get to know him over the coming months.

The others were standing at the window, lingering over a 'government issue' buffet lunch of dry sandwiches and lukewarm sausage rolls. Perhaps the wine prolonged their conversation, or they needed a long break after the morning session. Four British scientists stood around a stocky Irishman. They were gathered in a small conference room in DEFRA, the Department for Environment, Food and Rural Affairs in its austere offices in Central London.

Stewart was tired. They had discussed the project since nine o'clock that morning, with only a short coffee break to interrupt his minute-taking. It would take a couple of hours to dictate the minutes of the meeting so far - and it looked like continuing for the rest of the afternoon. Still, the end was in sight. Eventually, after protracted discussions over many months, the group had blundered its way to near-agreement. He found it scarcely credible that the project could come off but, in spite of his scepticism, it now seemed that naivety had prevailed. This disparate collection of ill-suited academics would soon be heading for the African bush. God help them!

"OK folks! Let's get back to it," mumbled Hugo, leading the way back to the table. "We've still a bit to do."

As was his habit Stewart studied the man that he worked with so closely. Hugo Bamford was nearly bald and his round, pleasant face had grown fleshy over the years. At fifty-two he still sustained the frenetic workload he had maintained for over twenty years in the Civil Service. Stewart saw him most days so found it difficult to detect the creeping changes brought on by time, but suddenly he was starting to show his age. Five feet ten and about fifty pounds overweight, it was time Hugo focused on a healthier lifestyle. The Civil Service would continue long after the Bamfords of this world had their heart attacks or strokes and departed feet first, unmourned by those left to pursue petty career ambitions.

It has certainly been an interesting five years, mused Stewart, but I suspect old Hugo might have over-reached himself this time. I've got to hand it to him though, he smiled to himself, only Hugo could have browbeaten, cajoled and threatened his way to this point. How on earth had he managed to convince Brussels, Dublin and London that the taxpayers' interests would best be served by an African safari?'

He looked across the table at Brendan Doyle from the Irish Crops Research Institute. Presumably the fifty-three year old Dubliner had applied similar sales skills to get his masters in Dublin to accept the project. He was a confident and cynical individual. Stewart had met him many times, usually when Doyle sparred with Hugo on cooperative science. They were too alike ever to get along but fortunately for their working relationship they served different Civil Service masters - and could delude themselves about each other's motives and performances as it suited. Stewart had recently detected an almost imperceptible improvement in their relationship. Perhaps even these two super-egos had come to realise that this project was bigger than both of them. Careers were at stake this time and both knew they better deliver on the optimistic projections they had used to secure funding. Doyle looked deceptively sleepy but Stewart knew he was very wide-awake and switched on. Heavy-featured with a florid, drinker's face, thinning ginger hair and blue eyes, he had made a career of wheeling and dealing over the years.

He was diverted back to the business in hand. Doyle, in his over-emphasised Irish brogue, was winding up Hugo as usual.

"Now Hugo," he said, turning on his affable top-of-the-range charm factor, "you know my colleagues cannot stay on after mid-May. Sure how could they survive that long stuck in some Guinness-free zone in Uganda?"

Hugo's sense of humour was naive and slow-acting at the best of times but he managed an unconvincing laugh.

"The Guinness in Africa's probably green anyway Brendan!" he tittered, delivering his usual *non sequitur*.

Doyle groaned to himself. How have I tolerated this guy for so long? If we didn't need his backing I'd dump him right now.

"Okay, seriously. We must define a deadline for withdrawal," said Hugo.

He tended to use hard terminology instead of colloquial English. His phraseology on this occasion made Stewart recall those atmospheric images of the last hours of the US withdrawal from Saigon.

"I'm conscious that we have agreed a work schedule with built in slippage for unforeseen delays, but delays or not - unfinished tasks or not, I believe we must agree an absolute end date for withdrawal. It would be too easy to stay one more week to finish some ongoing task - or at least for some of the team to do so. The other principle inherent in what I'm proposing is an 'all in, all out together' policy. No way am I having part of the team remaining behind after some have left. Can we agree?"

"But Hugo, aren't you going to be jet-setting in and out from time to time?" Doyle quipped.

"Oh yes, but I'm talking about the core of the expedition, not the ..."

"Upper echelons?" Stewart volunteered, before he could stop himself.

"Right Hugo, I think that's a sensible proposal." Doyle interjected, rescuing Stewart with a 'naughty, naughty' glance. "But it's hardly an expedition is it?" he drawled, still trying to overcome his awful lunch. "I mean, I know it's not Shepherd's Bush, but a quick call on a cell-phone should bring the Cavalry homing in on our satellite navigation beacons!"

In spite of his simmering dislike of the man Stewart could not help being amused by his sarcasm.

Hugo flushed at the obvious put down but seemed reluctant to relinquish a mental image of hacking through dense bush, dabbing at a sweat-soaked brow and leech-infested backside. He blundered on.

"I think 'expedition' defines it admirably Brendan! We don't know exactly how it will go and while we've tried to cover all eventualities, there's still an unquantifiable risk involved."

"Risk, what risk!" Everyone round the table came fully awake. "This is the first time any risk has been mentioned!"

"Perhaps you should elaborate on that Chief?" Peter Rent carefully prompted Hugo.

What a crawler, thought Stewart - for the thousandth time! Rent still persists in calling him Chief! Chief of the Commanches or what? He suddenly wondered if Rent could possibly be winding Hugo up? He stared at him with ill-disguised contempt. Has he no self-respect at all?

Rent was a crop scientist but a career Civil Servant nonetheless. A tall man, his shock of straggly black hair detracted from the suave business-man appearance he so obviously intended to promote. A clever brain, he was renowned for his sarcasm and vicious tongue.

"Perhaps 'risk' was the wrong word," Hugo muttered. "However we must be aware of possibilities for difficulty."

Why doesn't he just say 'problems' like anyone else? Stewart was getting irritated.

"There is the potential for health problems – malaria, cholera *et cetera*, although we should be okay with the medication. Also, we'll have to manage our diets and drinking water - and of course solar radiation effects. "

Sunburn! Just say sunburn!

"We might also encounter wild animals, and the roads are less than ideal - to put it mildly."

"Oh we've had all this before," Doyle groaned.

"And there is a slight potential for civil unrest." Hugo dropped this little bombshell into the meeting.

"Bloody hell! What's this?" They all jumped in at once.

"Surely not! You must be joking!" Doyle exaggerated, knowing full well there was no real threat to them.

"I told you all before - last month in fact. There are some minor ongoing skirmishes with rebels. They're of limited extent, well away from where we're going and they're being easily controlled by Government Troops. I have the President's personal assurance that the press reports have been overly sensationalised - believe me!"

"Oh that's alright Hugo," Sheila said in relief. "I thought you meant things had escalated since."

Stewart's pulse quickened as she smiled at him.

"No, no, - no change. The expedition area is perfectly peaceful. Do you really think I'd ... that Brendan and I would even contemplate an expedition if there was the slightest risk to anyone?"

Now there's a rhetorical question, thought Stewart. Of course Hugo wouldn't dream of such a thing - not unless there was significant personal glory in it for him - in which case he wouldn't hesitate to send them in, dispassionately, like a cold Khmer Rouge General.

***

The meeting continued in desultory fashion throughout the rest of the winter afternoon. By a gradual process of attrition, rather than Hugo's skills of chairmanship, they managed to address all the salient points. Each expert was called upon to present their scientific work plans and for the first time Tom Nottes contributed to the meeting. In his late forties, Nottes was the strong silent type but a pleasant man nevertheless. He was looking forward immensely to the expedition.

It was late afternoon before final details of the expedition programme were settled and agreed. Hugo started to summarise the day-long discussion. Normally in such situations he was good at remembering the important points, although he had a strong penchant for maximising his role in things. Stewart was never quite sure if he did it deliberately, like blowing his nose, or if it was an unconscious habit, like scratching his scrotum. He knew how Hugo liked minutes to be written, (much as he imagined Vladimir Putin would want them to promote his personality cult), and he was familiar enough with the detail of the expedition to allow himself the luxury of sitting back, eyes glazed like the rest of the audience, to enjoy the show. He would dictate this bit later - in suitable style.

"Gentlemen, and lady..." Hugo began, with a pseudo-deferential nod at Sheila who smiled sweetly at him. "We'll need to prepare a Press Notice on the expedition for simultaneous release by both Departments."

Yes, Stewart thought. I think I agree with him. 'Expedition' rather than 'project' was by far the better term to use. It conjured images of charging elephants, a leech-infested Humphrey Bogart, Idi Amin Dada guzzling human ear fritters, Hugo being feted on a be-garlanded barge up the White Nile… 'Project', in contrast, invoked connotations of a pre-planned, well-designed and properly managed enterprise with its costs and benefits analysed - something which would confer tangible benefits on some sector of humanity. Oh definitely, 'expedition' was the apposite term.

"My office can draft a notice for your consideration Brendan, before issue." Hugo continued. "Something short and snappy will do…"

Like Sheila Wilson, thought Stewart.

"… sufficient to allow our Ministers to pick up on if they wish - for a photo-call or whatever. I don't think we would want to gild the lily at this stage. Better to wait until the expedition's completed and then launch a major Press Event."

Stewart, as was his habit, languidly made the mental translation. He means muggins here will write the damn Press Notice. Then he wants his picture in the paper but no more than that in case it all blows up in his face. Later, if things go well, we can bring out the band and have the thousands of accrued brownie points presented to him in public. I must stop doing this, he told himself. Just listen to what the man is saying…

"I take we are agreed on that?" Hugo asked the now comatose gathering who managed to signify feeble assent. "Today's the fifteenth of January and you're scheduled to depart London on the first of February. That's about… let's see… just over two weeks from now. So we'd need your clearance on a Press Notice by about the twenty-eighth, twenty-ninth of January Brendan, for issue on the thirty-first. Just check Bob. What day of the week is the thirty-first?" Stewart fumbled for his dairy.

"A weekday's best for press coverage…"

"It's a Thursday," Stewart offered.

"Good! Now just let me quickly run over things again - in case anyone's not clear on any points."

In spite of mild protestations he went over the logistics of the expedition once more. They were fast approaching burn out for this particular meeting but the group was reluctantly content to let him take them over it one more time. This was a final opportunity while they were all together to spot any points which might have been overlooked. In fact Hugo provided a good summary, demonstrating his formidable ability to gather, analyse and present complex facts.

Eventually he was finished, like his audience, and the end of the meeting was in sight. Stewart suddenly realised he would not see some of these people again until they met up in a mud-hut village on the shores of Lake Albert, Uganda.

"Right! That's about it everyone. I wish you all a safe journey and a pleasant and scientifically rewarding expedition. I hope to make my first visit on site sometime during the first two weeks. By the time I see you all again you'l

I be well sun-tanned and speaking Swahili like natives!"

"Hugo!" Sheila snapped. "That's hardly an acceptable way of putting things!"

"Sorry! No offence intended. I hope everything goes well."

***

The meeting broke up and they made their way out, tired after the long day but with a growing sense of excitement now that departure was fast approaching.

"Are you rushing off Sheila?" Stewart asked as they walked along the gloomy corridor.

"I'm afraid so Bob. Brendan and I are catching the eight o'clock flight back to Dublin."

"Oh that's a pity. I thought perhaps you were leaving in the morning. I was going to ask if you'd have dinner with me this evening," he said, nervously.

She was surprised. I didn't think he was that interested. Damn! Dinner would have been lovely.

Recovering quickly, she smiled sweetly at him. "That would have been very nice Bob, but I must get back home tonight." She wanted to end on a positive note. "Perhaps we can have dinner under the African stars?"

"Yes! We will. That's a promise!" he said and they laughed at the idea. "Well, take care. Have a safe journey home. See you in darkest Africa!" They shook hands and he saw her out the door to where Doyle was waiting on the pavement.

He watched intently as she walked away, Yes, this project is going to be much more interesting than I'd originally imagined!

Chapter 2

DEFRA Headquarters, London

1500 hrs, 15 January

Stewart and Bamford strode purposefully along a gloomy corridor heading for a special briefing meeting. They were late. Stewart realised Hugo was distracted when he saw him smile at a passing typist. Such 'lower forms of life' were usually beneath his notice - there was no prospect of personal advantage by communicating with minions - unless of course he wanted a rush job done, when a few minutes of what he imagined to be his 'human touch' invariably worked wonders.

Does he not realise that bullying abuse of his rank is what makes people kowtow? It certainly isn't admiration. Stewart told himself, for the umpteenth time.

Most of his colleagues disliked Hugo - and those that saw a lot of him disliked him most. Indeed, it was true to say that a few positively hated his guts. He rode roughshod over people, usually good, hard-working staff that on occasion stood in his way over some issue, and then experienced his megalomania at first hand. Invariably, they grew to detest him, profoundly. Many were uncomfortable in their detestation, at the secret hoping for his downfall, because real, deep loathing of a fellow human being is a rare condition in civilised society. Some people are hard to like, sure, but contact with them can usually be avoided. No effort need be expended therefore, no time wasted, no sleep lost over them. But Hugo was something else. With quite breathtaking ease he could engender instant dislike - and in some cases deep, everlasting hatred. Stewart had studied him over the years. At times he thought he had him typed, at others he realised stereo-typing was impossible. He knew with certainty however, that he was an egotist of colossal proportions. A man who only with great difficulty stayed within the bounds of acceptable behaviour - but a man who would love to let himself off a self-imposed leash to burst forth into his true colours of thuggery and dictatorship. Oh yes, given the right circumstances, or in another time and place - say in the early part of this century, in the Weimar Republic - Hugo could have aspired to true barbarism.

From time to time an apparent chink, more a defect, in his brutishness could flare briefly. He had been known, for example, to arrive laden with good wines and choice cheeses for the office Christmas party. This type of aberrant behaviour fooled a few, those who met him only seldom. Stewart came to recognise such behaviour for what it was - a further mechanism to impress, rather than a genuinely kind reward to staff at the end of an exhaustive year. His inconsistency was the give-away. Some years he just did not bother - when some other, more pressing claim on his self-seeking time diverted him.

What was his childhood like? Was it the consequence of upbringing or genes - or a complex interaction of the two. Did his father drive him too hard? What made him so power-hungry, so publicity-seeking - so impervious to the feelings of others? What path of social interaction did he blunder along through life that led him to think that success - as he defined it - was the goal at any price? Who or what had sold him that comic strip idea? Had he no concept of how his colleagues felt about him? Or, tragically, perhaps he did? Did he go to sleep each night, content with his day's performance - the 'I showed them again today' syndrome - when in reality people wrestled in their beds, fantasising about shoving red hot irons up his rectum. Stewart laughed aloud at the thought.

Hugo had waylaid Jones of Finance Division for a quick word and assumed that Stewart's sudden guffaw was a result of some witticism he had uttered unconsciously in discussion - as all great men are apt to do.

"Yes, old Bruce had no answer to my proposal! How could he?" Hugo laughed, missing the heavenward roll of the eyes Jones managed behind his back.

He resumed close discussion with the unfortunate Jones, who had been ambushed just short of the sanctuary of the toilet. Roy Bruce, the Departmental Accountant, was not normally a man to be browbeaten, especially not by Hugo. Bruce was another colleague, foe rather, of Hugo's who had tried hard over the years to drop him deeply, abyssally in it - with some limited success to date.

I wonder what Roy's hatching now Stewart wondered? It's not like him to let Hugo off so easily.

He paid closer attention to the continuing diatribe being inflicted on poor Jones, who was beginning to perspire and edge further across the doorway into the 'Gents'.

Can't he see the poor bugger's dying for a pee? Stewart glanced down, looking in vain for Jones' urine dripping onto Hugo's shoes.

"Then he said he couldn't guarantee funding into next year!" Hugo was getting incensed as he related the previous day's meeting.

"What does he know about funding?" (This of the Departmental Accountant.) "I've brought more external funding into this Department than anyone!" Hugo bore on. "I don't need a pen-pusher like Bruce to tell me how to manage it!"

That's exactly what you need, thought Stewart who understood the depths of Hugo's hatred of financial constraints.

"He kept saying that I would have to budget on the assumption that no further funding would be available next year. What way's that to run a scientific programme? If I'm to continue to underpin the science base I must have freedom to plan for the future."

Stewart had a mental flash of a naked Hugo on hands and knees hammering rusty nails into a tottering cupboard full of dusty test-tubes. Underpin the science base! How many times have I heard that idiotic phrase? What on earth does it mean?

Jones forgot the state of his bladder for a moment and asked, "So you have secured all the funding?" He groaned inwardly at his own stupidity. I'm going to wet myself!

"Oh yes, I'm quite certain I have secured all necessary funding required to extend the Uganda Project well into next year. We just can't afford to let finances dictate our actions."

Stewart watched in amusement as this last remark penetrated Jones' brain and saw a look of total incredulity develop his face.

Surely the man can't mean that? He could almost read Jones' thoughts. We can't let finances dictate our actions? Where has he been for the last ten years?

The astonished look slowly transformed itself into something akin to pity as Jones closed his gaping mouth and narrowed his eyes at Hugo, (who, naturally, took Jones' near-fainting fit to signify outright wonder at yet another of his verbal master strokes).

"Let me get this straight." Jones said in a rare display of firmness which caused Hugo to take a half-step back, so removing his gut from contact with Jones' hip.

Hugo, consciously or unconsciously - Stewart could never quite decide which, always made a point of invading others' space when conversing and threatened them from the outset by shoving his presence right into their faces. He knew of only one colleague who made a point of standing his ground, usually forcing Hugo to back off. Poor Jones had no option at present, pinned against the door jamb.

"Are you telling me Bruce actually confirmed next year's money then?"

"Well no, but he made no answer when I insisted it was needed to complete the project." enthused Hugo.

"I see." said Jones, twisting around in anguish and stumbling towards blissful relief at the urinal. "Let's hope you're right." he shouted over his shoulder as the door closed on its spring leaving Hugo with a perplexed expression.

"What does he mean by that? The money's secured I tell you, Bob."

As they continued up the corridor Stewart's sense of unease grew. How typical of the man to translate the encounter into another browbeating victory for himself. This time Stewart wasn't so sure. It wasn't like Bruce to let matters drop like that.

I wonder what he's up to? He continued to develop his analysis. What would be the implications for the project if no money was available after the thirty-first of March - the end of the financial year? Surely the Department would have to continue funding until the project team returned home? As widespread as hatred of Hugo was, the Department could hardly leave them all stranded abroad. No, there must be something else brewing. He decided to have a quiet word with Bruce - if he could get him to talk. The trouble was, if Bruce had found some administrative means of emasculating Hugo at last, he might not run the risk of letting me in on it, in case Hugo escaped the noose. Actually, come to think of it, Hugo's build would be ideal for a eunuch.

***

"Gentlemen!" Hugo began, bustling to the front of the room to address the small gathering of DEFRA Under-Secretaries. Joe Roomer and Peter Rent were also present.

"I'm sure you've been wondering just what we've been up to over this expedition, why we're sending a team to a small remote village in western Uganda? Well, as promised, I and my colleagues Doctors Roomer and Rent will now present an overview, covering the rationale, funding, the proposed work programme - and of course the potential benefits."

He outlined the European Union programme which was providing part funding, the United Kingdom and Republic of Ireland collaboration, and referred to the intended scientific work.

"Joe Roomer will make a short presentation on the fisheries work and Peter Rent, who's standing in for Tom Nottes today, will summarise the crop work for you. But first of all let me give you the broad overview."

He presented impressive statistics about Lake Albert that Sir Samuel White Baker discovered in 1864. The shallow lake lay at an altitude of two thousand feet on the border with the Democratic Republic of the Congo. It was around one hundred miles long and some twenty miles wide. The great lake was fed by the Semuliki River which drained Lake Edward and the Victoria Nile flowing from Lake Victoria. It was drained at its northern end by the Albert Nile. He explained they would be based in a small village on the south-west shore of the lake, in the Semuliki Wildlife Reserve Reserve, about 20 kilometres from border with the Congo. He summarised the local fisheries and the potential to greatly improve catches, so long as the lake was not already over-exploited.

"Perhaps you would tell us a bit more about it Joe?" he asked, settling his generous frame to concentrate on the speaker now making his way to the lectern.

Of medium height and build, Roomer was an Ulsterman who had obtained his PhD in Zoology from Queens University, Belfast. His Belfast accent had softened over the years he had worked in England - at the DEFRA Fisheries Research Directorate in Lowestoft. He first met Stewart at Lowestoft while he too was employed there as a fisheries scientist. Approaching forty and balding, Roomer had a rugged face and his blue eyes gleamed as he reached the front. As usual he was relaxed and confident both of his own ability and in this case the audience's ignorance of the subject matter.

"I will have to assume that not all of you have an understanding of fish population dynamics." Roomer began, knowing full well that no-one else in the room had the slightest idea about the topic.

"It's really a complex concept, but you will be glad to hear that I am not going to lecture you on the detailed theory. A summary of the practicalities will suffice. Actually, fish population dynamics evolved from studies on whales. These were the first scientific attempts to quantify the dynamics of aquatic populations and to try to understand how exploitation by man was impacting on the population of each whale species."

His audience fidgeted in apprehension.

"That's the first important point to bear in mind - that we must treat each population separately and that fluctuations in one population may not be reflected in another. In other words each exploited fish species in Lake Albert - providing there is a single breeding population of that species - will have to have its own sampling programme devoted to it."

A grey Under-Secretary in a grey suit interrupted. "Is it known how many different fish species are in the lake?"

"Well, it is believed that there are around ninety fish species, but of course we will be mainly interested in the species being exploited - or those that might be exploited - and there are a dozen or so of these. However, I fully expect to come across some species in the unexploited stocks which will be new to science - not yet described in the literature."

"Are they all mixed together throughout the lake ?" Someone else asked.

He was irritated by the quick interruptions but was careful not to let it show.

"Yes and no. Some co-habit in the same areas - indeed some are predators on others. Some species inhabit different areas of the lake, for example in shallow water, some in deeper water - and all this can vary seasonally since most fish migrate to specific areas to congregate and spawn."

Realising that he was being dragged into more specifics than he intended, Roomer addressed the room.

"Look, I'll just summarise the practical sampling programme we've planned, and leave how we'll interpret and analyse the results to another day. I intend to investigate first of all how the villagers exploit the fish populations at present. I'll need to see them in action, see what gear they use, how often they use it and what they catch. My understanding is that most fish are taken by gill-netting and I hope to experiment with some long-lining."

He dimmed the lights and projected photographic slides as he talked, explaining the various fishing techniques and showing shots of local fishermen and their catches.

"Their boats are quite interesting, and I detect some external influence in their design, perhaps through missionaries in years gone by."

He showed slides of brightly painted fishing boats, some afloat, some beached on a dried mud foreshore.

"It's not unusual to have quite severe storms on the lake you know and the boats need to be able to withstand some choppy conditions from time to time. Notice their high prows and nice lines - not unlike a Yorkshire cobble. Oh, by the way, the rainy seasons are from March to May and from October to November. We'll be there from February onwards, so will experience some rain."

His audience found the talk surprisingly interesting, and began to appreciate the scale and magnificence of Lake Albert.

"I expect to be out on the lake nearly every day soon after first light. We'll be working a grid of sampling stations covering the area which is normally in range of the village boats. There'll be two boats always, working together - partly for safety reasons but also to work the sampling gear. We'll have portable echo-sounders, satellite navigation and two-way radio of course to keep in regular contact with village HQ. It seems the cell phone network is a bit patchy in the region so we'll rely on two-way radios. We'll return each day for on-shore analysis of the catch. Without large-scale deep-freeze facilities we'll have to analyse each day's catch before we go out again the next day. The whole exercise is really only a beginning. The lake is far too vast for us to study its entirety. Even if we could, we would need quite a few years of extensive sampling to even begin to build up a picture of the aquatic ecosystem."

"What *will* you achieve?" Hugo asked mischievously.

"The objective is simply to get a first estimate of the type and extent of exploitable fish in the lake within reach of the village. We may be able to exploit other species which currently the villagers can not, and hopefully show them how to do this after we've left."

"What are the prospects of that?" queried another listener dubiously.

"Well, the locals only set their nets in the morning and lift them around midday. There may be a valid reason for this, but we could try setting nets overnight to see if different species can be caught which aren't available in daytime. Also, nets can't be deployed easily in shallow water or in strong currents so I'm hoping that long-lining in these areas will give positive results. Each experimental fishing boat will have a crew of two or three villagers and Doctor Paul Moriarty from the Irish Department will be in charge of one boat and I will be on the other, in overall charge of each fishing voyage. Doctor Moriarty and I will have the support of two undergraduate students - I'm not sure exactly about these yet - the Ugandan National Agricultural Institute is providing these for us. So there will be a total complement of five or six on each boat. We'll have a 'wet fish room' on shore to weigh and dissect fish each evening and also to preserve samples for further study back home."

Roomer completed his twenty minute talk efficiently and snapped on the conference room lights as he returned to his seat.

"Thank you Joe, that all seems very clear." Hugo beamed, rising to address them again.

"It's nice to know that while your colleagues will be slaving in their London offices all day you will be having balmy lake cruises!" he chortled, and a polite titter of amusement went round the room.

"Now if I could ask Peter Rent to summarise the crops project for us."

Rent began somewhat diffidently, surprising in someone so arrogant.

"The essence of the work which Doctor Nottes of our Crop Science Unit will be leading, is to determine how the village can enhance its crop yields without adding unacceptably to present costs and effort. Currently, their main crops are potatoes, cassava and Soya beans but they grow other crops such as bananas. Virtually all of these are grown by traditional farming methods and most are grown for their own consumption - although they do grow a little coffee for market. We don't know if they've been practising crop rotation, how they select and store their seed - if at all, if they fertilise fields and how many crops a year are possible. We want also to look at pest and disease control. We intend to trial some newly developed varieties which have been produced elsewhere."

He took them through some of the detail and after a few questions he too resumed his seat.

Hugo rounded off the briefing by explaining how both the shore and lake-based aspects of the expedition would depend heavily on satellite navigation instrumentation and computerised data loggers to capture field measurements for downloading into laboratory computers for daily data analyses. He informed them that the Irish Department was providing a computer technician to maintain the expedition's hardware and software. Stewart hoped the young girl they were sending, Ethne Dunne, would be able to manage. Doyle had assured them she was very capable and, to be fair, she impressed him as being very efficient on the one occasion he met her.

"Well." said Hugo. "That's about it. I think everyone now has a fair idea of all aspects of the overall programme. Now if Dr. Mwanga would appear we could address some further logistics and get the show on the road."

Right on cue the door opened and a tall, well-dressed African was shown into the room. Taking in his surroundings quickly, he strode, hand out-stretched and smiling, towards Hugo who rose to meet him.

"Welcome, welcome Shaban." he gushed. "Glad you could join us. Did you have a good trip?"

"Fine, no trouble. Glad to be here." replied Mwanga in a rich bass voice.

"Good, good. We'll get you a coffee and then perhaps you would be kind enough to summarise the input of the Ugandan Agriculture Department."

As Hugo fussed over him, Mwanga glanced around the table and realised that the other occupants of the room were studying him intently. He smiled as Hugo began the introductions.

Mwanga then had his time at the front. He explained the logistics of transporting the team and equipment to Lake Albert, and how the Ugandan army would continue to supply them and keep in regular contact.

"As Director of the Ugandan National Institute for Agriculture, I am instructed by my Government to say how much Uganda values the collaboration and potential inherent in this project. We are very pleased to be able to facilitate it logistically, and also to provide assurance for the expedition's well-being."

"Doctor Mwanga," began one of the Under-Secretaries, "I understand there is a level of civil unrest in Uganda at present. Can you update us on the situation please?"

"Yes, there have been some reports of minor skirmishes but these have been on the north-western border with the Congo- not in the expedition area. You will realise sir that, while we are continually striving to develop and modernise, there are parts of the country where tribalism still exists..."

Like Kampala, mused Stewart.

"... and we do get a little inter-tribal skirmishing from time to time. However this seldom gets into the newspapers, even in Uganda, so there need be no fears for the safety of the expedition - none at all,

I assure you."

This seemed to satisfy his questioner and Mwanga resumed his seat.

The best bit of 'inter-tribal skirmishing' in Uganda that I've heard of involved that nice young man called Idi Amin Dada, Stewart recalled. And of course old Milton Obote did his share of stirring things up after that.

Eventually the meeting drew to a close and Hugo was left to entertain Mwanga for the rest of the day. Stewart assumed he would take the poor man out for dinner that evening, to one of the many restaurants he frequented, and subject him to the usual egotistical tirade of his career exploits. He hoped Mwanga had a strong stomach.

Suddenly Stewart was very tired. He decided to leave early to beat the traffic.

Chapter 3

The village

0700 hrs, 6 February

Alone in the early morning quiet, Stewart breakfasted alfresco, gazing across the compound at expedition HQ.

It's strange, he thought, how everyone regards the radio tent as headquarters. He supposed it was because the radio was their day-to-day link with the outside world. Always an early riser, he guessed he would have about another ten minutes' peace before his colleagues awakened to their first full working day. I should have had a lie-in myself, he told himself, especially after all the exertions of yesterday. But, as always, his built-in biological clock was unaffected and had switched him on promptly at six-fifteen a.m. as usual. It's going to be another scorcher, he reckoned, then laughed at his European-ness. Every day is a scorcher here! I'll bet the locals never discuss the weather the way we English do!

Yesterday had been an exhausting saga. He'd left his Kampala hotel at dawn to be driven recklessly to the army base on the outskirts of the city by a very laid-back young conscript. He had flopped out of his conveyance like a wet rag to be confronted by organised chaos as the base personnel checked and loaded supplies aboard a well-worn, but apparently still serviceable, Sikorsky helicopter. In the general hubbub of activity he managed mostly to get in the way. The Army Captain in charge was well briefed and a lot of planning and preparation had obviously gone into this aspect of the expedition. A huge store of supplies was under close guard in a large warehouse depot and he realised that, was it not guarded, the stores would disappear overnight in a country where thieving was endemic. He just hoped all went well on this front, since for three months the expedition would be totally dependent on being supplied from base. The Captain explained that there was to be an initial period of intensive supply flights to build up sufficient food and other stores in the village to last for a month, with a weekly flight thereafter. He saw the logic of this. If for some reason problems occurred with the helicopter flights or, God forbid, the depot supplies were stolen or damaged, then the expedition would have at least three weeks supplies on site to last them until the regular supply line could be restored. The weekly flight would maintain physical contact with the expedition and could fly the occasional visitor in and out.

Stewart's arrival had coincided with the final day's flight in the initial build up. After the eleven o'clock sortie there and back - a six hour round trip - there would be no further flights until the following week, except for emergencies. A regular schedule of radio contact had been arranged, each morning at nine and again at six in the evening, for status reports and to confirm all was well. In spite of initial indications, everyone's cell phones had proved useless as there was no network available at all. This was a big disappointment for Stewart as it meant he could not really keep up to date on the Premier League football scores - and his team in particular, Tottenham Hotspur. If a need arose, the expedition could radio at any time outside pre-arranged times and they had a satellite phone for use in emergencies, so long as they could keep it charged via the camp generator.

The supplies build up had continued for a week but, before that, Ugandan technicians were flown in as an advance party. With the help of local village labour they erected the dining tent and two large laboratory tents. Then generators, water pumps, fridges, gas bottles and other laboratory equipment were flown in. Once all these had been set up, including the main radio and field kitchen, the stores build up began. About mid-way through this phase, when camp beds, toilets and showers were in place, it was time for the Europeans to go in. Stewart's colleagues had been in the village now for the past three days.

After a long, hot and very noisy helicopter ride jammed in amongst supply cartons, Stewart too had eventually arrived in the village at three o'clock yesterday afternoon. Everyone was pleased to see him and keen to show him what they had achieved so far. It was great to see them all again, especially Sheila of course. He had been really looking forward to seeing her again. She'd looked terrific in shorts and seemed pleased to see him too, although he soon realised she was very tired.   Around five o'clock she suggested he familiarise himself with the overall site by climbing the hill south of the village. He agreed enthusiastically but then, mischievously, she insisted on washing her hair before dinner, so he made the climb alone. He reached the top in a quiet, windless calm and was overwhelmed by the panorama beneath him. Planning for the expedition had taken so long it was difficult to take in that at long last he was sitting on a hill in the wilds of Western Uganda.

The village below was truly beautiful in the late afternoon sun. Thatched mud huts extended for a half mile or so along the lake, some close to the shore, others inland of well-tended fields. Strong greens, browns and blues assailed the eye. The grey-green of wild grass complemented an emerald green of trees and irrigated crops. The red brown soil of East Africa, a duller brown of mud huts and the straw colour of thatched roofs intermingled across the whole canvas. A wide swathe of grey mud beach dominated the eye, extending behind the village in a curving sweep from left to right, reaching to the forested slopes of the lake's eastern and western shores. The darkening, intense blue sky was unblemished by even a small cloud and Lake Albert lay undisturbed in the windless calm, a metallic blue mantle stretching out of sight to a far shore many miles distant. Flocks of birds were dotted across the lake-scape, pale pink flamingoes some distance off and less exotically coloured waders at the water's edge. Evening meals were being prepared and grey blue columns of smoke rose lazily from the huts.

Figures moved slowly here and there, tending cooking fires. Small groups of five or six strolled leisurely along field margins, heading home at the end of another day's labour under an intense tropical sun. The faint sound of voices carried on the evening calm. A farming smell permeated the air, a not-unpleasant aroma of cattle, fodder and wood-smoke. This was a prosperous community, well-organised and stable, and its members sustained what they regarded as a good standard of living. In spite of geographical isolation, the village traded regularly in a market town some thirty miles north along the lake's eastern shore. The community owned and maintained a small fleet of outboard-powered fishing boats which they also used to transport crops and goods to market. Around a hundred and fifty people lived here. Members of the Baganda tribe, they had developed a profitable farming lifestyle based on low-cost traditional methods. Infant mortality was much lower than the norm for the region. This was due in large measure to the sustained availability of a nutritious local food supply. Due to the influence of the Africa Inland Church, AIDS was not the scourge it was across the rest of the country. This was a Christian village, now largely self-supportive in terms of its economic, social and religious affairs and the Ugandan Government now recognised it as a jewel in the general dross of the wider community. This was a village to boast about to the world, a model for the rest of rural Africa.

***

Before the short twilight fell he scrambled back down to sort out his personal gear. He felt obliged to help Nottes with some final tidying in his laboratory tent and then he was ready for a shower and dinner. Everyone was tired and there were few attempts at conversation during the meal. They had all gone to bed early. In spite of the heat he'd flaked out like a light, waking as usual at six-fifteen this morning. Now, as he looked around, he became more and more impressed by what he saw. The gleaming white tents shone in the early morning light. Everything was neatly set out. Grey electric cables were suspended above head height from regularly spaced poles running in straight rows from the diesel generator some distance away, to minimise noise. Bright blue water pipes ran to and from a large black plastic header tank perched on a support frame. He traced the line of the input pipe bringing pumped water from a well and the outgoing pipe from the tank to the wash areas.

Those technicians have done a really magnificent job, he thought. It's very impressive the way they've sorted out all these systems. Everything is running well and the pre-planning seems to have paid off. We're all set to go!

He looked left. Sleeping huts extended in an arc round the edge of the compound. It was a good idea to 'rent' local huts rather than sleep in tents. Huts had more living space and were much cooler during the day. With camp beds and a few other home comforts installed, they reminded him vaguely of an austere Austrian guest house.

Soon, his companions appeared, sleepily in ones and twos, stilled tired from the exertions of yesterday.

"Did you sleep?" he asked Nottes, assuming from his appearance that he had not.

"Not very well. Did you?"

"Well yes, I did. But yesterday tired me out."

"Tell me about it! I was whacked too but I tossed and turned all night long. Did you hear the noises?"

"What noises?"

"Wild animals. Hyenas, baboons and a few more besides! At least I think that's what they were. Ben says they're further away than they sound. They're no threat. I suppose he should know, but they sounded pretty close to me!"

"Were you worried?"

"No. Not really. No, I wasn't. It just takes a bit of getting used to!" Nottes laughed. "It's not like Hounslow you know. Actually, I'm looking forward to seeing big game close up. Once we settle to a routine here maybe we could organise an occasional safari, although I hear poaching has cleaned out nearly all the big game."

"Yeah. That would be great! Have you talked to the technicians at all?"

"No. Not yet. I want to concentrate on the job in hand first. It'll take all my efforts to get the field programme up and running. Maybe next week. Would you be keen Bob?"

"Of course I would."

Nottes frowned. "I wonder if these lads know how to go about it?"

"How do you mean?"

"Well... they're city lads, from Kampala. What do they know about safaris or big game? They might pretend to know it all but would they be okay? Would we be safe?"

Stewart was surprised. "I hadn't thought of that. I suppose that's my ignorance showing... or is it my bigotry?"

"Bigotry?"

"My assumption that all Africans are tribesmen - you know, just pretending to be city slickers but in reality just down from the trees."

"Oh I see what you mean!" Nottes laughed. "You're being a bit hard on yourself Bob. I wouldn't worry too much about your attitude, or about doing the right thing *vis-à-vis* our African colleagues. Relax, hang loose! I know you're not a bigot! I find the best thing to do in these situations is to treat people exactly as you find them - or would find them at home. If some 'know all' technician at home acted up you'd soon cut the tripe out of him and not give it a second thought. Same thing here - and *vice versa*. That's what I'm going to do. I'm sure it's the best way."

"Oh really!" Sheila interjected, sitting down with her cornflakes. "That's extremely patronising of you - if you don't mind me saying so!" But they could see she was joking.

"Patronising! How is it patronising Doctor Wilson?" Stewart played along.

"Of course it's patronising to ..."

"To what? To treat people here as you would at home? What's patronising about that?" he smiled.

She flushed with embarrassment. "Oh... Is that what you were saying? I'm sorry. I took you up wrongly... not fully awake yet..." she babbled on, eyes fixed on her cereal bowl.

He realised she'd been partly serious in her criticism and tried to put her at ease.

"It's too early for all of us. We're out of sorts too."

Nottes poked his bacon around the plate during this exchange, then changed the subject adroitly.

"Bob and I were talking about arranging a bit of a safari sometime, to see if we can spot some big game"

"That would be fantastic!" she cried and her eyes lit up at the prospect. "Do you think we could?" she gushed, turning to Stewart for an answer.

"Well, it's not up to me ..." he mumbled, and could have cut his tongue out as the lameness of his knee-jerk answer cast a shadow of disappointment in her animated face. "... but I'll make damn sure it's organised as soon as we're ready to go!" he finished on a note of bravado.

"Wonderful Bob! That's great! Count me in as soon as it's organised!" She gathered up her dishes and took them to the wash-up.

Oh oh! I hope I can deliver on this. He saw Nottes smiling at him.

"What's so funny?"

"Oh nothing Bob, nothing. Just enjoying the view."

What did he mean by that?

Everyone was breakfasting now and to an external observer the general hubbub of gentile conversation would have seemed incongruous in its rural setting. The villagers were up and about and many were setting off for work in the fields. A group of able-bodied men gathered at the edge of the expedition compound. This was the group who were hired to work in the experimental plots and on the fishing voyages. Studying them, Stewart wondered what on earth they must think about this circus of foreigners who brought tents and gadgets into their rural world.

"Tom. Did Hugo have much of a problem selling this venture to the villagers?" he asked.

"How do you mean?"

"How did we get them to agree to this enterprise... the invasion of their village... and their privacy! I wonder what on earth they make of us? They must see us as some sort of Gods... with all our high-tech gear... or as utter idiots, wealthy idiots!"

"Who knows!" Tom laughed. "But you can rest easy on the general point. Old Hugo and Shaban Whatsisname spent a long time setting this up ... together with the Director of the Agricultural Research Institute in Kampala. Hugo was out here last year, twice in fact, talking to the village elders... "

"... You're kidding! Hugo was here last year? You mean before the project was agreed?"

"Yes. He came twice... once last March, and again in November I think it was. I'm not sure exactly about the second time, but I know the first time was March - the seventeenth in fact."

"I don't believe it! Typical of the man! Secrecy for its own sake! What for?"

"Oh now Bob, you're too hard on him! He just forgets to mention things."

"Forgets my ass! He knows I'm not gonna say 'Gosh! Gee Hugo! That's terrific!' whenever he bums and blows about his achievements... that's why he doesn't tell me!"

"Well then, you have your answer."

"Eh?"

"Why he doesn't tell you everything."

"Anyway Tom, how come you're so well-informed?"

"Well, I happen to remember it was March the seventeenth because that's our wedding anniversary."

"I don't follow."

"I was away on our anniversary!"

"So... I still don't follow."

"Oh Bob, really! I was here too, with Hugo!"

Stewart was astounded. "Tom, I'm astonished. I'd no idea!"

"There's no reason why you should have heard. We seldom see each other these days since the Crop Institute was re-located..."

"Why did Hugo bring you Tom?... Sorry!" He laughed. "I didn't mean that the way it sounded... I meant was there a specific reason?"

"For the Swahili."

"I beg your pardon?" He was perplexed once more.

"For heaven's sake Bob! I helped translate at the meetings with the elders."

"You mean you speak Swahili?" he asked incredulously, wondering what further surprises Nottes had in store.

Could he be a closet transvestite?

"I thought you knew? I grew up in Kenya. My parents lived there most of their adult lives. It was a bit rusty but it soon came back to me."

"The Swahili?"

Nottes nodded.

"But what about Mwanga? I thought you said he was here? Couldn't he do all the translating?"

"Of course he could, and so could the Institute Director for that matter."

"Then why you?"

"Oh think Bob! Hugo, quite rightly in my view, wanted an independent interpreter on hand... one he could trust. Of course we were careful not to let them know I was a fluent Swahili speaker. I summarised everything privately for him after each meeting... any conversations in Swahili between the Ugandans that is. They still don't suspect that I can speak the lingo. Hugo wants to keep it that way for a while, just to see how things go, so I'm depending on you to keep this to yourself Bob. Okay?"

"Yes, fine. I'll keep it quiet... of course. Well, did you pick up anything dodgy by the way... anything they didn't want you to know?"

"Oh no. They were pretty straight and above board about everything - at least the way we would be if the shoe was on the other foot!" He smiled and leant forward to whisper. "There was one thing they said though."

"What?"

"At one point the villagers referred to Hugo as the great hippopotamus!" he chortled.

"And I suppose you told him?"

"What do you think?"

Well, well, Stewart mused as they finished breakfast. You live and learn! What else don't I know about this expedition?

***

"So Bob, how are you this lovely morning?" breezed Doyle as he sat down.

"Fine, fine - but a bit tired after yesterday. All the travelling and unpacking seemed to go for me. I see you're dressed for action Brendan!" Stewart laughed, looking him up and down. Like everyone else, he was wearing a 'safari suit', in his case khaki shorts and short-sleeved matching shirt, socks and tan-coloured suede leather 'safari' boots. Doyle being Doyle however, he had added a wide-brimmed white hunter's hat to his ensemble, complete with fake leopard skin hat band. In the few days on site he managed to get all his exposed skin sunburnt to a boiled lobster colour. All in all he looked like a lottery winner on tour from the north of England or some such cultural wasteland.

"Sure I couldn't resist it for a laugh. Got it at the airport but actually it'll do the job very well. The wide brim keeps the sun off my head and neck."

"I must say it doesn't look like it Brendan!" Nottes exclaimed. "You'll need to watch it or you'll be laid up with bad sunburn or heat stroke even. Haven't you been using sun block? Remember what we were told about working in this sun?"

Doyle became serious. "Yes I know Tom. I should be all right if I'm careful from now on. You won't believe it but I came here determined to be extra careful about the sun. With my red hair and complexion I know from bitter experience that the sun and I don't get on, but in the general excitement I completely forgot to put on any cream! I remembered eventually and slapped some on. I've used it religiously ever since. I caught it just in time I reckon. This might look bad but I'm fine really. The sun block has kept it from getting any worse. It should be well faded in another day or so."

"Let's hope so. So what are you up to this morning?" Stewart asked.

"Tom and I are about to take charge of our squad of locals and head for the fields to do some planting! Ideal job for an Irish peasant don't you think?"

"Oh right! I'd forgotten you two were working together. Are the plots ready for planting - or do you have to clear them?"

"Already cleared my man - in true efficient manner! No, we arranged for that to be done over the last few days while we were setting up the lab and things."

"So that's it then?" said Stewart. "Nottes and Doyle just mosey down the track, hands in pockets, and supervise their African colleagues sweating under the tropical sun..."

"No..."

"... and then, potatoes planted, you come back here - drink Pimms all day with your dipsomaniac associate for two months..."

"Three months!"

"... and then, just before the Learjet comes to whisk us all back to civilisation, the pickled pair crawl back to a by now ten foot high jungle wilderness - to supervise their merry band once more as they hack out an enormous crop of truffles - which you then sell on the gourmet market at exorbitant prices!"

"Damn. You've rumbled it!" they cackled. "Surely you didn't think this venture was anything to do with science or altruism did you?"

"You're one to talk Stewart!" said Doyle. "What are you supposed to be doing - apart from the obvious?" He glanced at Sheila as she strolled across the compound, thankfully out of earshot. Stewart passed the remark off lightly but it riled him. He got up as the rest of the team headed towards the laboratory tents.

He stopped to speak to two of the Ugandan technicians, Ben and David, that he had met last night.

"Good morning Doctor Stewart!" they replied, apparently full of enthusiasm for the task ahead.

"Will you be in the fields today?"

"No Doctor. We're lake sampling this week with Doctor Roomer and Doctor Moriarty."

"Oh yes, sorry. You told me that last night. I haven't got all the names and faces sorted out yet."

"Don't worry Doctor. You'll soon get to know everyone!" David smiled.

 "When do you think you might join us on the lake Doctor?" Ben asked.

He had not given much thought as to precisely how he would split his time between the two halves of the expedition but, now that he had arrived, the prospect of getting out on Lake Albert was exciting. A keen angler since childhood, especially when he lived in Cape Town and caught yellowfin tuna most summer weekends, he intended to pay particular attention to the lake sampling aspects. He had brought a couple of spinning rods with him for that very purpose!

"I'd better familiarise myself with the crops work to start with. It'll help me get my bearings around the village. But I'm very keen to go out on the lake as soon as possible. I'll talk to Doctor Roomer about it this evening. Maybe in a couple of days time?"

"Fine Doctor. We look forward to seeing you." They beamed.

As they went down the track to the lake he called after them. "Hey! I thought the boats were supposed to leave very early each day?"

"Yes. That's right Doctor - but not this morning. This is the first day. We're just trying out the routine today!"

'I'd better get organised,' he thought. 'I can't wait to get out on the lake. There must be some whacking big fish out there!'

Chapter 4

The village

0545 hrs, 8 February

"Rise and shine! Rise and shine!"

Roomer woke with a start as Moriarty, all business and bursting to get going, marched gleefully into the sleeping area.

"What time is it?" he slurred, still struggling to get his brain moving. Where the hell was he…?

"Time we were out on the lake my boy - up you get!"

With a groan he recognised his surroundings - the dark, dusty hut and alien smells. He struggled out of the mosquito netting and swung his legs off the bed. It took him a moment to come to, head in hands, elbows on knees, allowing the African pre-dawn to seep gradually into his being.

"Oh come on Joe! We're ten minutes behind schedule as it is - and this is day one!"

Roomer shuffled outside for a quick wash and most of the stiffness in his joints had eased by the time he finished a wet shave. Moriarty fussed around at the edge of his vision checking lists and packing his 'day bag' as he called it. He watched him vigorously rubbing sun-block onto his face and forearms. It was Moriarty's idea that they should each carry a small rucksack, their 'day bags', for all the smaller bits and pieces needed for the day's work.

The technicians had risen a good half-hour earlier. Ben offered fried eggs and bacon under the canvas awning and, for a split second, Roomer resented his cheery black face.

"This will do you good Dr. Roomer Sir! No man should face the day without a hearty English breakfast!"

He glanced at him but saw no hint of mickey-taking in Ben's smiling face. The food was good, and with orange juice, toast and black, freshly-ground coffee they tucked into the most delicious breakfast they had had in years.

They tidied up quickly. Ben washed the breakfast things and the others sorted their day bags, charts and weapons. Roomer had a Beretta automatic pistol and Moriarty slung the heavy 0.308 Mauser rifle over his shoulder as they set off on the short walk to the lakeside. The question of weapons had been a contentious one but, based on Mwanga's firm advice, they had eventually accepted that the risk of attack from hippos was a real though remote possibility. Roomer didn't rate their chances of deterring an enraged hippo in a sustained attack but, what the hell, they would carry the weapons nevertheless. In a body of water the size of Lake Albert there should be plenty of scope to give hippos a very wide berth - which was precisely what he intended.

Stewart was coming with them this morning.

"Where's Bob?" Roomer asked.

"Been and gone! He's an early riser. He had breakfast half an hour ago and wandered on down to the beach. We'll see him there."

They approached the shore as dawn was brightening a clear sky. In the faint light the village seemed surreal, almost two-dimensional. They heard people stirring in most of the huts as they passed. At the boats Stewart, two villagers and David the other technician were already preparing to launch.

"Good morning." Moriarty said softly, not wanting to intrude on the surrounding peace.

"Good morning Doctor Moriarty, Doctor Roomer, Ben. We are just about ready I think." David replied and the others flashed quick smiles of greeting.

 The lake stretched away into the gloom, no wind stirred the air and Roomer shivered in the pre-dawn chill.

"You haven't touched anything since last evening have you David?"

"Of course not Dr. Roomer - everything is just as we left it - nets, ropes, bins, spare outboard..."

"And fuel?"

"Yes, I've checked again this morning and I am sure all is in order Doctor."

"I'm sorry David. I know you have. It's just me flapping - first day and all that! Too late when we're twenty-five miles away to discover we've no pencil!" he joked. "I dare say we'll all get used to it once we've settled to a routine."

Roomer's questioning stimulated Moriarty to make a last check himself. He panicked for a second when he couldn't locate the hand-held sat-nav instrument but soon found it in the side-pocket of his day bag.

"How are you this morning Bob?" Roomer asked, "Raring to go?"

"I'm fine thanks Joe, can't wait to get out there!"

"Good. Right everyone, all aboard! Let's go!"

The locals insisted that the expedition members embarked and sat amidships before launching. Stewart and the technicians were in one boat, Roomer and Moriarty in the other. Pushing on each side of the stern, the men launched the first boat into deepening water, jumping neatly onto the gunnels before clambering easily on board. One villager went quickly to the tilted outboard and locked it in its vertical position. The other man was already using a crude wooden paddle off the bow, to keep them moving ahead. With a quick flourish their helmsman whipped the engine into noisy life. The second boat was launched and its engine also fired easily. As propellers bit the water, both boats 'sat down' slightly at the stern, quickly gained speed and in a matter of seconds were travelling side by side at ten knots through glassy dark water.

Bending to stow some gear, Roomer studied Moriarty's face. He knew from their first meeting that he would get on well with this quiet Irishman. They had hit it off from the start. He assumed Moriarty would have assessed him too as they would be working and living closely together for the duration of the fisheries project. So far, he liked what he saw. He had an in-built, almost sub-conscious, bias against the Southern Irish in general and Irish scientists in particular. He'd met too many bluffers not to be sceptical. However, Moriarty was different. Quiet and unassuming, he knew his science inside out but was content to recognise Roomer as the senior man. Roomer was careful not to abuse his role for he knew how crucial it was for the two of them to get along well, at both the personal and scientific levels. Looking at him now he saw a fresh, youthful thirty-five year old. Unkempt brown hair partly obscured finely chiselled features. Tall and lanky he carried himself with a slight stoop. He reminded him facially of Claude Raines and, come to think of it, he had as fine a speaking voice as the famous movie actor of the forties.

Neither man broached the subject of Irish politics. It just did not come up.

Not like that bastard Doyle, Roomer thought, always getting digs in about the English. Why is it that most Irish Republicans make sure you know their views in the first five minutes? Who the hell cares? Don't they realise that nobody gives a toss what they think, least of all the English? Why don't they stay at home and stew in it, instead of inflicting their out-dated ideas on the rest of us? Don't they know the world's moved on? Time they did!

He realised that thoughts of Doyle had riled him, and this annoyed him even more - that Doyle had intruded on the first day out...

"Well Joe, here we go." Moriarty said quietly, as if he sensed his friend's agitation.

"Yes, I can hardly believe we're actually on our way." He smiled a reply at his companion and his irritation melted away.

With a growing sense of excitement they began their first experimental fishing voyage on the immensity of the great lake.

They had studied what charts were available. In 1929 a British Survey expedition had charted the lake but no reliable soundings had been taken since. However they expected to find little change from the earlier survey. They had hand-held satellite navigation instruments which gave their position to within ten metres. They also had portable echo sounders to provide depth profiles. Using the two technologies in tandem, they intended to make a rapid survey of each experimental area in advance, by alternating fishing days with survey days. They would survey an area of the lake one day, work up the results and produce depth contour charts that evening. They would then use these to plan and carry out experimental fishing the following day. In fact they expected to be fishing about three days to every survey day. It would depend on the survey results as to whether it would take one or more days to cover an area with different fishing gears. It should be possible to cover quite a large area while surveying and if it turned out to be complex - say with a wide variation in depth - then it could take several days fishing to make sure they had covered the area adequately.

On this first day they intended to survey an area five kilometres by five kilometres at the far side of the island. The island was about a kilometre long, low-lying and covered in scrub with a good stand of trees. It was situated some two kilometres offshore from the village and obscured a view of the wider lake from the beach. Anyone wanting to see further afield would have to climb the hill behind the village.

They had tested the survey gear yesterday in the stretch of water inshore of the island. Everything seemed to work well and they had no trouble translating the data into a depth contour map. This nearby area was not fished much by the locals any more. Apparently heavy fishing had nearly fished this area out, and the survey had shown it to be quite shallow - only one to two metres deep. The team had decided not to conduct any experimental fishing there, at least not at first.

The far side of the island was being fished by the villagers at present and catches were quite good considering how close it was to the village. It apparently made economic sense for fishermen to accept a lower catch rate when they were fishing close to home and therefore used less fuel travelling to and from more distant fishing grounds.

They had calculated that an area five kilometres by five kilometres would take most of a morning and early afternoon to survey. There would always be two boats for safety reasons and two boats would allow them to survey this size of area in a working day. They had defined today's starting point for each boat and the plan was for them to run in straight lines, parallel to each other at five knots, about two hundred metres apart, from one side of the five kilometre square to the other. Each would run its echo sounder continuously and note their position every five minutes using the sat-nav instruments. So long as they noted the precise time at each navigational fix and kept a constant speed, they could create depth contour maps on shore later. When both boats reached the opposite side of the square they would turn at right angles to run along the side of the square for one kilometre, before turning at right angles again to make another survey run back across to the other side of the square, five kilometres away. In this way they would gather data at precise points along a series of parallel transects across the width of the survey square. That would allow them to produce a depth contour map adequate for them to plan experimental fishing sites over the following day or two. Once that area had been experimentally fished they would move on to survey the next five kilometre square.

Roomer and Moriarty would not normally be together in the same boat but they agreed it would be best on this first survey day. Moriarty would monitor the echo-sounder and Roomer would take the sat-nav readings. They intended to swap roles later so that by the end of the first day they should have ironed out any practical wrinkles for the future. Stewart and David were carefully briefed last evening and would carry out the same sampling procedures from their boat. With his fisheries background Stewart should have no difficulty in handling his part of the operation.

"Put it on!" Roomer shouted across to Stewart, pointing to his own bright orange life-jacket that he was wearing.

Stewart waved to say he understood and bent to locate the life-jacket stowed at his feet. Roomer had been most insistent that everyone, including the villagers, wore life-jackets at all times. They would be working in a potentially hostile environment and some of the work would be unfamiliar even to the locals. Surprisingly, it had taken little persuasion to convince the villagers to wear them. There was no way he was going to lose a man on this project Roomer told himself.

Stewart now had his jacket on and was giving him the 'thumbs up' sign, grinning foolishly.

Half an hour later they reached the starting point for the day's survey and without undue fuss or difficulty began the routine work. At first they found the work intense. There was no time for relaxation. Readings had to be taken every five minutes and occasional course adjustments to be conveyed through Ben or David to their helmsman. Stewart had been unsure what to expect from the fishermen. They might have been difficult to work with, especially if they didn't understand what was going on or if for some reason they resented the entire enterprise. He was pleasantly surprised at their efficiency, their obvious interest in the survey and their general good humour and co-operation. In a very short time everything settled to a steady, if exacting, routine. The work brought back memories for Stewart. It had been a long time since he had sampled the North Sea.

Soon after they started, an incandescent sun rose into an aquamarine sky. The lake turned to chrome, twinkling and flashing as they ploughed its surface. The glare was intense. Stewart envied the local men who seemed untroubled by the conditions. They had no need of ultraviolet-blocking creams, Polaroid glasses or wide-brimmed hats. However they were wearing what seemed to him to be an excessive amount of clothes. He had been amused to see this throughout the village since his arrival. It was a habit that he had also noted in the Western Cape.

After an hour or so they had completed two legs across the square and came alongside each other for a break and to compare notes on how things were going. They had talked intermittently on the radios but Roomer was not in favour of this developing this into a regular habit. While he was willing to be lenient on this first morning in an alien environment, as they tried to establish a working routine, he was concerned about conserving battery power. The handsets were fully-charged but he thought it prudent not to over-use them. There was no real need for much chat during this intensive phase and regular breaks would let them talk face-to-face. He had no particular expectation of things going wrong. There was always a risk associated with small boat work and even though these were stable twenty-five-footers, a man could trip and hurt himself, perhaps go over the side. He had seen it happen more than once in his career, even on ocean-going research vessels. Today's programme was low risk but when they began deploying and hauling fishing gear over the side then the dangers would be increased. He was insistent on the life-jackets rule and was surprised how easily the locals were persuaded. They actually seemed very keen on the idea, once it was explained to them. He imagined, wrongly, that they must have seen magazine pictures of European yachtsmen wearing them and wanted to look the part. The men in fact appreciated the safety aspect immediately and wore the jackets solely for that reason, as any sensible fishermen should. Many European trawler men thought the wearing of life-jackets was unmanly and their safety record was so appalling that sea-fishing far out-ranked mining on the list of dangerous occupations. He made a mental note to donate the jackets to the village at the end of the project.

They talked between the boats, Europeans having one conversation, educated Ugandans a second and uneducated Ugandans a third. Hot coffee from flasks tasted superb, especially with the mild cheroot Stewart smoked. He decided not to offer any to the locals, not out of meanness but because once he started he could hardly desist later and his finite stock of cheroots would quickly be exhausted. The men seemed quite content with the self-roll cigarettes they smoked constantly throughout the day.

By lunch time they needed a substantial break to recuperate. The work was not physically arduous but its intensity and the need for close concentration was quite demanding. They agreed on a half-hour break for lunch and then a last push to finish up and get ashore, away from the heat and glare as soon as possible. The boats wallowed side by side about a hundred yards off the island, as their occupants devoured a variety of packed lunches, made the previous evening by Ben and David to individual tastes, and fresh from the cool boxes.

***

In a lull in the conversation Stewart suddenly announced, "Right gentlemen! The time has come for me to demonstrate my prowess with a spinning rod."

He produced a shining carbon-fibre rod from beneath the seat and stood up to fit it together. This caused general hilarity and prompted Roomer to tell him that he could have only five minutes or so to 'fool around' before they would have to resume work.

Stewart ignored what was going on around him and concentrated on tackling up. He hadn't been sure which rod to bring today - he had three different rods in camp, ranging from a light one he sometimes used for trout, to his nine footer that had once tossed heavy six-inch lures into the waters off the Cape, for yellowtail, katonkel and tunny. He fitted together a seven-foot, medium-weight spinning rod, a lightweight ABU multiplier reel with a hundred and fifty yards of ten pounds test nylon monofilament line. He selected a three-inch German sprat lure from his tackle box. The chromed lure was a good weight for casting with ten pound line.

He pulled on the line with the gears engaged to check the reel drag, to satisfy himself it was correctly set so that a heavy fish could strip line off him automatically without risk of the line breaking. Bracing himself, feet well apart across the boat, he got ready to make his first cast. He twisted to the right, rod held horizontally and pointing behind him, the lure dangling some twelve inches below the rod tip, a foot or so above the polished lake surface, on the other side of the boat. Everyone was quiet, waiting for the first cast - keeping a weather eye out for the vicious treble hook on the end of the lure. He heard the silence, not even a bird called, and tried to make sure he got it right in front of them all. He held the rod butt in his left hand and with his right gripped just below the reel, right thumb holding the now dis-engaged spool. With a quick movement and a skill acquired by many years' practice, he whipped the rod into action, simultaneously twisting his upper body in the direction of the cast. The whoosh of it and the whirr of the reel engrossed them as, frozen in the post-casting position, he watched the German sprat arc high through the air and splash down with an audible plop some fifty yards from the boat.

"Good cast!" someone said as he engaged the reel and began winding to retrieve the lure at spinning speed.

He was opening his mouth to reply when something big struck the lure viciously. Instinctively, he jerked the rod to strike the fish, to drive the hooks into its mouth, realising as he did so that the take was so powerful the fish must be already well-hooked. The rod bent alarmingly and, just when he thought the line must snap, the drag released line as the fish charged off on a fast run, the reel singing once more. Now it was seventy yards from the boat, unseen but near the surface. His heart was thumping with surprise and excitement.

"Bloody hell!" he shouted. "First blinkin' cast!"

The others cheered when the fish struck and one or two stood looking towards to where the fish must be, hands shading eyes from the glare.

"Careful now everybody!" Roomer called. "We don't want anyone falling in!"

He could tell from the shape and feel of the rod that there was a powerful fish on the line. He didn't know what he had hooked but it was big, although he had no real idea of the fighting characteristics of the local fish. It hadn't broken the surface as yet. He began a gentle pumping action, trying to regain some line. The fish stopped after its initial burst for freedom and now 'sat' broadside in the water to present as much resistance as possible to the pull of the line. Steadily he raised the rod tip as high as he could and then, by rapid winding, winched the rod down quickly to the surface, regaining a few feet of line in the process. By repeating this well-used manoeuvre time after time, he was able to pump the fish about twenty yards nearer the boat, to about the distance at which it had first taken the lure.

"What is it Bob?" asked Moriarty.

"I've no idea, but it's a good fish!"

The rod tip danced now as the fish began throwing its head from side to side in an effort to dislodge the hook. He held it steady, letting the fish fight, making no attempt to regain line, knowing it would stop and quieten again soon. Without warning the fast predator charged towards the boat, the line lying slack in the water as the distance between angler and fish shortened rapidly. Caught napping, he began to wind in slack as fast as he could, tensioning the line onto the reel by winding it through thumb and forefinger of his left hand, above the reel. When the fish had reduced the range to about twenty-five yards it suddenly flipped into a right angle turn and hurtled off to his left. He hadn't caught up all the slack at this point and, worried that the strain might be too much when the line came tight again, he quickly eased off the drag a quarter turn. Sure enough, when the line tightened, the rod was whipped to his left and the fish began stripping line once more. He managed to get the drag tightened down a bit again, and as soon as he did this the fish stopped once more, about forty yards off the starboard bow. He felt the sweat beading on his forehead and the strain on his back and forearms was beginning to tell. He shifted position to face his quarry.

"Come on Bob! You can do it!" they laughed, and he saw they were as excited as he was.

The locals had seen nothing like it and were even more excited than the others.

The fish fought him as he tried to pump it once more, and he contented himself with keeping a tight line. Any slackness would give it a chance of throwing the hook. Thank goodness we're in open water, he thought. I doubt if there are any underwater snags to foul the line. The tussle had lasted for nearly ten minutes now but Roomer had forgotten his earlier concern about time-keeping. Gently, Stewart pumped the fish again, conscious that the breaking strain of his line was on the limit with this monster. He got twenty yards on it and thought it was tiring. Suddenly it ran again. This time it headed straight out from shore and he clambered across onto the other boat holding his rod high in the air as the fish stripped line relentlessly. This run was the fiercest so far and took back all the yards gained earlier.

"Phew! This is a killer!" he grunted through his teeth and pumped again.

This time the fish stopped only briefly before it began a steady swim to his left, bringing it round in an arc and closing the range on the boat. For a few minutes he was able to gain line on it, winding in as the fish swam at an angle. Still none of them could see it. Its fight was spectacular but still it did not break the surface, let alone jump clear of the water as a trout might. He remembered the great yellowfin tunny off Cape Town. His last one was his biggest - a smashing one hundred and fifty-four pounds of sheer power. It took a good half-hour to bring that one to the gaff and it had lifted him out of the fighting chair several times! If you were fortunate you might see tunny hit the lure astern of the boat but after that, the first you saw of them was when you gaffed them aboard. He remembered too how they learnt not to rest when the tunny rested. After surging runs which could strip line off big 8/0 Penn Senator reels like an express train, the secret in overcoming those fish magnificent fish was to pump them whenever they wanted to rest. He saw exhausted novice anglers having to hand their rod over to a friend. They let their fish rest and recover too often during the fight so that the angler, not the fish, succumbed. This fish was not big enough to physically exhaust him but he could certainly feel the strain of the fight so far.

It was closer now, within twenty yards. Suddenly it caught sight of the dark underbelly of the boat and for the first time dived down and away, heading for the bottom, some thirty feet below. He held steady, allowing the spring in the rod to tame the fish. He pumped it towards the surface, lift and wind down, lift and wind down. It was definitely tiring now. So am I, he thought! It shuddered and fought for a few seconds but he was able to pump it again.

"Any sign of it?" he gasped to Moriarty, crouched beside him with the gaff.

"Not yet."

"Ever gaffed a fish before?"

"Oh yes!" he laughed. "I've poached quite a few Irish salmon this way!"

He pumped the fish slowly to the surface from slightly under the boat. Moriarty leant out over the gunnel, straining to catch a first sight of it in the brown, almost peaty water.

"It must there now!" Stewart grunted in frustration straining to raise the rod tip.

In that instant the fish made a last dash for freedom. It charged in a final headlong burst, flashing out from below the boat, tail pounding the surface, splashing great gouts of water and spray into the air. They shouted in surprise, both soaked by spray.

"Did you see it?" Stewart yelled.

"No! I just got a flash of something for a second! The spray blinded me!"

The fish ran only a few yards. It was exhausted by the fierce fight it had put up for over fifteen minutes.

"Okay. This time you bugger!" He grunted to himself, beginning to get angry with it. He began to pump vigorously.

"Steady Bob!" Moriarty hissed, for he could see he was losing patience and he wanted to see this brute landed.

In a few more moments it was beaten.

"I see it! One more pump Bob... Steady... lift a bit more... come to me baby..."

He grunted as he sank the sharp, chrome gaff point into the fish's shoulder and in the same movement swept it high and clear of the gunnel to dump it unceremoniously in the bottom of the boat. A general cheer went up.

"Well done Bob!"

"Well done to you too Paul! Thanks. That was well gaffed."

They crowded round to examine the magnificent specimen which lay quivering, its silvery sides gleaming in the bottom of the boat.

"Is it a Nile perch?" Stewart asked uncertainly.

"Yes! Genus *Lates*, the Nile perch. I'm not sure which species yet. Look out for those teeth!" Roomer warned. "It's a small one as these go! They can run to well over a hundred pounds or more. I'd say this one was about ten or twelve pounds, a real beauty. Let's hope we see a lot more good fish like that when we start work."

"It certainly put up some fight! That's the best fight I've had from a fish since Cape Town!"

He carefully examined the vicious teeth which marked this species as a predator. It was hooked in the roof of the mouth, close to the front of the jaw. It had been biting on the metal of the lure during the fight, otherwise it would easily have bitten through the nylon line. I must use a wire trace for these in future, he noted.

"Joe. Should we dissect it when we get back?"

"Oh why don't you let them cook it for tomorrow evening's dinner? So far as I know they're nice to eat. There should be enough meat on it for everyone. Let's leave the dissecting until we bring back our first proper catch." He smiled at the others. "Okay everyone! Fun's over! Let's get on and finish this survey and get home."

With simulated groans they sorted themselves out and in a few minutes were steaming along in formation, heading for their turning points for the next leg of the survey. Roomer estimated they would be finished in a couple of hours and should be back at base by about four o'clock. Apart from Stewart they soon forgot the excitement over the Nile perch as the demands of the survey imposed once more. However, Stewart replayed the action several times, smiling with relived pleasure. One cast one beauty! Unbelievable! He watched the glassy waters slide past and wondered with a thrill what other adversaries lurked beneath. He could hardly wait to be out on the lake again when they were actually using the fishing nets. Then there would be plenty of time to try the rod again while they stooged around between setting and lifting the gear.

He wondered how Sheila was getting on. She would be pleased with his catch!

Chapter 5

The village

2130 hrs, 14 February

Stewart had been in camp nine days now. Time had passed quickly; day following day in a blur of work. It had taken until now for the Europeans to acclimatise. Stewart in particular was only just beginning to feel himself again. He always found it difficult to adapt to a change of environment, even in Europe, let alone East Africa. He could never quite put his finger on what his problem was. It happened every time. He just felt once-removed from reality, physically tired and his mental ability was below par. At last, now that he had managed a few nights' sound sleep and his body had become accustomed to all the physical exertion in the boiling heat, he was nearly back to his usual self again.

His companions seemed to have similar problems. This surprised him. He usually found that other people had much less difficulty and adapted quickly. During this past week however, everyone in camp was lethargic, slow to rise in the mornings, grumpy over breakfast, with poor appetites. They felt tired all day and crashed into bed as soon as possible after dinner each evening. He wondered if the anti-malarial pills they were taking could be a factor. In a way he was pleased the others were also afflicted. At least nobody seemed to notice that he in particular was badly out of sorts. He thought it best to stay out of Sheila's way as much as possible, without giving her the impression he was trying to avoid her. He was glad she too seemed to prefer her own company during the first week. There'd been no real opportunity to be alone with her since their brief conversation back in London, when he asked her to dinner. He wondered if she remembered their joke about having dinner under the stars? Anyhow, in his disorientated state, it had suited him well enough to postpone having a private conversation with her. She would have thought him a cloth-eared idiot if he had!

The days out on the lake were very exciting and he had great sport catching strong fighting fish on rod and line. It certainly was impressive, so vast, so majestic. He discovered too that he really liked the lake sampling group. Roomer and Moriarty were so different as individuals and yet they obviously liked and respected each other enormously. Ben and David too were likeable young men, enthusiastic about the work and amazingly tolerant of the Europeans who knew so little about their country. Stewart was particularly fascinated by the local fishermen in the team. He studied them closely as they worked – though not too obviously he hoped. It was a bit difficult conversing with them although they spoke some English, but he managed well enough to develop a burgeoning respect for their knowledge and experience, above all for their dignity and pride in their village lifestyle and values. He suspected their tolerance of this invasion by 'mad' scientists was infinitely greater than his would have been in reciprocal circumstances.

That evening, they finished a fine dinner of cordon bleu chicken, admirably defrosted and microwaved by the technicians, accompanied by a glass or two of chilled Frascati. Now he was enjoying an after-dinner cigar with his black filter coffee. The conversation around him was going well - quite a change from earlier in the week. It seemed his colleagues had finally emerged from their lethargy. They settled into more comfortable seats after dinner and he slumped in a canvas chair against the base of a big Acacia tree outside the mess tent. He was slightly apart from the others, far enough away that cigar smoke would not irritate the non-smokers.

"Hello. How are you?" He jumped as Sheila spoke behind his back.

"I didn't hear you there! You made me jump! I'm fine Sheila. How are you? Will you join me?" He got up and pulled another chair over, closer to his own. "I hope you don't mind this cigar?"

"No. Not at all. I like the smell of cigars. My Dad used to smoke them."

"Oh?"

"He died last year."

"Oh, I'm sorry Sheila. I'm very sorry to hear that."

"Thanks. We were very close my Dad and I… I suppose I was a real Daddy's girl." she laughed, then more seriously, "He was a really nice man and I miss him."

He let a few moments pass in silence.

"What would he have thought about you being out here I wonder?"

She laughed. "Yeah, he'd have been very interested in all of this. I miss not being able to tell him about things." Then, with an effort, she brightened. "I'm sorry Bob. I didn't mean to be so …"

"… No. It's okay. I understand. I do really. I think it's fine that you think well of your parents. I know I do of mine."

She changed the subject. "How did you get on today?"

"It was terrific! I really enjoyed it. We caught lots of exotic fish and they even let me catch some on rod and line!"

"Yes, I heard you are a keen angler!"

"Did you?" he said, pleased that she had discussed him with someone. "Who told you that?"

"I think Brendan mentioned it." He was disappointed, finding it hard to imagine Doyle having something nice to say about anybody.

"How was your day?"

"Fine thanks. It went well. I'm pleased with the way the work's going so far. I really wasn't feeling up to scratch until today. I must have been jet-lagged or something. It's taken me a long while to settle in. Did you find that?"

"Yes, as a matter of fact I did. I think everyone's had a battle to acclimatise. Actually, today's the first day I've felt fully up to the mark"

She looked gorgeous in the light from the nearby tent. There was so much he wanted to know about this woman. Conscious of the others nearby, he wondered when he was going to be able to have a private conversation with her. He could hardly ask her to go for a walk in the pitch dark of the village, could he? An invitation back to his hut for a drink would seem far too pushy to this lady. She would very likely refuse, and he would hardly blame her, in full earshot of the others.

As luck would have it the problem solved itself. Doyle too was starting to feel like his old self again and invited everyone back for a night-cap to the hut he shared with Nottes.

"Come on folks! I've an unopened bottle of Jameson, ready and waiting!"

"Come on Sheila and Bob. Fancy a night-cap?"

He was about to get up with the rest, not seeing how it could be avoided, when Sheila said, "If you'll forgive me Brendan I won't. I'm not feeling great. I'll just sit here for a few more minutes - that's if Bob will keep me company - and have an early night thanks."

"Oh spoil sport!"

He could not believe his luck and as Doyle herded the others off towards his hut he looked at her. "Are you not well?"

"I'm fine!" she laughed. "I don't take to that man and besides, I want to sit here and talk!"

"Me too." he smiled. "To be honest I was wondering how to get you alone for a decent conversation."

"Just so long as you keep it decent!" They laughed together.

"I assumed all you Irish stuck together. I mean, I'm surprised to hear you're not keen on Brendan."

"Not keen! I think he's a dreadful man, always shoving his political ideas down everybody's throat. He's the sort of Republican that gets us Irish a bad name. It really annoys me. He typifies the way the Irish are portrayed in books and films! People just don't realise that the vast majority of Irish people, both North and South of the border, are just like their fellow Europeans. Decent people trying to make their way in the world, trying to provide secure and comfortable homes for their children and to make sure they get a decent education and turn out right. I promise you, it's only a few who are what we call 'stage Irish', like Doyle. Everyone has their political and religious beliefs of course but they prefer to keep them between themselves and the ballot box, or between themselves and their Maker."

"I'm not sure I agree with you there." he said cautiously.

"Oh?"

"Well, so far as I can see, in England at least, having a religious belief is becoming a rarity and, from what I've read, the Catholic Church in Ireland is rapidly losing its influence with more and more people, especially young people, having no religion at all. And as regards political belief, well you've only got to look at the percentage turnout in elections, both in Ireland and the UK, to realise that about half the electorate just don't bother to vote any more."

She sighed, smiling at him. "You're right of course. I was being a bit too simplistic. I'm not in the mood to give you a debate on the statistics, but my general point about people just minding their own business and getting on with life still holds true."

"Yes, I know. I was only nit-picking… Do you have a faith Sheila?" he asked, hoping she would not be offended.

"Well I believe in God but I'm not a regular churchgoer. I was brought up a Catholic, but to tell you the truth I'd run a mile if a priest tried to preach to me!" she laughed. "But yes, I do have a faith. What about you?"

"I was brought up C of E - Church of England - but I suppose I'm about the same as you." he smiled.

"Do you think it's our scientific education that's done it?" she wondered. "You know, made us less susceptible to a blind belief because there is no proof."

"I've sometimes wondered about that, but I don't think so. After all there can never be any proof that God exists. I always knew that from an early age. Becoming educated didn't change that. Faith must always be blind. That's part of its definition."

They talked on, enjoying each other's conversation. It flowed naturally between them, without any sexual undertones. She preferred serious conversations and it was so nice that this man seemed to talk the same language. She found she didn't mind what he said or what opinion he offered, she just enjoyed his company, his way of talking. He didn't boast, didn't 'bum and blow' as her father would have said, and seemed genuinely interested in her and what she had to say. He was a good listener, which was a rarity these days. In her experience most people were so wrapped up in their own affairs that they had no time for anyone else's. People just pretended to listen when really they only kept quiet for a time, while you spoke. Then when you stopped they launched into more expositions on their own affairs.

"What made you become a botanist?"

"Oh, it's hard to say now." she said thoughtfully. "I always enjoyed the subject at University."

"...Where did you go?" he interrupted.

"UCG." Seeing his blank look, she laughed. "University College Galway. I come from Galway, a town called Oughterard in fact, near Galway City."

"Spell it?"

"Oughterard? O-U-G-H-T-E-R-A-R-D."

"Ock-ter-ard." he offered.

"Nearly, but not quite!" she laughed. "Where do you come from?"

"I grew up in Shrewsbury, in Shropshire, and went to the University of East Anglia. They have a tie-up with the DEFRA Fisheries Laboratory in Lowestoft and that's how I drifted into Fisheries Biology."

"So you're not an administrator by trade?" she asked in some surprise.

"Oh no! I spent most of my early career as a research scientist at Lowestoft actually. It's only about five years ago that I made a sideways move into administration at DEFRA HQ in London."

"Don't you miss research?"

"Not really. I was always involved in administration to some extent, even when I was doing research. I found I liked it just as much, so when a job came up in the Chief Scientist's Group I applied for it. By that time I'd had my fill of working on research vessels at two in the morning in a howling North Sea gale in February!"

"Didn't you mind the move into London?"

"No actually. At least not at first. It was part of the attraction at the time. I had no ties and quite fancied the idea of a bachelor pad in the metropolis!" he laughed. "I'm not sure I'd be so keen now though. I mean, I would be tempted to move back to the country but it would cost a lot and there'd be all that travelling to work..." he tailed off wistfully.

She wondered, then, taking the bull by the horns, "Are you married?"

That brought him up short! Did she not know? How would she, he realised? I suppose she knows nothing about me!

"I'm sorry if I've ..."

"No, no, it's okay." he laughed. "I'm an idiot! Egotist more like! You threw me there because I've been arrogant enough to assume you knew a bit about me - but how could you?" Smiling gently at her, he went on. "I'd better give you a quick tour! I'm thirty-five years old, no wife - never been married - no kids either! Come to think of it no steady girl friend either. In case you're wondering I'm definitely heterosexual."

"Bob!" she said, in mock outrage.

"I admit to having had a long-standing relationship which, sadly, is no more. It finished about six months ago. So there you are!" he said, brightening.

"I'm sorry. I've opened an old wound."

"No, don't be silly Sheila. It's water under the bridge now. I'll get... I've got over it, but it took a while I must admit. I haven't rushed into anything since. That must sound bad!" he snorted. "As if I can just pick and choose from a host of women queuing up for me!" He laughed "You know what I mean. Now, Doctor Wilson..?"

"Right. I owe you my potted history don't I?"

"Only if you want to, really Sheila. I was only joking."

"I want to tell you Bob." she replied, holding eye contact with him.

His heart began to beat slightly faster. Be careful Stewart. You don't need any more drama for a while...

"Well, here are the salient points!" She began with a titter. "I'm thirty-two but if you tell any of this bunch my age I'll have you put in a cooking pot! Single, never married - and in case you were wondering Stewart," she threatened playfully, "no children! I have a boy-friend in Dublin, but it's not a serious relationship."

I hope that's fair on Liam, she reflected for a moment.'She decided it was.

He was very relaxed with her. It was the way she talked perhaps. Nothing she said jarred with him, as most women's conversation seemed to do recently, but maybe that was a hangover from his breakup with Judy. She wasn't pushy either. Scientific research was still mainly a man's preserve and women could have a tough time gaining recognition. Some of them over-reacted to this, became too sensitive about it, and further entrenched male attitudes every time they opened their mouths. Sheila didn't seem to have a problem. Obviously she knew her field and was confident enough about her work not to feel she had to push. He had seen her *curriculum vitae* along with everyone else's, when he was working up the funding application to the EU, for the expedition. Sheila Wilson's name appeared regularly in the scientific literature and she had published in good international journals.

She talked a lot about her family in Galway, her mother and three sisters. He liked that too. He had his fill of hard-boiled macho types who pretended social self-sufficiency in life. Who did they think they were kidding? She was a good listener and seemed genuinely interested in what he had to say. She could draw him out and he felt no reticence or embarrassment in talking about himself. Indeed, he realised he was telling her things about himself that he had either forgotten or hadn't mentioned to anyone, even Judy, for many years.

"Sheila, I have a nice bottle of white wine chilling in the fridge. Let me get a couple of glasses."

"Mm. Sounds great." she purred mischievously but when he returned and began to pour, "I don't drink much Bob." she said quietly.

"Good. I'm glad to hear it!" he said seriously, and meant it.

That put her at ease again. "You have another smoke if you want."

Smiling to herself she watched him light a cigar. This is a lovely man you've discovered. Not at all like first impressions.

The more they talked the more she warmed to him. She liked his gentle smile, his total lack of bullshit. He seemed interested in her too. It was easy just to be herself, as if she'd known him for years. She felt safe with him. But not too safe she hoped!

In a while the others started getting ready for bed. One or two of them were messing around in the compound with towels and toilet bags.

"Well, maybe we should think about turning in Bob."

Before that lout Doyle shouts over something lewd, she thought.

"Yes, we've another tiring day ahead. I'll re-cork this for tomorrow." He got to his feet stiffly. "I must be getting old!" he laughed, flexing his leg. "Well, goodnight Sheila. I've really enjoyed our chat. I'll keep my eye on you to make sure you reach your hut safely!"

"Make sure you do! Goodnight Bob. You must come to our field plots soon. I'll show you round. It's really very interesting."

"No fishing?"

"There's more to life than fishing!" she laughed back over her shoulder as she jogged across the now deserted compound to her hut.

You can say that again, he thought, watching her dark hair swirling from side to side as she ran.

Chapter 6

The village

1500 hrs, 15 February

It was three o'clock and the village lay baking under the afternoon sun. At this time of day there were no obvious signs of the expedition's presence. The fishing group was not due back for another hour and the scientific field plots were deserted. The silence was broken only by an occasional dog bark or a distant bird call. Villagers were still out in the fields but here too the day's work was drawing to a close and they would soon drift homewards.

Stewart lay in his bunk trying to summon enough energy to get up. Everyone else had resumed work half an hour ago.

This is ridiculous. You may be an early morning riser but in this heat you could easily become a malingerer!

He swung his legs off the bed and sat upright.

I suppose these siestas are a good idea but it's hard to get going again afterwards.

The team had quickly discovered the energy-sapping power of the tropical sun and that they were not able to work in it all day long. A daily routine had soon evolved. Early rising at seven o'clock and a light breakfast was followed by field work from eight-thirty to noon with copious water intake to prevent dehydration. There was time for a quick shower before lunch at twelve-thirty and then a siesta had become the usual practice. After three o'clock, the remainder of the afternoon was spent in the laboratory so it was possible to maintain performance by having a short, energy-building sleep just after lunch in the relative cool of the huts.

Stewart was not needed for laboratory work in the plants project and, not for the first time, was glad he had not chosen Botany as a career. Still, his conscience was relatively clear because after the fisheries team returned home he always helped them process their samples between four and six o'clock.

Better get moving, he told himself. They'll soon be landing with another exotic catch.

He found the work fascinating and enjoyed measuring and dissecting the fish that were brought ashore.

I must go out with them again tomorrow. Maybe there'll be a chance of a really big fish on the spinning rod.

He had been out on the lake most days and although it was very hot and tiring he had thoroughly enjoyed the experience.

Across the compound the crops team were working in one of the laboratories. They did this every afternoon, analysing data, examining and identifying pests they had collected, growing plant disease cultures. He found it difficult to maintain much enthusiasm for this type of work but Sheila and the others seemed excited. It takes all sorts, he smiled to himself.

He became conscious of a faint, rhythmic thumping sound.

What was it?

'Thump, thump, thump ... ' it was growing louder by the second.

Suddenly he realised what it was and rushed outside. Sheila, Ethne and the others were emerging from the laboratory and he hurried with them to the clearing outside the compound. A camouflage-painted army helicopter swept into view from the south, flared, tail down, and settled on the roughly marked landing pad. It had flown in only two days ago on the first of its weekly supply runs. In the normal course of events they would not have expected to see it again until next week. However, this morning's radio call to Kampala had revealed that VIPs would be visiting them today.

The crescendo of noise abated and the helicopter dust storm eased. Stewart watched with amusement as Hugo Bamford blundered out of the aircraft and stumbled towards them, bent at the waist, camera bag slung on his shoulder. Doctor Mwanga followed close behind. Stewart was immediately reminded of those Second World War images - Reichsmarshall Hermann Goering reviewing the troops in white designer uniform, Field-marshal's baton clutched in pudgy hand like a child with a stick of candy, fat smiling face exuding cruelty and depravity, flunkies grovelling around him as he strutted double-chinned to glorious Wagnerian music tainted forever by its association with the Third Reich. Hugo further emphasised the imagery by passing along the line of those waiting to greet him, shaking hands and smiling, a word here, a word there, as if they would die for him should he, Goering-like, order them into battle. Some of them would indeed die for him, or rather because of him, but that was unimaginable on this peaceful afternoon as the group strolled back to the compound. The technicians were left to carry the rest of Hugo's kit which had been unloaded from the now-departed helicopter.

Hugo and Mwanga were shown to the 'guest hut' where they unpacked a few essentials. Stewart stayed with them to explain about the facilities and the expedition's routine. The others returned to their laboratory duties to finish the day's analyses on schedule. Hugo was keen to take photographs before evening so Stewart showed him and Mwanga round the expedition compound and the wider village. They decided to wait until morning to climb the hill-side above the village.

Stewart found Mwanga to be a pleasant character, not at all overshadowed by Hugo, and his excellent English demonstrated a subtle, slightly sarcastic sense of humour which appealed to him. The two of them struck up an easy relationship almost immediately. He found himself explaining everything directly to Mwanga but Hugo did not seem to mind as he concentrated on taking pictures of everything, from every conceivable angle. Photography was a hobby that he had taken up quite recently and, typically, he went into it in a big way. He seemed to have a number of different lenses, some telephoto, some for close-ups and he regularly inter-changed these as he photographed insects, flowers, trees and other scenery.

Thinking he had better make some reference to photography Stewart asked, "Have you plenty of flash cards with you Hugo? There's lot's more to photograph you know. You won't run out?"

Hugo laughed. "I've brought about ten cards!" Seeing his surprise he added, "I've got two stills cameras and one camcorder."

"Oh I see."

At about four o'clock the three went down to the lake to meet the fishing group. As they neared the beach they could see, and hear, the two boats approaching at full speed about a mile offshore. Hugo photographed them through a telephoto lens. Soon the leading boat beached in front of them and Roomer and the others greeted Hugo wearily. They had had a long hot day and for once even Hugo realised they were tired. He tried not to get in the way as they off-loaded samples and trudged up the track. When they reached the lab, Stewart noticed that Hugo gave them peace to get on with their analyses so that they could finish in time for dinner. He wandered into the crops laboratory next door and took pictures of the continuing activities there. Now he was full of questions, in his usual aggressive mode. Stewart had long supposed he used this interrogative technique to maintain dominance over others. He 'grilled' people, piling question on question so that, no matter how experienced or well-versed the victim was in their subject, Hugo usually managed to reduce them to a level of uncertainty. This generally manifested itself as a tendency to bluster, slightly red-faced and sweating, as his questions eventually succeeded in getting under the victim's skin.

Hugo began putting Nottes through his paces, rather like a head waiter would have done with a new recruit.

"How many replicates for each treatment are you doing Tom?"

Tom told him.

"And have you allowed for spatial variation in soil type?"

Tom explained there was virtually no variation in soil type from west to east across the breadth of the continent at this latitude but the irony appeared to be lost on Hugo.

"How do you ensure there's no cross-contamination between samples?"

Tom told him that too.

And so he went on, probing for a weakness in the sampling or laboratory regimes. He did this, not because he wanted to satisfy himself on the validity of the work, but because he hoped that his questioning would reveal a shortcoming that no-one had thought of previously. Thus his superior intellect would have been publicly exhibited once more, his ego massaged.

Did he really believe that he was doing anyone a favour by this, Stewart asked himself for the hundredth time? Surely he must realise that in flushing out some minor shortcoming he so alienated colleagues that they would vehemently oppose anything he might suggest?

Nottes was no longer bothered by Hugo's technique. He had seen it so often before that now he let it wash over him like foam from a cheap shower gel. He had discovered a long time ago that the best defence against a Hugo onslaught was attack. So long as you kept off Hugo's own specialist subject, (on which he had been known to argue for hours on end until protagonists usually let him win for sanity's sake), he could be fended off relatively easily by a few telling questions. He decided that Hugo had had his obligatory two minutes to play boss and began his reactive strike.

"What did you make of that paper by Smith and Alcock?"

"Which one?" Hugo replied warily.

"It was in last month's issue of 'Plant International Journal'. I thought their analyses demonstrated quite clearly how to allow for spatial variation in a situation such as ours. Didn't you see it?"

"Er... no, must've missed it." Hugo muttered.

Then, before he could get going again, Nottes hit him with a second strike.

"I'd like you to spend the whole of tomorrow with us in the field Hugo. You'll really enjoy it!" he lied. "We can go through the experimental design in detail once you've seen the layout on the ground. It'll be over a hundred in the shade so you'll need to prepare for a long hot day. What do you think?"

"We'll see Tom... We'll see how my schedule develops."

Content that he had once again deflected Hugo's aggression, Nottes waited with some curiosity to see who he would select as his next victim. In fact no-one was unfortunate and he contented himself with a quick tour of the lab and a few words over everyone's shoulder as they worked at microscopes or other apparatus. He spent quite some time with Ethne Dunne and she was pleased by his genuine interest in her computer logging and analysis set up. She was always ready to discuss computing with someone who had a basic grasp and interest. Unfortunately many scientists, while they used computer technology in their work, remained a bit in awe of it and preferred not to show their ignorance by discussing the topic in any depth. She was pleasantly surprised at the depth of Hugo's understanding and both of them enjoyed a short but intense discussion on the hardware and software being used.

While Hugo was otherwise engaged, Stewart studied Sheila's profile as she and Doyle pored over their work. Suddenly, she looked up and caught his eye and smiled. She came over leaving Doyle to finish whatever they'd been doing. Stewart ignored his suggestive wink behind Sheila's back.

"Hello Bob! Have you come to see where the real work is going on?"

"Of course! I just couldn't stay away." he laughed.

They chatted on, oblivious to their surroundings and he looked closely into her brown eyes as she talked. He had no difficulty in giving his total attention to a woman who was fast becoming the centre of his existence. The more he saw of her the more beautiful and attractive she became. For her part she had stopped fighting her natural reticence to becoming emotionally involved with a work colleague. Sheila had not fully realised it yet, had not admitted to herself that her feelings for Bob Stewart were deepening intensely.

Hugo was now talking to Rent who, when he wasn't acting like a sycophant, was enthusiastic about his work and had a rare ability to make it sound interesting to others.

"How long are you staying Hugo?" Rent asked.

"I can only stay five days. I'll be leaving again on the next scheduled supply flight next week."

"Oh that's a pity." Rent lied, since he too preferred Hugo in small doses, if he must endure him at all. "Still you'll be able to get a good overview of progress in five days. I suppose you'll be spending a day in the fields with us?"

"Yes... I hope to." Hugo said uncertainly, with a growing realisation that he could hardly avoid wasting a day in such a way. Botany was such a deadly subject!

At last, in a final flurry of picture-taking the day's work came to an end. There was just time for a quick shower before dinner. Leaving the technicians to tidy up, they dispersed to their huts, Stewart and Sheila parting reluctantly, to freshen up for dinner. The fisheries group was also finished and Ben and David were cleaning and preparing to dump any unwanted fish carcases outside the village perimeter where the local carrion-eaters made short work of disposing of any remains.

Later, cleansed and refreshed, they gathered again for dinner at eight o'clock. The sun set soon after seven and darkness fell quickly in the tropics, just north of the equator. Gas lights at dinner changed the scene dramatically. Stewart and Sheila sat beside each other paying little heed to the conversations going on around them. The meal was really quite good. After a starter of fresh locally-grown melon they were served a delicious dish of steamed lake fish in hollandaise sauce, with fresh sugar beans and boiled potatoes. An acceptable white Burgundy went well with the meal which finished with fresh fruit sorbet and rich freshly-ground Ugandan coffee. Hugo tried to dominate matters for a time but eventually the day's travelling caught up with him and he became very fatigued. At around nine-thirty he excused himself and went to bed. Mwanga gave him a few moments head start then he too retired. As usual, the rest sat outside for a drink but, to avoid disturbing Hugo and Mwanga, the after-dinner conversation was subdued and they broke up around ten-thirty.

Stewart and Sheila's chats were commonplace now and the others, including Doyle, had ceased any good-natured banter some days ago. Lingering for a moment after the rest had gone Sheila rose and without a word walked towards her hut. Stewart walked beside her. Neither spoke. As they strolled across the shadowed compound he gently took her by the hand. She squeezed his hand firmly without looking at him. At the hut doorway he stepped into the deep shadow of the porch roof and gently, a hand on each shoulder, turned her round to face him. Still without speaking he drew her slowly to him and gently kissed her parted lips. She moaned softly and clung to him tightly. He could feel the length of her body against him and his senses reeled with the scent and feel of her. They both knew at that moment they were born for each other. This would be no quick fling. They had built this carefully from the beginning, studying and enjoying each other's company before risking physical contact. It was too important to spoil in a moment's thoughtlessness. The slow, delicious build-up could continue for a while yet. He admired her so much he wanted their relationship to develop at precisely the pace she wanted. As if reading his thoughts she disengaged herself slowly and holding his face in both hands she smiled at him.

"Goodnight Doctor Stewart." she murmured huskily. "Be careful out in that boat tomorrow." Her face became serious with concern. "Make sure you come to see me as soon as you get back. Promise?"

"I will, of course I will." He kissed her gently again.

"Sheila... "

"Shhhh... I'll talk to you tomorrow. Goodnight Bob." Then, afraid of not being able to hold herself in check any longer she blew him a kiss and stepped quickly through the curtain into the dark interior of the hut.

He walked slowly back across the compound, not hearing the animal cries in the bush, not noticing the scorpion that scuttled across his path.

They lay awake thinking about each other well into the night and it was a several hours before either of them managed to get to sleep. They would be ill-rested to face the rigours of the coming day.

Chapter 7

The village

0645 hrs, 16 February

Another equatorial day dawned, quietly but magnificently, on the shores of the lake. Almost none of the local populous noticed the beauty of early morning. They were too busy preparing for another day's labour, another day's hardship. Even those who came to experiment in this environment and who might have been expected to be more aware of the wonders of their surroundings were too busy this morning. Like the indigenous population, they too were preparing for work in red-soiled fields. Their preparations were becoming acrimonious.

"I'm telling you Brendan, Ethne assured me the data loggers were all set up and ready to go!" Rent was furious and getting more and more worked up.

He tried to keep a rein on himself in front of Doyle. That drip of a girl couldn't have sorted the machines out properly as she'd promised last night! Their whole day would have to be aborted if the data-loggers couldn't be set up!

He berated himself for letting her take the day off before he checked that the loggers were ready. So now, while Miss Dunne was out on the lake sunning herself with Roomer and his team, she had left the shore party in disarray!

"What's wrong with them?" Doyle asked, uncertain as to the precise nature of the problem.

"I can't get them to boot up! Their batteries are flat. If we can't get them to work we can't complete the day's sampling - in fact there's no point starting it at all!"

"Surely we could write down the results and put them into the computer later this evening, after Ethne gets back?"

He could hardly believe what he was hearing.

Doyle was talking rubbish!

With a shock he realised the man had no conception of the crucial role the data loggers played in the sampling routine. He obviously had not the slightest notion how much they depended on the computer programs to define their sampling. It was not a matter of having a pre-planned sampling strategy and sticking to it no matter what. On the contrary, they had to be sure the samples reflected any variations in particular field plots. By using data loggers as sampling progressed, any natural variation they encountered could be allowed for by adjusting sampling while they were still working in the fields. Without this facility they might discover later, after they analysed the data back in the laboratory, that a plot was not sampled in a statistically valid manner. This would mean they would have to repeat the sample the next day, which would itself cause further problems in comparing results which were all supposed to be obtained on the same day. Repeat sampling also played havoc with the overall schedule. No, it was better not to sample at all if the computers were unavailable, to avoid the risk of wasting the entire day. It would be better to get on with some laboratory work instead, and postpone sampling until another day.

In a rare moment of charity to his fellow man, Rent decided not to point out Doyle's supreme stupidity to him. No, on reflection, this was too good a point to waste just now, he thought. Better to trot it out at dinner in front of the others. He imagined how he would draw Doyle into the trap. A subtle question or two should do it, then he would drop him right in it in front of his peers! He was almost gleeful at the prospect in spite of his continuing frustration with the computers.

"Er, no Brendan … it just wouldn't be practical to write the data down…"

He became aware of Sheila approaching.

"Morning Peter, Brendan!" she said cheerfully, then noticed Rent's frown. "Anything wrong?"

"It's these bloody data loggers!" he said through his teeth. "Ethne was to leave them all set up but of course she's waltzed off for the day and… "

"That's not like her." She said in some concern, bending to examine the machines. "What's the problem?"

"Flat batteries." Doyle explained, glad to be able to contribute something he understood.

Why was Rent so worked up he wondered? He must have got out on the wrong side.

"Both of them?" She exclaimed in some surprise. "That's very odd… "

She straightened, smiling.

"Peter. I'm surprised at you! I knew Ethne wouldn't be so careless! They're still on charge you duffer! Unplug them from the generator supply and then boot them up. You should find they're okay."

Rent realised immediately that she was right. He did as she suggested and, sure enough, the machines both 'booted' perfectly, ready for action.

Good grief! I'm as thick as this fool Doyle, he smiled bitterly to himself.

"Thanks Sheila!" he laughed sheepishly after her as she strode off towards the lab and rolled his eyes heavenward at Doyle to cover his embarrassment. He was very relieved to have the problem sorted out. Imagine having to explain it to you know who! Hugo was the main driving force in the introduction of data loggers to the work, and he would have been particularly annoyed at the foul up.

Soon the field party, as they referred to themselves, organised their equipment and lunches for a day's work in the experimental plots at the edge of the village. They were to be assisted by four village labourers under the supervision of technicians Adam and John. This support group began the half-mile walk along a well-trodden track which meandered away from the lake through village fields to the experimental area. The Europeans did not deign to walk such a distance in this environment. If truth be told none of them would contemplate such a walk either here in East Africa or in Shropshire or Kildare - wherever their work was located. Walking to work had gone completely from their culture, at least from the educated classes - apart from a few keep-fit fanatics who deluded themselves they would live longer, (when in fact it would only seem longer). No, this party travelled by Landrover. Nottes fired its engine and they began loading. Hugo wandered up to join the group and of course took the front seat leaving Rent and Doyle to clamber into the back with Sheila.

"Everyone okay back there?" Hugo shouted over his shoulder, not caring in the least how they were jammed in.

They rattled and swayed their way along the track in the battered vehicle. Sheila assumed it was quite a few years old but in fact it had been acquired new by the Ugandan Institute just over two years ago. Its present condition was testimony both to the state of the local roads and the lack of a proper servicing regime.

"Where's Doctor Mwanga this morning?" Doyle asked Hugo, having to raise his voice above the engine noise.

"Oh he's seen the plots before." Nottes replied on Hugo's behalf.

"He has some work to do in the lab today. He'll be able to make the daily radio call from camp for us. I'll give him a buzz on a hand-set later. It'll save me having to drive back up to use the main radio."

Soon they were disembarked and preparing to start sampling. Nottes remained behind the wheel and Hugo spoke in through the open window.

"Now tell me exactly what we're doing here Tom. I want to be able to help as much as possible but, as I told you, I'll want to take pictures from time to time - for the record!"

"Just a moment Hugo. I want to run the Landrover in under the trees, otherwise it will heat like an oven in the sun. Won't be a tick!"

He revved the engine and, leaving the others standing, bumped across fifty yards of rough ground towards the forest of tall trees which extended southwards from the village. Hugo watched the Landrover disappear as it went down into a deep hollow at the edge of the trees. While he waited for Nottes to reappear, he looked around him. He realised the immediate area was far from flat. Hummocks and hollows extended in all directions and he wondered what affect these would have on their sampling. He hoped they had allowed for them in the experimental design.

In a few minutes Nottes was back and in response to Hugo's questioning explained how the field trials had been set up, the different crops that were sown and how they would sample each plot. He described the various treatments that were being applied and the number of replicates of each. Listening to this, Sheila realised that Hugo was quite familiar with the principles of valid scientific design, the need to build in and allow for natural variation that occurred in all biological systems, so that statistically significant results could be obtained.

They spent an intensive few hours. Sheila with Nottes, Rent working with Doyle and Hugo quizzing, snapping photos and making a general nuisance of himself. Rent in particular was having great difficulty in keeping his temper in check. It was bad enough having to work with an imbecile like Doyle, but to endure Hugo was an almost unbearable additional burden. Common sense told him that the man would not endure a second day of this. Indeed, looking at him, Rent realised that he was already losing interest in what was a hot, dusty and unglamorous day's toil. Obviously, even Hugo felt unable to duck out of participating in at least some field work. If he had come, as he said, to inspect the work of the expedition then he had little option but to spend at least one day with the field party.

For his part Hugo found it incredible that educated beings could sustain an interest in grovelling on their knees measuring leaf widths and other minutiae for hours on end. It was amazing! They actually seemed enthralled by it and at times got quite excited by a leaf here or a stem there! Not for the first time he reminded himself that it took all sorts in this world!

Just when he was beginning to feel that enough was enough Nottes called a welcome halt.

"Okay everyone! I think that's enough for now. We'll take a break."

They walked slowly towards the out of sight Landrover and Nottes glanced back to see Adam and John still kneeling, engrossed in some measurement.

"Come on you two!"

"We'll come in a moment Doctor!" Adam shouted. "Two minutes will finish this plot."

He waved to them and lengthened his stride to catch up with the others, now out of sight at the Landrover in the hollow ahead. They set up a collapsible picnic table and chairs and in the relative comfort of the shade, relaxed with long refreshing drinks from the cool box. They concentrated on replenishing fluids lost during the morning and conversation was sparse. Sheila sprawled with her legs flung out, head thrown back, gazing at the tree canopy above. An occasional bird flitted from tree to tree but the monkeys that had entertained her yesterday were absent today.

Hugo also noticed the bird life and resolved to take photos when he finished his drink. Doyle slouched, red and sweating, smoking a cigarette.

Looking at him, Rent had to admire his stamina. With a complexion like that and two stone overweight I'm amazed he can stick this for more than ten minutes!

"It's time for the radio call." Nottes interrupted, standing to open the Landrover door, looking for one of the hand-held radios. Hugo remembered that the expedition was supposed to report to Kampala each morning at ten o'clock.

"Damn! I left the radios with Adam and John."

He had scarcely uttered the words when the shocking noise of automatic gunfire burst brutally upon their senses. Instinctively, they flung themselves to the ground, stunned and uncomprehending, drinks and chairs sent flying in the din. Sheila drew breath to scream as another savage burst was unleashed. Some instinct made Rent grab her and clamp his hand over her mouth.

"Quiet! Quiet!" he hissed at the others in the stunned silence after the second burst.

"What..."

"Shut up Hugo! Be quiet!" Rent hissed at him frantically.

They realised then, as Rent had somehow a moment earlier, that the shooting was not aimed at them. Whoever was shooting could not have seen them? The gunfire was over at the plots. As if to confirm this, a scream of terror came from over the rise. It was brutally cut off by another burst of firing. This time small stones and soil sprayed onto the Landrover roof. This latest burst was in their direction but the hollow protected them. Sheila clung to Rent, burying her face in his shoulder, sobbing noiselessly. The others were dumbstruck. Doyle lay face-down in the dirt, hands on head. Nottes cringed, wide-eyed under the Landrover. Only Hugo was half upright, on his knees, head held high, scanning from side to side trying to make sense of what was happening.

"Get down Hugo! Get down you idiot!" Rent was almost screaming at him. "They don't know we're here!"

This seemed to make sense to Hugo and he crawled quickly under the vehicle beside Nottes. They stayed frozen in tableau as the gunfire continued, intermittent burst after burst. At times they thought they heard screams and shouting. Sometimes the firing seemed to be close. At other times it sounded more distant. None of them had experienced anything remotely like it. The terror and horror of it stupefied them, yet instinctively they understood two facts. They were not the target and, if they kept their heads down, the nightmare might pass, might go away. So they froze there, scared rigid, unheard and unseen in the midst of violent slaughter in the hot African morning.

After a while the gunfire stopped. Birds screeched in the trees above. Hugo spoke first, in a whisper, his voice trembling with shock.

"Anyone hurt? Everybody okay?"

No-one answered.

"Tom, Peter! Are you alright? Sheila, Brendan?" They nodded slowly or mumbled a reply.

"I'm okay."

"Alright."

"Okay."

Hugo slid slowly from beneath the Landrover, an incongruously awkward sight, and started crawling up the gently sloping side of the hollow. This time no-one hissed at him. Sheila disentangled herself from Rent and sat shaking, mesmerised by Hugo's slow progress up the slope. His heart was thumping and sweat ran down his face, stinging his eyes, dripping off his nose and chin. He tried to crawl quietly but could not control his heaving chest as he hyperventilated, close to panic. He neared the top. The crawl subsided to an inch by inch movement. With each fractional rise, more and more of the immediate horizon appeared in front of him. Now he could see the rough ground they had walked across. He scanned around, still terrified of what might happen. Nothing! At first he saw nothing unusual. The scene was just as he remembered it. He lay still, carefully studying the scene in front of him, and to either side. There was no-one, no movement at all. Suddenly he noticed the smoke. All at once he became aware of several pillars of grey-black smoke rising soundlessly, straight into the clear blue sky. Were they there when he first looked? He wasn't sure. It was obvious that a number of substantial fires were burning in the village, half a mile away up the track. On the ground in front of him he saw only red soil intermingled with bright green patches of vegetation. The ground sloped away from his position making it impossible to see the plots and the village track beyond. If he was to see further he would have to get higher. He thought about getting up on his knees and the idea nearly made him sick. Hugo was many things, but cowardice did not come easily to him. Over-riding his fear, he gritted his teeth and wrestled awkwardly to his knees.

"Aaghh!" he grunted and threw himself down and backwards in an involuntary reflex.

"What is it?" Nottes hissed, but Hugo, without looking round, silenced him with a vicious downwards slash of the arm. The shock of what he had seen began to ease and his heartbeat slowed slightly. He steeled himself to return to his vantage point.

Again he worked himself up the slope and knelt on the lip of the hollow to examine Adam's bloody, mutilated corpse lying stretched towards him. It was partially hidden behind a small hummock about ten yards in front of him. He realised that the burst of gunfire that sprayed dirt onto the Landrover roof must have been the one that cut Adam to pieces as he ran towards them, terrified. He had a flash of anger, then relief, when he realised how close they were to being discovered. If Adam had made it a few yards further, or shouted and waved at them as he ran...

Steeling himself, he craned higher and immediately spotted another body, sprawled and bloody, lying in the middle of the experimental area.

Dear God! It looks like the other technician.

He could see flames in the direction of the village beyond and, as he tried to make it out, suddenly saw distant figures through the smoke. He dropped quickly to the ground and slithered back down to the others as a burst of more distant firing echoed in the trees above.

"What's happening?" Rent asked. "Hugo! For heaven's sake!"

"They've been shot!" Hugo snapped.

"Who?"

"The two technicians have been shot... Dead."

Sheila sobbed in horror and the others sat back, stunned.

"There's some bloody gang out there. They've fired the village!"

His voice came in short, panting bursts as he struggled to keep control of himself.

"We're too exposed here. They could come back and spot us. We'll have to get under cover, in the trees."

"But... " Nottes spluttered.

"There's no buts about it! We're going into those bloody trees - and we're going now!"

He grabbed Nottes by the lapels and flung him towards the trees.

"Get going, all of you! And crawl! Keep down! Peter, get Doyle moving! Sheila! Hold on to me. Come on!"

They stumbled and crawled up the far side of the hollow. Doyle had not uttered a word since the first burst of firing and was all but dragged along by Rent. Sheila crawled close to Hugo, behind Nottes. He made them push on into the trees for several hundred yards. He had no idea how far the grove extended but there was no sign of the trees thinning out where they rested, grouped around the base of a large tree. They lay exhausted from the shock of it all. They knew the Landrover might be discovered at any minute. If it was, their discovery and violent death would soon follow. All they could do was lie there and pray, insides heaving with fear, minds reeling almost beyond control.

Hugo became aware of an excruciating headache.

***

They lay under the trees, well covered by thick undergrowth and hidden from any casual observer. It would take a sustained search of the area to find them but Hugo had little doubt they would be discovered once this gang of murderers became aware of their existence. He could not understand how they had been missed so far. It was now twelve-thirty by his watch. From time to time they heard distant yelling and screaming, with occasional gunfire, sometimes a single shot or two, at other times bursts of automatic fire. In between there was relative silence, only the sounds of birds calling in the trees around them.

Rent was calmer now and he too tried to analyse the situation. Looking around he tried to gauge the status of his companions. Sheila and Nottes sat hunched beside each other talking quietly. He could see that Nottes was doing his best to comfort her but she was very stressed, red-eyed and tearful. Doyle lay curled up on his side nearby. He had hardly moved or spoken since they had reached their hiding place. Rent supposed he was in shock. Sorry mate, you'll just have to hang in there like the rest of us.

Hugo looked okay. Now that they were not crawling around everyone had cooled down and, after the first shock of it all, they were calmer, breathing normally.

He crawled two yards to Hugo.

"How goes it?"

"Okay. Yourself?"

"I'm alright." He paused for a moment, watching to see Hugo's reaction. "I can't understand why they aren't looking for us."

"Who? The others or… "

"This gang of killers."

"I've been wondering that myself," he said grimly. "As I see it, this is a group of rebels who've come across the Congo border as part of an insurrection. You'll remember Mwanga gave us an assurance there would be no trouble anywhere near us!" He spat the last remark in disgust.

"Well the poor bugger's found out the hard way."

"Yes. I assume Shaban's been subjected to some physical abuse."

Rent thought it highly likely that Hugo's colleague had been shot some time ago, but said nothing.

"What's your assessment Peter?"

"I agree with you. From what we've heard, the village has been attacked. Judging by the heavy shooting earlier, most of the locals have either been killed or have run off. I shudder to think what they've been doing to any women survivors since."

"Yes," muttered Hugo. "There seem to be isolated killings still going on. I can't understand why they haven't realised we're in the vicinity. Surely if they've seen the huts and the labs - and all our gear - they must realise some sort of expedition is based here?"

"I've been puzzling over that too. They cannot know we are in the area or we would have heard them searching for us. They'd have found us by now in fact! No, for whatever reason, they don't suspect there's a group of us in the vicinity. The only logical explanation I can think of is Mwanga."

"Mwanga?"

"Yes. He must have told them we're away for the day. As you say our equipment is a give-away. He couldn't have denied there was something going on but somehow he's convinced them we're not around. I'm damned if I can think what he's told them."

"The boat party!" Hugo cried excitedly.

"Eh?"

"He could have convinced them we're all out on the lake and won't be back until later."

"I suppose so." Rent said doubtfully. "But don't you think we're getting a bit ahead of ourselves Hugo? After all we haven't the foggiest idea what really has happened. We're making a helluva lot of assumptions!"

"Look Peter, those two technicians were shot to hell and it doesn't take a genius to work out what all the shooting and burning has been about!"

"Okay, but I think it's time we tried to see what's actually going on. We need to find out. We can't hide here for the rest of our lives!" With a sudden thought he added, "And we'd need to do it before the boat party sail slap into the middle of it all!"

"Hell, you're right Peter! What time are they due back?"

"Around four, usually." He looked at his watch. "It's nearly one o'clock now. I've just had a thought Hugo."

"What?"

"It may be this lot's waiting for the boat party. Maybe that's why they're hanging around, why they haven't moved on by now."

Hugo groaned. "Okay, you and I will have to reconnoitre. We'd better tell the others."

They crawled over to the other three who watched, wide-eyed, as they approached. After repeating their conversation they began to plan a reconnaissance. They estimated they were about three-quarters of a mile from the village, about a quarter-mile into the trees beyond the hollow where the Landrover was, presumably, still undetected. Now that there was time to think, they realised that there was quite a bit of essential gear that could be retrieved from the vehicle. There was still a possibility that even if the vehicle itself was spotted they might remain undetected. The terrorists might not realise that the Landrover meant there were people hiding nearby. One way or the other they would need that gear to survive. There was a hand-gun, a rifle and ammunition and the cool-box with its food and drink. Nottes was fairly certain he had left a pair of binoculars too but, most important of all, there should be a sat-nav instrument and maps. The two radio hand-sets had been with the technicians. No-one discussed the prospect of trying to reach Adam or John's body to see if the radios could be retrieved - if they were still there.

Doyle began to emerge from his almost catatonic state and was very nervous about the proposal.

"Wouldn't it be safer just to sit tight Hugo? Until these bastards move off? If you're seen we're all dead you know!"

"I know Brendan, I know. But what choice do we have. We can't just hide here and wait for the boat party to be butchered... "

"We don't know that for certain... "

"Exactly! That's why we have to take a look!" Rent snapped unpleasantly and for once Hugo did not try to moderate.

"Right. It's one twenty-five by my watch." said Hugo. "I reckon if we move carefully and steadily we should reach the edge of the trees by one-forty at the latest. Allowing for, say, fifteen minutes to assess what we can see of the situation in the village and get what we need from the vehicle, Peter and I should be back here by... " studying his watch, "... by one-fifty-five, say two o'clock at the very latest. Now for heaven's sake don't move from this position while we're away. If we get separated our situation will be even worse. Right Peter, let's go."

They began to crawl and Hugo paused to take a long look over his shoulder at the vulnerable trio crouched in the scrub behind him. He let Rent get slightly ahead and off to his left about five yards. They crawled and slithered for a few minutes until their palms and knees began to ache.

Rent whispered, "We'd be better on our feet. We'd make a lot less noise walking!"

"Agreed." he hissed in reply.

They moved off again, separated as before by a few yards, Rent slightly ahead. Walking at the crouch and placing their feet carefully they progressed quite quietly through the light undergrowth. Rent began to worry about snakes. Then his imagination extended to carnivores.

'Did lions stalk in trees? There must be some risk,' he thought. 'After all, that was why they were advised to bring firearms in the first place! Anyway, to hell with it just now! Why worry about wild animals when there was every chance some illiterate black bastard would blow your head off at any second!'

Hugo signalled for a short breather, literally. Walking at the crouch and the general stress level had them panting once more. They must be near the edge of the trees by now, Hugo calculated. His watch said one-forty. Suddenly Rent froze and chopped his right arm downwards. Hugo inched forwards gingerly to join him and both sank gently to their knees, peering ahead through the foliage. They had come out almost exactly at the spot where they had fled in panic into the trees a few hours earlier.

The Landrover was as they had left it, in isolation in the hollow, shaded by the trees. Table and camp chairs were scattered around where they had fallen in the earlier panic. There was no sign anyone had been there since they left. Rent pointed beyond. From this vantage point they could see Adam's body and beyond it the body they assumed to be John's. Smoke still billowed in the further distance, in the village, but there was no movement in the indistinct scene up the track. Hugo realised this was the first sight Rent had had of the bodies. He gave him a moment to take in the scene. Now that he had more time to view the area, Hugo thought he could make out two more bodies lying side by side further back up the track. He had been wondering about the four labourers who were helping them in the plots. It looked like at least two of them were slaughtered as they fled. For the first time he felt a flush of anger at the scum who had done this. What cause could possibly justify such wanton slaughter?

Rent interrupted his thoughts.

"Come on Hugo. Let's get on with it before some of those bastards show up."

He slithered down to the Landrover and Hugo followed. They quickly located the rifle, cool-box and other items. Rent found the sat-nav and maps in a small case on the front seat. There were two 'safari' water bottles, both full, and they grabbed those as well.

"That's about it." said Rent. Hugo nodded his agreement.

"Let's get this gear back to the edge of the trees first."

"What do you mean first?"

"The radios." Hugo said, nodding in the direction of the plots.

"Oh ... right." Rent set off for the trees, glad to be heading for cover.

He felt very exposed even though they were hidden in the hollow. It took quite some effort by both of them to hump and drag all the equipment up the slope into the undergrowth. By the time they finished they were sweating profusely and breathing heavily. They sat just out of sight in the undergrowth, to recover.

"I don't know about this Hugo."

"Nor I Peter, but if those radios are there they could be our salvation." he paused. "I think on balance it's worth taking the risk."

"That's precisely my point! I don't think it is worth risking! If we leave now there's a good chance we can stay hidden until this lot move on. Then with the sat-nav maybe we can walk out of this nightmare. If one of us goes down there and is spotted then we're all dead! End of story!"

"You're wrong Peter! Without those radios we've no way of contacting the outside world. There's no chance of reaching the satellite phone in camp and these scum have probably found it - or smashed it - by now! Unless we can, we won't know in which direction safety lies! The entire area is probably overrun by these buggers. With the radios we might be able to call in a chopper to airlift us out... "

"... If they're still flying - and there's one within radio range!"

"And what about the boat party? We can radio them to avoid an ambush."

"Damn! Damn! Damn!" hissed Rent. "I'd forgotten them! I suppose we owe it to them to give it a try... Okay. Okay. I'm convinced. Where are you going?"

He tugged at Hugo's arm as the bigger man tried to struggle forward.

"I'll go Hugo."

His companion started to protest but he cut him short.

"Don't be daft! I'm much fitter than you are. Listen, if anything starts you get offside immediately! Okay?"

Hugo nodded and Rent slithered back down to the Landrover and crawled quickly up to the far lip of the hollow.

He lay examining Adam's body as best he could. There was no obvious sign of the radios. He realised they had dithered too long as it was. Every moment they delayed made it more and more likely someone would come down the track, or appear from any direction in fact. He made up his mind how to handle it, stood up and ran the few steps to Adam's body, throwing himself down beside it. He steeled himself against the sight and smell of the fly-covered wounds and avoided looking at the face. Kneeling, he rolled the body onto its back and quickly searched for a radio. Nothing, either in the pockets of the bush jacket or lying nearby. As soon as he was sure he had not missed anything he got to his feet again and charged towards John's body thirty yards further on. He threw himself down again and repeated the search. Nothing. Severely hyperventilating now, he gathered himself once more and charged back to the hollow, throwing himself over the lip to finish in a heap near the Landrover.

Hugo watched the whole thing in utter shock and amazement! He expected Rent to crawl slowly to the first body and make a careful search for the radios. When Rent charged off he had literally fallen backwards with surprise! Then he saw him manhandling the body like an abattoir worker and that too shocked him. He checked up the path with the binoculars while Rent continued his task, but there was no sign of anything, just smoke. He realised that Rent was right to do it all quickly but then his heart nearly burst from his chest.

Hells bells! He could hardly believe the evidence of his eyes. Rent was running towards the second body! Bloody hell! Hugo had never even contemplated trying to reach the farther technician. It was far too risky! No wonder Peter wasn't keen on the whole idea!

He started to sweat badly again. Come on Peter, get moving! Discarding the binoculars he couldn't take his eyes off the track, but Rent was in his field of vision too. He found himself mumbling, 'come on Peter, come on Peter, …' over and over again, only stopping with a great sigh as Rent slid to a heap in the relative safety of the hollow once more.

He knew without asking that there were no radios on the bodies. The disappointment that washed over him was tempered by relief that Rent was back safely, apparently undiscovered.

"Come on Peter." he said gently. "We'd better get back."

"Okay, but we should tidy up the furniture before we go."

"What?"

"If we leave it scattered around and they find the Landrover they'll know we were here and made a run for it!"

"I doubt it… but okay, let's stack it quickly!"

Then they clambered up the bank and, heavy-laden, headed back to the others. Hugo decided it was not a good time to say he had not meant him to check the second body. He was careful not to let him see the involuntary smile which came when he thought of Rent's pell-mell charge.

The topography made it relatively easy to re-trace their steps and they had no difficulty finding their way back to the others.

"Where on earth have you been?" Sheila hissed at them angrily, giving them a start.

"It's nearly half-two! You said you'd be back by two! We thought you'd been captured!"

"Sorry Sheila. It took longer than I estimated." said Hugo, un-shouldering the rifle and water bottles and slumping to the ground.

"Did you get everything?" Nottes asked.

"Yes." said Rent. "But no radios."

"Oh? But why not?" Nottes asked, and seeing Rent about to bite his head off added quickly, "I mean Adam or John had them. Definitely."

"Well neither of them have a radio now." Hugo said, not wanting to start a discussion of Rent's reckless body-searching episode.

"Well that means the terrorists have taken the sets off the bodies." said Nottes. "Or off whichever body had them."

They fell silent, not sure of the import of this revelation.

It was Doyle who broke the silence. "What do we do now?"

"Do? What do you mean do? What do you suggest we do Brendan?"

Rent quizzed him aggressively not bothering to hide his contempt for the Irishman.

"Well it seems to me we have no choice at the moment." Doyle answered with surprising firmness.

"It would be obvious lunacy for us to barge out of the trees straight into the middle of this gang of butchers. They'd shoot us on sight, at least us men." He glanced at Sheila who flushed as the horror of his meaning dawned.

"Do you really think... " she whispered.

"Sheila." said Hugo firmly. "Let me say this once, out in the open, just so none of us is under any illusions. If we're caught I have little doubt we will all be killed. We may be shot, or we may be tortured and shot. Peter and I believe that women villagers have been raped and killed. I'm sorry to have to say this Sheila, but I see no reason why you wouldn't suffer the same fate."

"Why *did* you say it?" she hissed at him. "Is that supposed to make me feel better?"

"I'm sorry." he said gently. "I wanted all of us to be absolutely certain of the position. There is a reason why it's crucial for us all to be aware." he said, looking around the group.

"I'm giving Sheila the hand gun, for her personal protection and... " he began to mumble, "to use, *in extremis*, as she sees fit."

Reaching into a pack at his feet he handed her the Beretta Eighty-four and a box of nine millimetre ammunition. They had all been given a short basic training course on firearms and she applied this unconsciously, checking that a full clip of thirteen rounds was in the weapon and the safety was on. She belted the holster round her waist and broke open the ammunition box to shake the rounds out loose, putting half in each front pocket of her 'safari' jacket. She was immensely saddened by it all. Frightened of course, trying hard not to crack up, but above all desperately over-burdened by the nightmare that had come upon them.

She couldn't get Bob out of her head. Where was he? What would happen to him - to all of them? Dear God keep us safe, she prayed. She wanted to be with Stewart. She wished desperately that he was with her now, to hold her tight, to keep her safe.

Doyle continued. "As I was saying, we have no option but to stay put, keep our heads down until we're absolutely certain this gang has left."

"And then what?" Rent snapped. "What about Joe Roomer's group? Do we just lie here and wait for them to be butchered?"

"What else do you suggest?"

"He's right Peter." said Hugo, thinking aloud. "We may not like it. It may seem an appalling course of action - inaction I should say, but what else can we do? We can't take on this mob with a hunting rifle and a hand gun. It would be suicide! We can't warn the boat party. We've no radio, or any other means of signalling. We'll just have to let things take their course. There's nothing else we can do."

In his heart Rent knew they were right but he turned to Nottes in frustration.

 "Tom! What do you think? You've been very quiet so far."

"While you've all been arguing I've been assessing our resources. Hugo and Brendan are right of course. It's as plain as a pike-staff Peter. We sit where we are and try to trek out when it's safe to do so. Further discussion is a waste of energy."

Nottes was way ahead of them. He had seen the only possible conclusion some time ago and had been sorting through the gear and provisions.

"Alright. Alright. I accept the situation." said Rent quietly. "I have one suggestion for action however... " He held up his hand as Hugo started to interrupt. "... let me finish Hugo, please! I'm forced to agree we stay out of sight and let the boat party take its chances. Incidentally, they're bound to see all the smoke long before they come into firing range."

"Yes, I'd thought of that Peter." said Nottes. "Unfortunately I can't see why the smoke would warn them off. In fact it might well make them return at high speed if they thought the village was on fire. They'd have no reason to expect violence, certainly not gunfire. The village has been quiet for quite a while now. No shooting I mean, to warn them - even if they were within earshot."

They realised there had been no shots for a long time.

"That brings me to my point." Rent continued. "It's high time we saw our enemy. All this theorising has been done in a vacuum. We'll have to get a look at the village to see what's actually going on. We've too many assumptions and precious few facts! We need to know how many are in this gang. Have they butchered everyone or not? Is the village destroyed? I for one am not trekking off into the bush unless I know for bloody sure what's going on and what the scale of it all is! Some of us will have to stalk to the edge of the trees and do a recce."

He felt a slight twinge of embarrassment at the gung-ho army slang.

"Peter's right." Nottes said firmly. "I was going to suggest the same thing myself."

Hugo saw the logic of the proposal. After a short debate it was agreed that Rent and Nottes would attempt the reconnaissance and, in spite of their attempts to dissuade him, Hugo insisted on going too. There was no way he was letting Rent take charge if he could help it! Who did he think he was – Arnold Swartzenegger?

Chapter 8

The lake

1400 hrs, 16 February

Far out on the huge lake, the two boats motored side by side on their way back from the day's experimental fishing. It was a smooth run home on a glass calm. At ten knots the boats caused a big disturbance to the surface. Standing at the stern, Roomer gazed at the wakes extending and intermingling for a considerable distance behind. The Evinrude outboards were very noisy, running at full power.

It's a shame we have to disturb this paradise with our noise and waves, he thought. However, the overall impact was insignificant in a water mass as immense as Lake Albert.

He glanced down at the fisherman at the helm. He sat to port of the engine squinting ahead into the afternoon glare, right arm on the steering bar holding the twist throttle at maximum. Like all professionals, the man seemed integrated with the boat, relaxed and at ease with his task. The line of the wake testified to the perfectly straight course being steered but, more for something to do than any lack of confidence in the man's ability, Roomer slipped the hand-held satellite navigation instrument out of its pouch. He checked their position and asked the instrument for a track plot back to village HQ co-ordinates which it held in memory. He confirmed they were exactly on course as usual. After only a few days on the lake he had come to trust the villagers' innate navigational skills. Without compass or other modern aid they seemed particularly adept at finding their way accurately around the lake, no matter how far they were from 'home base'.

He looked across at the other boat forging along ten yards to starboard, its bright blue bow reflecting in the calm water. Moriarty sat facing astern, engrossed in his clipboard, going over the sample data. Stewart was stretched out along the seat amidships, apparently asleep. The crews of both boats were still working up in the bow stowing nets and ropes.

Roomer estimated another hour to reach the island and a further fifteen minutes from there to the village. It was two o'clock now. By the time they landed and got the samples to the lab it would be close to four o'clock. Allowing an hour or so to process the catch, he and Moriarty should be showered in good time for a relaxing sundowner before dinner. Ah, this was the life! He wondered with scant sympathy how his other DEFRA colleagues were enjoying the February weather back in London.

It was Paul's turn to call base. "Paul!" he shouted across. "Radio HQ and give our ETA!" After a couple of attempts he managed to make himself understood and Moriarty nodded his agreement.

"Group 1 calling HQ. Do you read me? Our ETA should be around three fifteen on the beach!" Moriarty began talking into his hand-held radio.

Roomer's attention wandered and as Moriarty made the call, he sat down to look for a stick of gum. The two boats ploughed steadily across the vastness around them. He watched young Ethne carefully packing away the oxygen/temperature meters and other electronic gear. He was pleased at her overall efficiency. She was a very pleasant young woman and seemed to have thoroughly enjoyed the day.

Suddenly, the two helmsmen started shouting in Swahili. Something up ahead was the focus of their attention. He swivelled round to see. At first he saw nothing. The lake expanse extended uninterrupted into the medium distance and although the sun's glare made it difficult to pick out any detail he could see no reason for their obvious excitement. By this time those in the bow were also looking ahead, shielding their eyes from the sun.

"What is it David?" he shouted. "What do you see?"

He could not make out the shouted reply and, realising this, the young technician clambered his way back to the stern.

David shouted in his ear. "There seems to be a fire in the village Doctor!"

"A bush fire?"

"It looks like it - but it's hard to tell from this range!"

Roomer grabbed for the binoculars and peered ahead through the glare at the island some ten miles ahead. Now that he knew what he was looking for he saw a long smudge of grey-blue smoke between the island and the more distant hills on the shore beyond. He thought too, he could see it at higher altitude, dirty brown against the bright sky. It certainly looked like it was near the village, if not in it. The trouble was they would not know for sure until they reached the island, lying two miles this side of the village and directly in their line of sight to the village on this course.

By this time both helmsmen were standing at their tillers and were jabbering away with the other men who were obviously very concerned about the situation up ahead. He looked across and saw Moriarty still hunched over the radio. Stewart was wide awake now and stood looking towards the village.

"I can't raise them!" Moriarty signalled.

"Whatd'ya mean?"

"I can't raise anybody at base!"

"Is the radio okay?"

"Yes, it seems to be. I've checked it - it was okay two hours ago when we last reported in."

"I'll try this one!" Roomer reached for his day bag.

David, and Ben on the other boat, were getting the message across to the locals that the radio was an obvious way to check out what was happening in the village. Both throttles were eased in unison until the boats glided along slowly, side by side, engines just ticking over.

Roomer began to call.

"Group 1 calling HQ. Group 1 calling HQ. Do you read me? Over"

"Group 1 calling HQ. Do you read me? Over."

Faint static came in reply.

"How long were you trying?" he asked Moriarty.

"A good five or ten minutes on and off. They're supposed to listen for us five minutes either side of the hour."

"I know."

"This set's okay Joe - at least I can hear you clearly on it. Can you hear me? Over."

"Yeah. I hear you fine. The sets are okay. There's nobody answering at HQ. They must be dealing with the fire," he muttered.

Both men looked worried as they reviewed the situation. David and Ben translated for the locals who listened intently.

It must be quite a big fire if our team is tackling it along with the villagers, Roomer thought. I hope the labs aren't in danger.

"Joe! What do you think is happening?" Stewart asked anxiously.

"I don't know. Paul, we should turn off our sets to conserve the batteries. There's no point wasting time calling any more. What can we do anyway? Let's just run on in as fast as we can!"

"Okay! Let's go!" Moriarty shouted, signalling for full steam ahead.

They sat down as the boats resumed their full speed course. Conversation which was difficult over the engine noise became almost non-existent as each man's worries and impatience grew. Their speed seemed agonisingly slow and the day was hotter than ever. Gradually the minutes passed and Roomer checked his sat-nav instrument as the others looked on. The instrument was continuously displaying the intervening distance from their present position and HQ.

After a moment to double check he shouted, "I make it nine point four nautical miles!"

"What's the distance between HQ and the eastern end of the island?" Ethne asked.

"I estimate it at two miles - so that leaves seven point four miles... seven point three now..." checking his instrument, "...until we can see the village."

"Yeah. That's about right." she agreed. "You clocked these boats at almost exactly ten knots the other day, didn't you?"

"Yes, but we have a load of samples on board now to slow us."

"But less fuel." she replied.

"Okay, let's say ten knots. So, roughly, I'd say we'll round the point in about forty minutes from now... say, ten to three - which is about what we'd estimated earlier."

They lapsed into silence, not greatly worried, but concerned that the fire might cause some disruption to the expedition.

This must happen this from time to time here, Roomer thought. The villagers should have some experience in handling a bush fire? Why didn't I think to ask them?

"David!" he beckoned.

"Can you ask them if they've had a big fire before?" He nodded over at the fishermen.

They had a lengthy conversation before David clambered back.

"They're quite worried Doctor. They've never had a bush fire before. Nothing big anyway. They've no more idea about it than us, I'm afraid."

"Thank you David." he said, thinking it was a very lengthy conversation if that was all was said.

On and on they droned and gradually the island grew more distinct as it emerged from the glare and distance. Even with binoculars they could make out little. The island was no more than a mile ahead now, long and thin, sitting at right angles to their track. Low-lying, six or seven metres at its highest point, it was surrounded by a muddy beach which shelved gently. Much of it was covered with lush green scrub. High thorn trees grew along its length and a proud Baobab stood here and there. At this distance it was still impossible to see the village and the island masked all sounds from the shore behind. They would not see anything until the very last moment when they rounded the point.

***

They were all on their feet staring intently at the lake shore sliding into view as they approached the point. The smoke rose in billows high into the sky. It seemed to be rising from several different points but Roomer thought it had lessened compared to earlier. His boat was now thirty yards ahead of the other. A slight speed differential between the two was no longer being adjusted for at this stage in the run in.

Suddenly, almost before he realised it, they were rounding the point. Their course altered to starboard as they curved into the bay beyond. The shock made him sag at the knees as he registered the scene of utter desolation which swept into view.

Every hut in sight was ablaze. Just the huts were on fire - had been fired! This was no bush fire. They had been systematically set alight!

"Dear God! Dear God!" he moaned and his companions wailed with despair.

Those in the second boat saw it now and they too shouted in disbelief. They forged on in at full speed towards the landing, still over a mile ahead, straining to see through haze and smoke which almost obscured the shore.

What in hell had happened? Roomer thought he heard timbers crackling in the flames nearest the shore. Was that people running on the beach?

He couldn't quite make it out as smoke billowed around in great gouts of grey. All at once it cleared momentarily and he saw the landing and shore. Three figures, two African men and a child were running hard, straight down the beach for the lake. It cleared some more and they all saw a group of five or six men in pursuit, some fifty yards back up the beach. As he tried to make sense of it, he saw a pursuer drop to one knee. Suddenly the three runners pitched headlong - cut to ribbons by a burst of automatic fire. The crackling sound of gunfire arrived faintly above the engine noise, a half second or so after the victims fell. Behind him Ethne screamed in horror. Shock surged through him again, like an express train. The enormity of what he had witnessed, the absolute gut-rending brutality of it stunned him totally.

The helmsman reacted rapidly. As the others stood transfixed with horror, some instinct made the man react in a way which undoubtedly saved their lives. He threw himself on the tiller and, without slackening speed, heeled the boat hard over. They grabbed for a hand hold as the engine battled to drive them out of the turn and back the way they had come.

Looking astern Roomer saw the scene on shore fade rapidly as smoke drifted across to obscure the view once more. Moriarty's boatman, whether instinctively or not, also swung hard over and his boat too was now driving hard, back for the point. Now that they were turned Roomer started to doubt if they had done the right thing.

What about the people in the village? Shouldn't they try to help? What about the rest of the expedition?

"Turn around! Turn back!" he shouted but the man gave no sign that he heard.

Suddenly, twenty yards to port, he saw the lake surface boil as a burst of gunfire erupted in the water. A distant crackling noise arrived a split second later.

"They're shooting at us! They're shooting at us!" he yelled in panic.

"Get down!"

They dived for cover below the gunnels. He quickly realised that the gunmen must be shooting blind from the shore.

Thank God we veered off. If we can't see them for smoke then they can't see us! We must be nearly a mile and a half offshore now. Out of range?

He had no idea.

Dear Jesus let the smoke hide us, he prayed, as they raced for the safety of the point.

There was another burst of gunfire. This time there was no sign of it hitting the water.

Peering astern over the crouching helmsman he saw them cowering in the boat behind. At that instant its stern was engulfed in a spray of gunfire. Wooden splinters flew off in all directions and the helmsman pitched forwards out of sight. The burst lasted only a second but inflicted mortal damage. The boat lost way rapidly and slewed off course to port. A moment later Moriarty moved quickly from the bow to take over the tiller. Stewart was standing at the bow. An enormous wave of relief washed over him.

They're okay!

He saw the boat start to regain speed, coming back on course for the point. Then black smoke billowed from her engine which suddenly cut out. Her bow settled lower in the water as her speed dropped off rapidly. Roomer tugged at his boatman's arm and pointed astern. Again the man reacted instantly and began a tight turn back to the disabled boat.

Afterwards he could only remember events and images unfolding like a dream - coming alongside, the boat awash, water pouring in where she was holed, blood everywhere, three bodies - Ben and two locals - wallowing in the reddening water, bloody wounds gaping.

Moriarty held the two boats together as the surviving local clambered, terrified, into the arms of his friends in the other boat.

"Are they dead?" he heard himself ask, throat so dry he could hardly speak.

"Yes! Yes, they're dead! Shot to bits!" Moriarty gasped, clambering aboard with his day bag and shouldering the rifle.

Stewart too climbed over, hunched and unspeaking, deep in shock.

"Let's go! Let's go!"

They drove on again leaving the still-floating hulk awash in their wake. They heard no more gunfire and rounded the point in stunned immobility. The helmsman ran them straight in on the beach out of sight of the village on the far side of the island. Judging the depth well, the man cut the engine and let them ground gently on the shelving shore.

The engine noise died and Roomer became aware of the panting and sobbing of his companions as they tried vainly to take in the nightmare.

***

The boat lay in a foot of water, grounded on mud and listing to port. Its frightened occupants still slumped, unmoving. The roar of the engine, the screams and shouting and the gunfire had all stopped. An eerie silence now dripped and ticked in the calm afternoon.

Stewart was the first to move. Gently, so as not to frighten her, he disengaged himself from Ethne who was clinging to him in near-hysteria, her head buried in his chest. She looked at him dumbly, tear-stained eyes still wide with shock, blonde hair straggling down her face. He whispered her name. She nodded vigorously to say she had got herself together - at least for now. He looked at her carefully. She seemed okay, considering. He suspected she was a lot tougher than she seemed. He wrestled off his life-jacket and unearthed a cheroot. His hand shook slightly as he lit it. Around him the others began to stir.

"Dear God! Sweet Jesus... " Moriarty began.

"Shut it! Just bloody shut it!" Stewart shouted, surprised at the intensity of his reaction.

The need for action was overpowering. He stood up and went to vault over the side, intending to wade to dry land. The locals were yelling but too late! He landed with a splash, plunging thigh deep into gelatinous, black mud. It scared him but he had the presence of mind to grab the gunnel, twisting awkwardly to reach it with both hands. The others rushed over to help and the boat listed further towards him.

"Watch it! Watch it!" he yelled, cracking his chin on the gunnel when his hands slipped sideways.

Roomer made the others stay back and, one to each arm, he and Moriarty tried to haul Stewart back into the boat.

"Easy! Easy! I'm losing a boot!"

They waited while he struggled to pull his boot clear of the mud. At last it came free and the three of them lay gasping in the boat.

"Sorry Doctor." said David. "The men tried to warn you but you jumped too quickly. There are soft patches all around. They didn't see it until after we landed. We must push off and come in again further over, on harder ground." He pointed along the shore.

It was Moriarty who tried to articulate what everyone was thinking. "David, we're so shocked about Ben..."

All David could do was to nod and turn away, still in shock, his eyes filling. Stewart stared at Moriarty who sat hunched over, head in hands, looking at the floorboards.

Roomer forced himself to break the spell. "Come on everyone, let's get over to firmer ground."

It proved difficult to get the boat off the mud but eventually, after the boatmen made themselves understood, everyone went to the stern and she slipped off, engine roaring in reverse. They let the helmsman select his spot and he ran ashore once more killing the engine as they grounded, this time on firm foreshore. They pulled the boat far enough up to be sure it could not float away and trudged wearily across thirty yards of foreshore to where grey-green grass grew at the edge of the trees. The late afternoon heat was oppressive and the air was moving with thousands of tiny insects. They sprawled on the grass like a battle-weary platoon of soldiers, taking long overdue drinks from their water bottles.

Roomer again broke the silence.

"David. I want you to translate for the locals as I go along." David nodded and sat up. He continued, "I know we've been traumatised by what's happened but we can't just sit here. There's been some sort of terrorist attack - obviously..." He took a deep breath and began again.

"Is everyone okay? Ethne? Bob? Nobody hurt?"

They shook their heads, the villagers too.

Before he could go on the four boatmen began to argue but David managed to quieten them. "They want to go to the village Doctor," David said. "Their families..." There was no need to finish the sentence.

"I know. I'm sure they do, but we can't go back there yet surely?"

He began to speak softly to the villagers in Swahili, telling them that he understood how they must feel but that it would be best if they all continued to plan and act together as a group. As he spoke he saw it register on their faces when they realised he was a fluent Swahili speaker. He looked at his watch. Four-thirty. It would be dark in ninety minutes. Stewart saw surprise flicker briefly on the faces of Ethne and Moriarty too but it was a mild reaction. After what they had just experienced this revelation of Roomer's linguistic ability was of minor import. A sudden thought hit him and his heart missed a beat.

"Joe! Paul! They could be coming after us!" he yelled, struggling to his feet.

Everyone jumped up.

"Sssh! Quiet!" Roomer hissed.

Silence.

"Hell no! I don't think so. We'd have heard a boat by now. But you're right Bob, we'd better find out what's going on. I'm not sure about the radios Paul. Should we try to raise the village?"

"Yes! Of course! Why not for heaven's sake? I'd forgotten about them." he answered excitedly.

"Well we'd need to be careful." Stewart said deliberately. "The radios in camp could have... could have fallen into the wrong hands... I mean we don't know who will hear us if we call..." he tailed off.

Roomer cut through the discussion by lifting a radio to his lips. They froze in alarm as he called.

"Expedition HQ. Calling Expedition HQ. Can you hear me? Over."

A hiss of static was the only reply.

"Expedition HQ, this is Joe Roomer. Do you read me? Over."

Static again. He tried several more times without success.

"You'd better leave it Joe." said Stewart. "Maybe we're in a dead spot?"

"I doubt it. I'm afraid there's just nobody answering. We can try again from the other side of the island. David, get the binoculars from the boat. You and I and a couple of the locals will try and check out the village from the other side of the island." He pointed into the trees behind them.

"What about us?" said Ethne belligerently.

"There's no point all of us charging off." Stewart said, trying to calm her. "We'll check out the food and water. Sort out the boat."

He wanted to go with Roomer but a part of him did not. He was afraid of what he might see, how he would react.

'Sheila! Oh Sheila … '

He willed himself not to let his imagination run riot.

'Hugo and Tom are resourceful men,' he reasoned. 'If the village had any warning at all there was a good chance the field team were able to escape - or hide even.'

He had to hang on to that. The alternative was unthinkable. He promised himself that if Sheila and he survived this he would not hesitate any longer. He would make a life with her, immediately - if she would have him.

"Good idea Bob. You and Ethne sort out the boat." Roomer agreed.

"The island's only a couple of hundred yards wide at this point. It won't take us long to have a look. We'll be right back."

Ethne started to sob.

"Hang in there Ethne." Moriarty said gently.

"What about the others? What's happened to Sheila and Brendan and the others?" she wailed.

"I don't know. We'll have to try and find out what exactly has happened." Roomer said.

He and David set off into the trees waving a couple of the men along with him. The ground sloped gently upwards as they walked. Roomer estimated that the island was no more than twenty or so feet above lake level and perhaps a hundred yards wide at this end. The undergrowth was sparse and they had no difficulty skirting the few bushes in their path. Suddenly water glinted ahead. They ducked down to crawl on all fours to where they could lie side by side looking across water at the burning village some two miles away. At first he could see little but smoke and haze. Then, as his eyes adapted to the glasses, Roomer scanned the stretch of placid water in front of them. He saw only an unbroken expanse of water. He thought he would see the half-submerged hull of the other boat and, God forbid, perhaps bodies floating. There was see no sign of anything. He was relieved and yet frustrated - angry even! It was as if the lake had swallowed them without trace. Was life so cheap? Only a short while ago three fellow human beings had been slaughtered in front of him. Now they were gone - as if they had never existed. He scanned around to confirm there were no other boats in sight. Then he concentrated on the far shore and located the jetty area from where they had launched that morning.

He asked the men, "How many boats should be at the jetty?"

After a brief discussion they agreed that four other fishing boats should have returned by this time of day. They asked him how many he could see. He checked carefully.

Still holding the glasses to his eyes he said, "I see three... no, four boats." He paused. "I'm afraid they're all ablaze." he muttered, twisting round to look sadly at them.

They were stunned. This was a huge loss to the village economy. Roomer now realised that they were safe where they were, at least for the meantime. There were no other serviceable boats in the area. No-one else could reach the island.

"Can you see anything in the village?" David asked.

"I can't make it out. I suppose we should try the radio again." He rolled onto his side to extract the radio from a side-pocket of his safari coat.

"Expedition HQ. Are you receiving me? Over."

It was no use. After several more tries he switched off and put it away. He tried not to think about what might have happened to Hugo and the others. A clear image flashed into mind of Sheila laughing across the dinner table.

Dear God...

They lay a while longer trying to make out the village. Twice they thought they saw figures running through the smoke. The nearest huts still burned fiercely. They heard a short burst of gunfire. At that range it was a distant sound but Roomer felt his blood run cold.

Our team must be dead. There is no way they could have surrendered, judging by the slaughter they had witnessed earlier. Poor bastards. What a bloody nightmare!

He wondered if the boat party could make it to safety.

Eventually they withdrew and walked back to the others. Stewart and Moriarty were sorting out the boat and they trotted up from the shore when they saw them coming. He told them what they had seen. They agreed there was no time to do anything more that day. It would be dark in an hour. They would have to spend the night where they were. They could not risk going ashore anywhere else in the area. They could be attacked at any point along the lake. Who knew how big a gang was involved? It could be a whole army on the move. Where they had beached seemed a safe enough spot for the meantime. It would have to do. They hurried to carry all the food and water from the boat, along with their life jackets and spare clothing. They decided they could not risk a fire. The idea of it being visible for miles made them feel very vulnerable. They had nothing to cook anyway.

Sunset came quickly and they huddled together, dozing fitfully as they endured the night, shocked and bemused by what had happened.

Chapter 9

The trees

1430 hrs, 16 February

They moved sluggishly, trying to come to terms with the situation. Nottes made everyone drink plenty of water and eat the last of the sandwiches in the cool-box, before they spoiled. They could worry about more food sometime later.

Doyle was not in the least embarrassed by staying behind again with Sheila. Everyone accepted there was no point in him going far as he was the least physically fit member of the party. In any case, he felt a growing pride in his role of looking after Sheila who was still very stressed by the whole, gut-wrenching mess. Just now, she listlessly checked that the hand gun was within easy reach in her hip holster. The gun gave her no reassurance whatsoever but she reasoned there was little point in giving it to Doyle. It was hard to imagine him making a stand against a horde of charging terrorists.

She and Doyle settled down and the others started to plan what they would do. Hugo tried to organise the reconnaissance but Rent was having none of it. As each hour passed, the reality of their desperate situation became more obvious. There were other changes too. Hugo's position as 'Top Dog' was becoming less and less relevant. They had not consciously thought about this, but the new reality dictated that the previous pecking order was fast becoming redundant. In the meantime, no-one else had yet assumed overall command of the group. Out of habit, Hugo continued to boss them about but subtle changes were happening to the way they interacted. Rent certainly, and Nottes to a burgeoning extent, were now overtly questioning Hugo's opinions. This was an unconscious shift of attitude, so far. Each was a highly intelligent individual and a free thinker - a pre-requisite for a good research scientist. There were no macho types here, no dumb brutes with physiques and cretinous brains to match who would blindly follow orders. None of these men would be stupid enough to play Schwartzennager and die in a hail of bullets. They could all think for themselves, could analyse a problem and find the best solution for a given set of circumstances. In some ways this ability was a drawback. There was usually more than one practical option in every situation and, invariably, this group of intelligentsia identified alternatives and wasted time in reaching a consensus – and of course there would always have to be consensus. No-one was in overall charge, as Hugo would soon realise when he had time to stop and think. A Civil Service hierarchy was one thing, even an expedition hierarchy, but this had ceased to be an expedition the instant the first shots were fired. They were starting to realise they were in a fight for survival, so each one of them needed to understand all the implications of any proposed plan of action, to assess its pros and cons and to consider the risks to themselves and that of the group as a whole.

Crouched in the undergrowth, they debated what to do. Hugo wanted them to return to the Landrover as a group and reconnoitre the village from there. He was not keen on them splitting up and felt they would be safer sticking together. He argued there was more chance of one of them being spotted if they all went to different locations. Rent, and to a lesser extent Nottes, disagreed. Rent insisted that the main objective was to find out as much as possible about what was going on. A view from a single position, especially from the spot they were before, would tell them little. He wanted to split up, to work to the edge of the trees at different places to get a better picture of what was going on. Yes, the Landrover was near the village, but the terrorists could be spread throughout a wide area. Even if they saw nothing from a number of different positions that in itself would be worth finding out. They would know then there was a chance to escape in those directions.

Eventually, they agreed Hugo would go due east to the Landrover and Nottes would go north to the edge of the trees. They were uncertain how far north the trees extended but Lake Albert lay in that direction and should be no more than two or three miles away. Nottes was bound to reach it eventually and, while this would take him farther away from the village, they needed to find out the situation to the north. There was a risk of getting disorientated and lost in the trees so Nottes would take the sat-nav instrument. Hugo was confident he knew his way to the Landrover and back by now but they were worried about Rent who was to reconnoitre south. He insisted he could find his way there and back unaided. He would stay as close as he dared to the edge of the trees, keeping this to his left all the time. So far as they could remember, the tree-line curved eastward eventually, towards the hillside south of the village. The trees grew at least partly up the hillside and with the binoculars it should be possible to get a bird's eye view from higher up. Rent knew he would have to be very careful because, if they had any military prowess at all, the terrorists would have posted a lookout on the hill.

Nottes broached the subject they had all avoided.

"Look, if any of us is spotted I suggest we surrender immediately."

"You realise what that will mean?" Hugo said sombrely.

"Chances are we'd be dead meat. I know Hugo. But what we mustn't do is lead them back to the rest of us. I'll leave it to each of you of course. Depending on how it happens, if it happens, to try to avoid that if at all possible. I just wanted to make the point."

They nodded silently, each trying to make some mental provision for how they would handle it. Nothing more was said. Discussion over, they shook hands with some embarrassment, whispered quick goodbyes to Doyle and Sheila, and set off quietly in different directions. They planned to return by five o'clock at the latest, well before it got dark. Sheila checked her watch. It was three o'clock.

Hugo made good progress. It was hot and he was soon filthy from the dusty soil underfoot. He was thankful not to be wearing shorts as he crept around occasional patches of thorny vegetation. Luckily there were trails through the undergrowth and he was able to skirt most of the nasty stuff. After these detours he tried to get back on course again by checking his line of sight on large trees he used as route markers. He was able to keep his breathing under control this time, now that the initial terror was past. After a while he stopped to take stock. Alone for the first time a sudden feeling of vulnerability hit him. He became aware of animal noises, bird life above and around him and the sound of insects - cicada, he supposed. He wondered if the birds were making alarm calls as he approached. Would that give him away? Whatever, there was little he could do about it.'

They had joked yesterday about big game. It was a really strange feeling to be alone in the African bush. Was a big cat stalking him even now? Bugger it! What could he do? He had to press on regardless. He couldn't just crouch there indefinitely, trying to hear if he was being stalked. He probably wouldn't hear anything until it was too late anyway. This was ridiculous! Surely there was too much human activity for dangerous wildlife to inhabit this area, certainly not lions? He had heard no talk about villagers being attacked. With all the shooting surely there was even less chance of any predators being around? This was modern day, not the Africa of the Great White Hunters. Those days were long gone and much of the big game with them, poached out. Nevertheless, I'd better keep a weather eye out for snakes, particularly where I'm putting my feet. What about tree snakes?

He remembered hearing about the Boomslang, one of the most deadly of all. It was a tree snake and he had read it could move through the trees as fast as a man could run. He thought it was a Southern African species but wasn't sure. Anyhow, there was bound to be an equivalent local snake.

This won't do Hugo, he castigated himself. Get on with it! You've had your moment of indulgence, like a panicky schoolgirl. He blundered on once more.

He reached the edge of the trees once more, a few yards further along from where he and Rent were before. He decided it would be good policy not to emerge at exactly the same spot again so he crawled carefully under a low-growing bush to peer out over the hollow. He was a few feet higher than before, on a small mound, and had a good view of the Landrover which still stood as they had left it. From his higher vantage point he could see well down the track to the village beyond. He was shocked to see a number of vultures on the ground beside the bodies. He watched, mesmerised, as two more of the vile carrion eaters glided in to land, then flapped onto Adam's nearby corpse. They tore at the flesh with vicious beaks and he squeezed his eyes shut in revulsion. Steeling himself to look beyond, he saw smoke still rising from what he assumed were burning huts, although these were out of sight round a bend in the track. He was surprised the fires were still burning. Surely the tinder-dry dwellings would have burnt out some time ago? Perhaps it was the mud walls?

He checked his watch. Three-forty-five. He decided to stay put until four o'clock. If nothing moved by then, he would go back to Doyle and Sheila. Exhaustion washed over him and he inched back under the bush and rested his head on his forearms. He was not prone to self-doubt, arrogance being his usual frame of mind, but even he now took time to consider the immediate future. So far they had reacted to events. There had been little opportunity to think very far ahead. Things were bad, as bad as they could get, he reckoned.

He wondered if the outside world knew what had happened. In this decrepit country would they know about the terrorist activity? Was there any hope that the Ugandan Army would mount a rescue mission - were they capable of doing so? He just didn't know.

He began to accept that he might be killed but, as this realisation dawned, he could not identify precisely when the concept had first occurred to him. So he joined the ranks of those who have knowingly faced death - and he crossed, never to return, the chasm that defines this categorisation of the human race. Surprisingly, he was not unduly affected. A tiny part of him, the internal energy source, the incandescent spark that made him the competitive spirit that he was, still flamed brightly. If he was to be killed, he was to be killed. If, finally, he found himself trapped and there was no escape, then so be it. But there was no rule that said you had to submit meekly. Oh no! The Hugo Bamfords of this world would plan, scheme and fight to the end and this particular example of the genre would be no exception. Self-delusion was the key. Find some ember of hope, however faint, to latch onto - to use as a talisman. That was the secret. It was so easy, yet so many were not privy to the technique. Hugo no longer realised he still used the technique. It had become automatic over the years. Perhaps long ago as a day-dreaming boy he was aware of the usefulness of the ploy, but long term usage had dulled his awareness of it. It may have begun with a clinging hope for a new cricket bat or some other toy that was parentally refused. The technique demanded an assumption that his wish, his will, would eventually prevail - that he would get his cricket bat after all. Once this concept was sown in the mind it could be nurtured, bolstered carefully over time, until it grew to virtual certainty. It had no effect whatsoever on any practical outcome, at least not directly, but the approach did confer significant benefits. Firstly, in a child, it prevented sulking - the great thief of precious boyhood. So it made for a cheerful demeanour which adults prefer in children, especially boys. Indirectly, this could result in a change of heart, a reward for good behaviour - a cricket bat. However, true understanding and application of the technique did not link the original assumption with any eventual success. The core of it was the assumption *per se*. Most often final success could not be measured - there was no external outcome. It was the internal impact that was crucial. In adulthood the need for self-delusion was infinitely greater. In Hugo's case he used it to convince himself that a disastrous performance at a meeting was a triumph, that everyone was not bursting with barely contained mirth but rather were glassy-eyed in awe. It greatly helped too in not taking no for an answer. No need to be disappointed at being turned down, perhaps scornfully. Some nuance, any nuance in delivery of the refusal could be latched onto and fanned into a mental denial of the facts. That was precisely what he did now, automatically, lying in the African dust. He did it really well this time. A real beauty of a concept. In a flash of inspiration he saw a news conference. All the world's media were there, interviewing him, the hero who brought them all to safety. In that second Hugo knew with absolute certainty that, either he would die there or he would be an international celebrity. There would be no half measures. If he died, there would be no condemnation to endure, no questions as to why he organised the expedition, why he brought them all out here to die. And if he survived? Well, if he survived it would be against all the odds, a triumph of endurance and intelligence. The rationale for the expedition would be forgotten. No-one would think of criticising, at least not until long after the euphoria of rescue faded. If he could lead everyone to safety that too would guarantee a positive outcome. Every colleague that died would push the pendulum away from adulation towards the mid-point and beyond to castigation. Already he was beginning to fan the glimmer of the delusion. The logic might be flawed just yet but he was working on it… He let his imagination off the leash.

***

He burst awake to a tremendous din. A great, blasting roar was above him and gunfire came from all directions. His heart surged as it tried to cope with the adrenalin spike in his system. Damn! Damn! What was happening?

He twisted this way and that but saw nothing. Then he caught a glimpse of the helicopter banking at full power up and away over the trees behind him. The firing stopped. He heard it flying away, ever more distant, and listened until the noise faded and was gone. The entire episode was over in moments. Silence rushed in once more.

Where did it come from? Who was it? Why did he not waken earlier? Had he missed a rescue opportunity?

The thoughts tormented him and he tried to get himself under control. He checked the time. Ten to four. He was stiff, thirsty and very tired. Nothing moved in the area in front of him, except for the vultures, re-settling after the disturbance. The scene was as before. He decided there was no point in lying there any longer. There was nothing to see. Short of him strolling down to the village, and he wasn't that stupid, he would learn nothing more from this vantage point.

He gathered himself to wrestle up and start back. Suddenly, two heavily armed men walked into view thirty yards away. He froze, rigid with shock, then very slowly eased himself back down until he lay prone, and he hoped hidden, at the edge of the bushes. The men ambled slowly, coming from his left and heading away from him down the track towards the village. He heard them talking faintly but could not make out what was said. Both were Africans, dressed in shoddy, camouflage-patterned combat fatigues. Their bare heads sweated in the heat. They were well-endowed with ammunition belts slung on their shoulders and around their necks, brass casings twinkling in the sun. The shorter of the two shouldered an automatic weapon but Hugo was not experienced enough to identify this. He realised it must have been these two who had fired at the helicopter! It gave him a very strange feeling to see them. Enemy in sight at last! He grew angry at their strolling arrogance and had a strange inner deadness - a feeling he had never experienced before. Was that how people felt when they caught a glimpse of death?

He was greatly disturbed, even after the men passed out of sight round the bend in the track. He could not understand where they came from and tried to work it out. Eventually, he decided they must have been at the tree-line further along to his left, and had fired from there at the chopper. He hoped they were not searching for them? No. From the way they ambled along, it looked like they were just wandering around aimlessly. He certainly hoped so!

That's enough excitement for one day Hugo old boy, he told himself. Better get back to Sheila and Doyle. He began the careful stalk back through the trees, wondering how Nottes and Rent had made out.

He weaved through trees and scrub, very tired and struggling to keep going on the soft, dusty soil underfoot. He was forced to stop often to rest, slumped against a tree. Sweat ran down his face and seeped profusely from his back and chest. His shirt was drenched and he began to worry he might actually collapse. Fear of this gave him added resolve to push on. Earlier on, he had sunk to his knees to draw great gasping breaths, to give respite to his pounding heart. It was such an effort to get to his feet again he decided he'd better not risk any more rests or he might never make it back.

It would be dark soon. The thought of a night alone in the trees spurred him on once more. He wondered why he was so exhausted. Sure, it was frightening - terrifying - but through all that had happened so far he had been able to cope physically. He was not a fit man but was pleasantly surprised at how well he had managed so far - at least until half an hour ago. Perhaps the sleep had relaxed his body sufficiently for adrenalin levels to return to normal. When the helicopter startled him at the edge of the trees maybe his physiology was taken unawares? No, he realised that was rubbish. I've pushed myself too hard and now it's all catching up with me. He had not eaten all day and realised he must be very dehydrated by now. Sweating was adding to the problem. Calm down Hugo, he told himself. Take it steady and you'll be alright.

"Hugo! Over here!" Sheila called, a few yards to his left.

"Good grief! What's wrong? Are you okay?" She was very concerned when she saw his condition.

"I'm alright." he gasped, trying to get his breath back. "I'm okay, just winded."

He let her lead him the short distance to where Doyle stood over the gear. They handed him a water bottle and he took long, life-saving swallows, sitting against a tree.

"Where's Tom, and Peter?"

"Not back yet Hugo." Doyle answered. "But I'm sure they'll be back before dark. We've heard no shooting or anything from their direction. What was the racket in your direction? Was that a helicopter we heard?"

Hugo had recovered to an extent and told them what had happened. They listened quietly, not wanting to interrupt. As he spoke, Hugo checked the status of his companions. Doyle seemed more like his old self now, more confident. He had lost the haunted look of a few hours ago. Sheila too was more collected. She had fixed her appearance, combed her hair. Somehow this made them all feel better. If she was concerned again with her appearance their situation must have improved in some subtle way? It had not of course, but they felt a fraction better about it - just a fraction.

It was starting to get dark by the time Hugo finished explaining.

Suddenly Nottes called quietly. "Brendan, Sheila. Are you there?"

"Over here." Both Nottes and Rent stumbled into view a few seconds later.

"We met just now." Nottes gasped as they grabbed water bottles and sank to the ground.

Doyle and Sheila gathered the gear together and they prepared as best they could for a night in their make-shift camp. The hot, humid atmosphere made any effort difficult. All of them were badly in need of a wash. Their hair was lank and red dust from the forest floor soiled their clothes, hands and faces. Angry scratches on their arms and legs itched. Rent seemed to have suffered most in this respect. In the gathering gloom Sheila noticed a bad scrape across his forehead.

"Peter, that cut on your face looks deep. You'd better let me try to wash it. It could become infected. Let me..."

"No! In a minute." he snapped.

It was only then she realised he was wired up. What were those stains all over his clothes? Good grief, was it blood? She could hardly see him in the gathering gloom. No-one else seemed to notice.

Prompted by Hugo's questioning, Nottes described his sortie. He had made his way north-westwards with little difficulty, stopping regularly to listen for sounds of terrorist activity. He heard only the sounds of the forest until, after an hour and a half, he reached a point where the trees grew right down to the lake. The sat-nav told him he was about two kilometres west of the village but the topography of the shoreline at that point prevented him from having a view eastwards. He decided not to risk going any further east for a view of the village. Two kilometres was quite close enough! The objective was to find out whether or not they could reach the lake safely. He rested for half an hour, lying under bushes right on the shoreline. There was no activity out on the lake itself. The island offshore stretched east and west in front of him and he saw no boats or any human activity on the water. It took him over three hours to travel to the lake and back.

They discussed this for a while. It seemed a viable option if they decided to try to escape in that direction.

"What's your opinion Tom?" Hugo asked.

"Well, it's clear we could get there safely, at the moment. The question is what do we do when we arrive? I can't see an escape route beyond that point Hugo. There are no boats or anything, and it would be a hell of a trek westwards along the lake, away from the village."

"What else can we do?" Sheila asked.

"I've been thinking." Nottes replied. "Our only sensible option, if we went to the lake, would be to work our way back east, to the village..."

"What!" Doyle started to argue but Nottes cut him short.

"Only if we were sure it was safe to do so I mean. If we could find out that those murdering bastards had moved on... had evacuated the village and gone on to wherever they are headed, then our best chance of survival would be to get back to the village and wait there for a rescue mission. I'm reasonably sure they will move on. If they're part of some rebel army they must have some overall plan to push further south, deeper into the country. I can't imagine the village is their final objective."

They bandied this back and forth. Rent took no part in the discussion. Sheila assumed he was exhausted. He sat, eyes closed, with his head against a tree.

"We can't just stay where we are." Hugo said. "We're out of food and getting low on water. One night in these trees is as much as we can take and we're all getting generally knocked about with scratches and lack of decent rest. We'll have to find somewhere to get food and shelter."

"I agree." Doyle said. "Sheila especially."

"Watch it Brendan!" she snapped. "I'm in the same state as everyone else, but don't think I'm any less able than the rest of you."

"Okay Sheila, okay," Hugo said gently. "Brendan's naturally concerned about you, like all of us. Put it down to male chauvinism," he smiled at her in the dark.

"If we're contemplating going back to the village why don't we just go from here?" she asked. "Why go all the way to the lake first? Surely we'd be much better able to check it out from this end - to see when they leave? It's only half a mile from here."

"We're going to the lake." Rent said quietly. They turned to stare blindly in the dark, in the direction of his voice and sensed immediately that he would brook no argument.

"What happened Peter? What did you see?" Sheila asked gently. There was no reply.

"Peter?" Hugo prompted. "I assume you found things pretty much as Tom did... "

"You assumed wrong."

They sat quietly, waiting for him to tell it in his own time. He began to speak. His disembodied voice made Sheila shiver in the blackness. She huddled between Nottes and Doyle as his tale of horror unfolded.

He had made good time initially although he tried to be as quiet as possible. The rifle was a hindrance, snagging occasionally as he weaved through the undergrowth, and he alternated between carrying it across his chest and slung on his shoulder. He followed the tree boundary, staying as far away from the actual edge as possible without losing sight of the open ground beyond. He saw and heard nothing until he estimated he was south of the village. At that point he worked his way cautiously to the edge of the trees. His dead reckoning was almost spot on. He found himself just thirty yards from the base of the hill. He stayed put for a good ten minutes, making a careful visual survey of the area. Open ground stretched in front for several hundred metres to more trees beyond. Red-brown earth was dotted with patches of green grass and scrub. There was no-one in sight, no human sounds. The ground to the left, towards the village, rose slightly preventing him from seeing far in that direction but smoke still rose against the blue sky. To his right the steep-sided hillside was bare in places but tree-covered near to him. It was just as he remembered it.

He began a careful descent of the hill, following the line of the trees as they crept up its western side. This was the most dangerous part. If this gang of butchers had any military training at all they would have stationed a lookout on the high ground. This hill was the most obvious one in the area. He made his way slowly through the trees, up and round the back of the hill, intending to approach from the side farthest from the village and creep up to the summit for a panoramic view. The trees were thinner now and there was less cover than before. He felt very exposed and his progress became slower and slower until he reached a point about twenty yards below the top of the dome-shaped hill. The summit was completely bare, only red-brown soil and stones stretched up in front of him to the top. He lay down beside a dense grey-green bush to recover his breath and summon his resolve.

He was struggling up to his knees when the sound of voices came from over the top of the rise. Instinctively, he clutched the rifle to his chest and flung himself sideways in under the bush. Thorns snagged on his clothes and tore his flesh as he wriggled desperately into the base of the bush. He lay there panting, hoping the violent movement of the bush would cease before he was discovered. He could just see through the foliage but only for ten feet or so. The voices were closer. He heard them clearly now, rough gutteral phrases - Swahili, he assumed. He tried to control his breathing. His heart was pounding. He was afraid to make the slightest movement.

Suddenly, a body was thrown to the ground a few feet away, right in his field of view. It was an African woman. A villager? She lay on her back, inert. She had been badly beaten. Her head was turned towards him and her battered face was bloodied and swollen. Blood streaked her naked torso. An emerald green skirt lay open, exposing her lower legs. Bright bracelets glinted on her right arm, flung out towards him. It was impossible to tell if she was dead or alive.

He caught the whiff of cigarette smoke as an intermittent conversation began. There were two of them, still out of his line of sight. He was transfixed by the woman and a sense of dread overcame him. The strain on his neck muscles was unbearable as he held his head up to stare at her. Careful not to disturb the foliage, he slowly lowered his head until it lay on the warm, dusty soil. He was lying on the rifle and it was hurting his chest. He had to move it. Slowly, ever so slowly, he rolled to his left trying not to shake the bush. Carefully, he eased his right arm forwards so that he could support himself in position and, with his left hand, tried to ease the weapon out from beneath him. He thought his lungs would burst with the effort of controlling his breathing. The woman lay unmoving and the conversation continued a few feet away. He froze each time the talking stopped and tried to synchronise his movements so that the voices covered any slight sounds he might be making. He wanted to get the rifle into a position where he would have a chance of defending himself. His full weight pinned his upper left arm and he could only move it from below the elbow. It was cramping with effort. He twisted his neck around to make sure that as he eased the rifle forwards it did not snag on a branch. He worried that he would push soil into the end of the barrel. If he fired it with the slightest obstruction there was a real risk it would blow up in his face. Sweat ran into his eyes and dripped to the ground. With a supreme effort of control he pushed the rifle stock as far forwards as his arm could manage, keeping a close watch on the end of the barrel. His arm and chest muscles shuddered in agony as he lowered himself on to his stomach again, his cheek on the rifle stock, the weapon pointing straight out in front of him, directly at the woman. He lay exhausted, waiting for his body to recover. After a few moments he eased off the ground once more, just enough to move the rifle into the firing position at his right shoulder. At least it was loaded. He had stalked through the trees with a fully-loaded ammo clip and a round up the barrel. Good job he had! He couldn't have worked the rifle bolt without the metallic noises being overheard.

Suddenly the conversation altered and he realised the men were going away. They called to each other, then it went quiet. Someone was coming back. A heavily-built, evil-looking African threw himself down beside the woman. He sat in clear view on the far side of her, side-on to him. The man was very drunk. As if to confirm this, the thug raised a half-empty gin bottle to his lips. Rent saw the sweat glint off his black face. He was dressed in camouflages, and wore an ammunition belt across his chest. The tableau continued for five minutes or more and he became convinced that the man's companion had left him alone on the hill with the woman.

Was this was the lookout? How was he going to extricate himself? He couldn't lie here until dark. There was no hope of crawling away unheard. What could he do?

The man finished the bottle and flung it away. He lit a cigarette, slumped in the classic drunk's position - head down, legs splayed. There was no sign of his weapon but it must be nearby. The woman moaned softly. The man lifted his head and stared vacantly at her. Then, grunting with the effort, he wrestled off his ammunition belt. Rent sensed immediately what was going to happen. The man struggled to his feet, reeling from side to side as he unzipped his trousers. He fell to his knees on top of her legs. She moaned in pain. He tried unsuccessfully to rip away her skirt, then fumbled at his waist trying to draw a knife. She tried to raise her head and lifted an arm, drawing up a knee in a feeble attempt to defend herself. Rent was sick with horror and a terrible rage possessed him. All thought for his own safety was gone. He was no longer in control of his actions but something in his subconscious told him not to use the rifle. A shot would be heard from below. He struggled up, straining to keep the woman in view. The couple was still not aware of his presence although the bush shook violently as he struggled towards them, tearing his arms and clothing on the vicious thorns. Just as he forced his head through the foliage the man, still kneeling between the woman's legs, twisted towards him in surprise. He held a six-inch knife in his left hand, the hand nearest to his charging attacker. Rent did not hesitate. He was way past the point of control and hurled himself forwards. He got good purchase a stride away from the man and launched himself through the air. The man flung up an arm in self defence and Rent ducked to avoid the knife. It sliced across his forehead as they hit shoulder to shoulder, both crashing off the woman to land heavily in a thrashing heap beside her. They were badly winded but Rent knew he must fight fast. He was no match for a fit terrorist, no matter how poorly trained. The man's drunkenness was his only advantage. He wrenched himself round on top and head-butted him, breaking his nose. All control gone, he punched in a frenzied attack, raining rapid blows to either side of his head. He remembered the knife and stopped punching to grab both arms, pinning them to the ground. The man was badly dazed, and lay with his eyes closed, snoring through his smashed nose. Rent sat on top of him sucking in great lungfuls of air. He looked around for the knife. There was no sign of it. He must have dropped it.

With a hoarse roar the man flung him off like a rag doll. His sheer brute strength terrified him. In that instant he knew he had no chance of beating him into submission. He landed heavily on his back and instinctively flung out an arm to break his fall. His right wrist hit the knife, almost buried in the dusty soil. The man was on him immediately. He spat bloodily in Rent's face and swung a vicious haymaker of a punch to the side of his head. Rent managed to get his forearm in the way to partially block the blow.

If one of those landed he was dead!

With the last of his strength he grabbed the knife and drove it hard and deep into the man's side. He screamed and fell forwards onto Rent's face. He stabbed again but the knife skidded off his back. He writhed in agony, reaching back to his wounded side. Suffocating, Rent used a strength borne of terror to roll him off. Without hesitating he gripped the knife in both hands and, from above his head, drove it deep into the centre of the man's chest. His body arched and he screamed again, clutching at the wound in his chest. Sobbing in panic, Rent drove it in again. The man went rigid, then convulsed violently. Rent lost his grip on the hilt of the blood-covered knife still buried deep in the man's chest. The death throes subsided and, horror-struck, he clambered off the body and crawled a few feet away. His mind dimly registered the bladder emptying at death. The stench of blood and urine was overwhelming. He sat hunched on his knees as with a final sigh the death rattle left the man's throat.

A few moments later, still dazed with shock, he crawled over to the woman. She was dead. He made sure by feeling for a non-existent pulse at her neck, trying not to look at her savagely beaten face. He forced himself to his feet and, exhausted, staggered over to retrieve his rifle. He lifted his water bottle from the dust. The terrorist's automatic rifle lay propped across a rock. He ignored it and, without a backward glance at the scene of horror above, stumbled down the hill back into the trees.

***

They were appalled, stupefied. Sheila became aware of Hugo trying gently to prise her hand off his arm. She had gripped it ever more tightly as Rent's story unfolded. She released her grip and shivered as Hugo took her hands in his to comfort her.

"Oh Peter." she whispered, letting him know she sympathised deeply.

The others sat silently not knowing what to say, analysing their thoughts, afraid of saying the wrong thing. Surprisingly, it was Doyle who broke the ice.

"Well done Peter! Bloody well done! Excellent. You did absolutely the right thing! Thank God you're safe."

Hugo and Nottes joined in, murmuring their agreement. Rent made no reply.

***

The night was warm and humid. They dozed intermittently, restless and disoriented in a pathetic, huddled group. Occasional rustling and forest noises disturbed them throughout the night. They were too overwhelmed by events to be much concerned about dangers from the forest itself. Rent's trauma had brought it home how close they were to violent attack, to being brutalised by a primaeval force so alien to their normal experience. Sheila and Doyle, each unaware of the other, prayed for much of the night. Doyle reverted to his ritualistic Catholicism, silently reciting Hail Marys and stylised liturgies remembered from boyhood. He swore on the Virgin Mary time and again that, if she spared him - brought him safely through - he would go to Mass every Sunday and give generously to the poor. That was all he had, no other prop, just this quasi-pagan belief based on icons and images, this deal-doing approach to his physical salvation. He thought nothing about his soul. Saving his skin took priority.

Sheila's reaction to fear and terror was changing as time went by. Her character refused to let her knuckle under. Her natural drive and fighting spirit had helped her through a male-dominated career area and now it re-asserted itself.

I am not going to fold here, she told herself. There must be a way out for us if we do the right things. She prayed to God to save her, to help her. Dear God forgive all my sins I pray. Please, look after me, protect me, protect Bob. Please God help me... She prayed directly and earnestly for help. No deals, no promises. She wanted salvation of her soul, the slate wiped clean so that if death came she would be ready, cleansed to go to her Maker. In contrast to Doyle, her prayers strengthened and reaffirmed her faith, renewed her strength to face the future. She wished Bob was with her. She prayed he was safe, but tried not to think about him. That way the panic beating of her heart was avoided, her terrified shaking for him was lessened. Dear God, bring him safely back to me...

Chapter 10

The Island

0530 hrs, 17 February

Dawn revealed another clear, calm day. It took a long time to work the stiffness from their limbs. Cold water was no substitute for hot coffee. They had discussed what to do during the long night. They would move from their present location to the western end of the island, a distance of about five miles. From there, they would check out the mainland carefully and, if there was no sign of terrorist activity, they would go across and land, hopefully undetected, a couple of miles west of the village. There was no other realistic course of action. Trying to get as far away as possible was not an option. The locals were adamant they were going back to the village as soon as possible. They insisted on finding out what had happened to their families. The Europeans felt the same. They could not contemplate leaving the area without finding out what had happened to Hugo and the others even though they feared the worst. In any event they were low on fuel. Each day's sampling was planned with a safe fuel margin but there was not enough left to go very far.

Roomer and Moriarty convinced the others that the two of them should set off on foot to explore westwards along the island. Then, if it was safe, the boat could be brought round. The further west they went, the further they would be from the village but they could check out the mainland as they moved along the island. There would be no point trying to land in an area that was alive with terrorists. While Roomer and Moriarty explored along the island, the others would keep a lookout on the village. The fires would be burnt out by now and the smoke should have cleared. It might be they would be able to see if the terrorists had left. Apart from all of this, none of them were keen to draw attention by starting up the boat engine. They knew how far noise carried across the lake. It would be better to explore first on foot. Then there was the mud. Roomer and Moriarty could check out the shore at the western end to find the best spot to beach the boat. They could keep in radio contact as they went.

The two men organised as best they could. They re-packed their 'day bags' with a share of what little food remained, some dried meat and fruit. Each had a bottle of purified water. Stewart insisted they took the rifle and hand gun. There seemed to be little immediate danger in their present position and, although the island was probably deserted, no-one could predict what they might encounter. Apparently the locals seldom landed on the island. There was little incentive to visit its muddy shore. Roomer politely declined a half-hearted offer from a villager to accompany them. He knew the man would much prefer to stay and keep a close watch on his village.

The men had grown more and more morose during the night. Stewart had seen it before in Africa. Instead of developing a healthy rage, a blazing need for action, they sank into themselves, allowing an overwhelming fatalism to engulf them. He hoped it was only a phase in the trauma affecting everyone. He suspected they might need a lot of help from these men if they were to survive and their present state worried him greatly.

While Roomer and Moriarty packed, Stewart trotted across the island to recce the village. Ethne insisted on coming with him. She had perked up considerably since yesterday and he was more convinced than ever that, beneath her mild exterior, she was made of strong stuff. They studied the entire area carefully but saw no sign of life in the village. A faint pall of smoke drifted skywards from still smouldering boats and burnt out huts. Nothing moved. They were about to go back when the faint but distinct sound of a long burst of automatic gun-fire crackled from the general area of the village. The sound made his heart beat faster and he flushed as the memory of yesterday's horrors returned. He sensed Ethne stiffening beside him.

"Come on Ethne. We'd best get back."

She got up quickly and, without a word, set off through the trees. He caught up with her and gently placed a comforting hand on her shoulder as they walked.

Roomer and Moriarty were waiting and ready to set off.

"What does it look like?" Roomer asked.

Stewart hesitated for a moment to let Ethne answer but, realising she was still shaken, he described what they had seen and heard. David relayed this to the men who digested it without any visible change to their lethargic state.

"So they're still there." said Moriarty, struggling a day-bag onto his back.

"Yes. I suppose you'd better go ahead as planned. It's early yet. If they're going to leave there's still a chance they'll evacuate the village later in the day."

"Right Bob. Paul and I'll get started. We'll give you a quick call every…"

He checked his watch. "Its nine-fifteen now. We'll call on the half hour and hour mark. Okay? First call at nine-thirty - just to report all's well."

He made to leave but turned back with a grin.

"Oh, by the way, don't call us. We'll call you."

He held out his hand and Stewart shook it firmly. They locked eyes for a moment. Moriarty shook hands. Roomer took Ethne by the shoulders, whispered to her quietly and gave her a peck on the cheek. Her tears welled quickly as Moriarty also kissed her and hurried after his colleague, adjusting the rifle slung on his shoulder. Stewart and Ethne stood frozen, watching as the two strolled off along the deserted shoreline. Moriarty stopped a hundred yards away, just before they disappeared around a curve. He turned to stare at them for a moment and raised his arm in an expansive, manly wave. They waved back and he turned quickly and loped off out of sight to catch up with Roomer. An unexpected burst of emotion swept over Stewart. It was so strong he almost sobbed. Ethne experienced it too and she clung to him.

"Oh Bob! Bob! Will they be alright?"

He could not speak. They hugged each other, then turned to David and the men.

"Right…" He cleared his throat. "Right David, let's get organised. Will you take a couple of the men to keep a watch on the village while Ethne and I finish sorting out the boat?"

He looked down at the four villagers huddled together in an almost catatonic state.

"On second thoughts… Ethne, would you go with David? Let the men lie there."

He nodded at the pathetic group and she agreed.

"You'd better take the radio, and keep in contact with Joe and Paul. They're due to call in ten minutes. Can you stick it over there for an hour or so? I want to go over the boat carefully to see if I can find anything useful. Maybe one of these boys will help me."

He nodded at the men again.

"Oh Bob, be careful. Don't stray far. I might need to find you quickly…"

"Don't worry Ethne. I won't go out of sight of here… I promise. Come back when you have to, and come back right away if Joe and Paul don't call in at any point. Understood?"

Reassured, she nodded and trudged off after David.

Stewart went down to the boat. The first thing that caught his eye was his spinning rod lying under a seat. Suddenly he had an idea.

***

Roomer and Moriarty set a moderate pace. It was easy going. The almost lawn-like Kikuyu grass carpeted the island luxuriously down to where the mud of the foreshore began. They walked on the grass for a while and Roomer wondered if it was being grazed by something. Bush pigs? There was no sign of life and with each passing minute their confidence increased. They still kept to the grass though. It felt safer than being totally exposed out on the mud. Roomer reasoned there was no point trudging through mud. They were not going to land the boat along here anyway. It would be important to check out the shore carefully at the end of the island, but not until then.

The shoreline meandered gently in and out but stretched more or less due west. They paused for Roomer to check their position on the sat-nav. They already knew the approximate dimensions of the island and the fact that it lay east-west. They had pored over the lake charts for many hours in the last few weeks and almost knew the topography of the area off by heart. Moriarty shielded his eyes to look northwards, out across the lake. In spite of his shocked state its immensity and the sheer splendour got to him. A heat haze was already playing tricks with the horizon where silver water merged with cobalt sky.

Still gazing across the lake, he said. "It must be time to check in Joe."

"Roomer to Stewart. Roomer to Stewart. Are you hearing me? Over."

Ethne's reply came clearly and immediately.

"Ethne here Joe. Receiving you loud and clear. Are you okay? Over"

"Okay here Ethne. Where's Bob? Over."

"He's at the boat. I'm watching the village... with David. Over."

"Okay Ethne. Better save batteries. Will call again at ten o'clock. Over and out."

"Understood. Over and out. Be careful."

They smiled thinly at each other at her minor lapse of radio etiquette.

"Shouldn't we try to raise the village again?"

"I'm not keen Paul. Don't ask me why. My instinct tells me not to at the moment. In fact I can't shake off the feeling those bastards are listening to us every time we're on air. We haven't heard anybody else on the radio - which tells me that Hugo and the others can't be using theirs. If they could hear us talking to Ethne surely they would have called us just now, if they could..."

He let it dangle.

"Come on, let's move on. If we keep going at a steady pace we should get to the far end in about three hours all told - allowing time to check out the mainland as we go."

"If the others spot those buggers leaving, they can come and pick us up by boat right away."

"I can't see that Paul. What are they going to see at long range that absolutely convinces them that it's safe to steam back to the village in broad daylight. Think about it."

He looked at his companion.

"No. Our best bet is to assume they're still there and sneak across to the mainland well west of the village, close to darkness if we can. Then we can make our way carefully on foot back towards the village and find out what the story is. Come on, let's go."

They set off once more.

***

The group of Africans lay moribund under a tree. Stewart got an occasional whiff of their home-grown tobacco, suspecting it was part marijuana, which grew locally. He became engrossed in setting up his spinning rod and forgot all about them. He realised he was ravenously hungry. None of them had eaten anything substantive since lunch-time the previous day. The shock of yesterday's events had left a hollow ache in their stomachs. They usually carried only sufficient food for the day's sampling and that was long finished. They had plenty of water and the means to purify as much as they needed. He gave silent thanks to Roomer's planning thoroughness. He could not be criticised as being too fussy this time.

He decided he could light a fire to cook something to eat, a few fish if he could catch them. They had to eat and when he thought it through, he could not see how a small fire would endanger them. So what if anyone saw it? What could they do? There were no serviceable boats in the area, except for their own.

Further along the shore, clear of the boat, he tucked his trousers into his socks and waded carefully out into the lake. He waded quite a distance before the water was up to his knees, soaking him up to the thigh. He looked down at his mud-covered trainers and tried in vain to remember his zoology. I should know the risks from water-borne parasites but I can't remember a thing. Still, that's the least of my worries.

He began spinning, tossing the lure in a curving arc of a lazy, well-practised cast. Spasmodically, he began retrieving - quite fast for a few turns of the reel, more slowly for a turn or two, then quickly again - trying to imitate with the lure the swimming motions of a small, injured fish. He half-expected a strike on his first cast. Not this time. There were no signs of fish at all. Cast after cast he tried, working the immediate area by casting in a slightly different spot each time. He glanced at his watch. Ten to ten. Okay, I'll give it five more minutes, then I'll take a break in case Ethne wants me to spell her on watch. He wanted to hear that Roomer and Moriarty were okay, when they radioed in at ten o'clock.

Bang! The fish hit the lure like an express train and he jumped with surprise. It seemed to be a good-sized fish, not as big as the very first one, but a pound or two in weigh, a nice size for eating. It fought well, making several strong runs for freedom. He set the reel drag quite slackly and the fish was able to strip line off him easily. This suited for the moment as he walked steadily backwards out of the water, rod held high. Without a landing net and someone to help, he would have to fight this one to the water's edge and make a grab for it. Soon he was playing the fish close to the shore. It was tiring rapidly. He guided it towards his feet, catching sight of it for the first time in the peat-coloured water. Nice one! About two pounds, he reckoned. Another Nile perch. He didn't care what it was, it was going on the fire! He brought it to the water's edge and, with his right foot, swept it out onto dry land where it thrashed noisily, glinting in the sun.

"Well done!" Ethne called, from a few yards along the shore.

"Did Joe and Paul check in okay?"

"Yes. They're fine. They called five minutes ago - at ten on the dot."

"What about the village? Did you see anything?"

He stood beside her holding his rod in one hand and the flapping fish in the other.

"I'm not sure I saw anything. It's so hard to make out in the haze and the glare. We can't be sure if the village is deserted or not."

She was probably right.

"I came to see what you were up to. I'll go back on watch in a minute."

"Are you hungry?"

"Gosh yes!" she exclaimed, with the first flicker of a smile since...

"Give me a hand to gather stuff for a fire."

"A fire? Are you sure?"

"Yes. It'll be okay." He smiled at her. "I just *have* to eat some grilled perch. Don't you?"

"Will I ask them to help?" She nodded towards the Africans.

He was beginning to get annoyed with them.

"No. Let them lie there. We'll do it ourselves. There's plenty of dry sticks lying around."

They tore paper from their sampling notes without a thought. They were a total irrelevancy now. His cigarette lighter got it going and soon a small fire was blazing on the beach. He made a mental note to conserve the lighter as much as possible. They would need it again.

Waiting for the flames to die down so he could grill the fish over the embers, he gutted it, slitting its belly and de-scaling it, then washing it clean at the water's edge. He found the aluminium container housing the oxygen meters and broke off the lid at its hinges. Cutting off the head and tail, he laid the fish on the aluminium lid and set it on the embers. In a few minutes it was cooked on both sides. Ethne turned it with a twig. Using his floppy hat he carried the hot lid over to the boat and they attacked the steaming fish with their fingers. It was delicious. Neither spoke as they sucked and blew at steaming pieces of hot fish.

Eventually she sat back. "That was one of the most memorable meals I've ever had! I'd no idea I was so hungry."

They finished off with a long drink of water. He carefully smoked a precious cheroot.

I may have to go onto marijuana when these run out, he smiled to himself. The thought of Sheila quickly wiped the smile off his face. We can't just sit here, waiting for something to happen! I hope Roomer and Moriarty keep moving.

Ethne headed back into the trees and he washed his hands at the lake edge. Might as well try to get a few more fish to cook, he thought. I suppose the men need food. We can take some round for Joe and Paul when we go.

He walked off with the rod again, glaring angrily at the group beneath the tree.

***

"Do you think it's okay?" Roomer whispered as they crouched at the edge of the scrub staring out across a wide mud foreshore.

"Depends what you mean by 'okay'. Anyway, we've no choice. We have to check out the mud before we call the boat round. The water must be a quarter mile away out there." Moriarty was hyperventilating as he hissed his reply. Roomer wondered why he was so agitated.

"Alright Paul?"

"Fine, fine." But he could see he was not.

"Right, let's go. Have you the pistol handy?"

"Do we need to lug the bags and the guns all the way out there? What's gonna harm us - birds?"

"Look Paul, this is a bloody serious situation and I'm not going to waltz out there in the open without some means to defend ourselves. I think we should bring all the gear. Give me the handgun if you like."

"No, it's okay. I'll bring it."

"And make sure you have a clip in, and one up the spout!"

"I know how to use it, okay?"

"Make sure you keep the safety on and don't wave it under my nose!"

"Look ! I said I know how to handle it! Let's go... what are you doing now?"

"I'm just checking the rifle."

"Good grief! Is all this really necessary?"

"I told you Paul - I think it is, and if you're not going to play ball then stay there and I'll go myself!"

He was astonished by this sudden display of belligerence from Moriarty. What the hell was the matter with him? Stress?

"Okay, okay- but don't point that rifle up my backside!"

"Paul ! Humour me. Please! If we carry on like this it's going to be a disaster. We all want to get out of this - so let's play it ultra-safe."

Moriarty heaved a deep sigh.

"Joe, you're right. I'm sorry. I'm all wound up I can't take in what's happened to us."

"I know Paul, I know. I'm wired up myself. Let's both try to calm down."

They emerged from the scrub and padded slowly across the grass towards the muddy shore. Subconsciously, they began in a crouch but with each step in the open, they gradually became fully erect. There was no-one to see them here.

The heat was intense and Roomer squinted at the far extent of the lake, lost in a blue-grey glare of heat, water and thermals. There was a varying drone of flies and other insects but no birds, either wading or flying. He glanced at Moriarty slightly ahead of him and was surprised at the amount of sweat soaking the back of his shirt. He was swivelling his head from side to side, as if checking for any sudden attack.

"Relax Paul." he whispered. "I thought I was the one who was nervous?"

"Why are you whispering? There's no-one within miles."

Ignoring the reply, Roomer paused and slowly stepped down the two foot bank onto the dried mud of the lake beach. Moriarty joined him and, with a grunt, sat down on the edge of the bank.

"This bank must mark the extent of the lake at the height of the rainy season." Roomer said.

The water's edge was several hundred yards away across a gently sloping brown mud shore.

"It looks firm enough Joe. Whatdya think?"

"I think we'd better walk out to the water's edge to make sure."

"Make sure of what?"

"To make sure it's firm all the way out to the lake and to see if it's firm underwater. It's such a gentle slope here we'll probably have to wade out quite a bit to get aboard the boat."

Moriarty got awkwardly to his feet and they set off once more, this time walking more confidently across the hard-baked mud towards the water's edge, gleaming up ahead.

Roomer checked the rifle's safety was on and carried it diagonally across his chest. Moriarty concentrated on placing his feet carefully as he walked amongst the scattering of stones half-embedded in the mud. There were extensive cracks in the mud, testimony to long days of exposure to searing heat. Roomer checked carefully, but there was no sign the mud was any softer closer to the water. He realised that, here and there along the shore, trenches - shallow channels really - ran parallel with them down to the water. The channels became deeper towards the water's edge. The channel they were walking along, Roomer on its left edge and Moriarty a couple of yards to his right on the othe edge, was a foot deep now, and deepening.

Neither spoke for some time, each engrossed in careful examination of their immediate environment. They reached the water's edge and stopped.

"This is ideal Paul. Look, the channel has nearly two feet of water in it now and yet we're still standing on dry land. We can bring the boat up the channel and it will still be afloat at the edge of the lake here. We can step into it from here."

He looked up to see his reaction and was mildly surprised to see that Moriarty had waded twenty yards on out into the lake. He was standing in about a foot of water, slightly stooped, peering intently down into the underwater channel in front of him.

"How deep is the channel out there? Does it run on out into the lake?"

Moriarty gave no indication that he heard.

"Paul?" he tried again.

In the same instant he drew breath to call him a third time, Roomer saw him galvanise into action, trying desperately to drag the hand-gun from his waistband as he started to back away from the edge. In the split second it took for that image to register on his brain Moriarty vanished in a maelstrom of spray and thrashing.

Shock hit Roomer like a thunderclap.

Reflexes took over and he stumbled towards the nightmare unfolding before his eyes. His right foot felt nothing out over the lip of the channel and he fell clumsily towards the surface of the water, dropping the rifle as he threw both hands up instinctively, eyes widened in terror, heart bursting with the horror of the snapshot in front of him as he went under.

The big crocodile's attack bite took Moriarty by the left leg and his kneecap was tearing off. He dropped the pistol and was holding frantically with both hands to the crocodile's see-sawing snout, his head thrown back in agony, screaming in terror.

Surfacing from his plunge, Roomer shook his head to clear his eyes and scrambled wildly for a purchase to lever himself up out of the channel, all the time trying desperately to keep sight of his friend.

The vicious impact had knocked Moriarty onto his backside, legs out over the edge of the channel, upper body in the shallows but being dragged inexorably into deeper water. The crocodile's powerful tail thrashed vigorously from side to side spraying great gouts of muddy water high in the air.

"Shoot it! Shoot it!" he screamed, flinging his head from side to side in agony.

"Paul! Paul! Oh God Paul!" Roomer moaned as he struggled to rise, feeling around him aimlessly in the mud for the rifle.

The crocodile suddenly snapped forwards, clamping its terrible jaws around Moriarty's thigh, trapping his right hand and wrist in the new bite. Still he flailed with his free arm but, more confident of the hold it now had on him, the crocodile made a supreme effort. In an irresistible flesh-rending twist, the beast flung its prey down and sideways and found enough purchase to drag him quickly and violently under the surface. One second the horror struggle was in view, the next it was gone, leaving only a bloody mud swirl at the surface, and a slowly turning floppy hat.

Roomer's right hand found the rifle barrel. He dragged it up clear of the water, managing to struggle to his feet at last.

He just could not take it in. His brain told him that any second now the struggle would burst to the surface and he would have to risk a shot if there was to be any hope of saving Moriarty.

He waited hunched, rifle at his shoulder, for what seemed like an eternity, a few feet away from where the animal had dragged its terrified victim below the water.

Nothing.

No sign.

No noise except his hyperventilating.

Eventually, very gradually, his unconscious logic took over and he sank slowly to his knees in the shallow water. His head hung down, forehead nearly touching the rifle across his legs. With a deep breath he threw his head back and screamed the loudest, most terrible scream of his life.

***

Stewart was worried. He could see Ethne was too. She sat astride the seat amidships, hunched forward, elbows on knees, fists clenched, head down, staring at the floorboards. Occasionally she twisted to glance over her shoulder at the shoreline sliding slowly past as they steamed westwards. She sat with her back to the shore, as if afraid to face it, afraid of what they might find.

It was two o'clock. They had heard nothing from Roomer and Moriarty since the scheduled eleven-thirty call. Stewart only realised they had missed a call at a few minutes after twelve. He was fishing away, picking up a small fish every so often, when Ethne re-appeared looking very concerned. Roomer and Moriarty had not checked in at eleven-thirty she explained. She waited for fifteen minutes and still they did not call so she tried but could not raise them. Trying not to panic, she decided to wait until the next scheduled call at noon. At five past twelve she came running to tell him.

He knew immediately they must be in trouble. They tried the radio again but there was no answer. He was aware that the effective range of their hand-held VHF radios was limited to only a few miles 'line of sight' but he would have expected Roomer and Moriarty to be well within range. They gathered all the gear back into the boat as quickly as possible and yelled at the men to get moving, surprised how they jumped to obey. David explained the situation to them and now they were in the bow, wide awake, scanning the shoreline intently. Their helmsman too squinted at the passing shore. Stewart and David used the binoculars every few minutes, sweeping the foreshore and the edge of the trees behind. He checked the time. Twelve-forty. He reckoned they had launched at about twelve-thirty. They were steaming at full speed about half a mile offshore. He stayed at that distance in case they came under attack. There was no sign of anyone else on the island but there was no sense in taking unnecessary risks. At this distance off, they should be able to spot their companions, unless they were in the trees or on the far side of the island, and yet they would have a chance to take evasive action if they were fired upon.

He glanced at the time again. Twelve forty-five. At ten knots he estimated they would reach the western end by about one o'clock.

The boat ploughed on, meandering slightly in an attempt to mirror the curves and indentations of the shoreline. It was almost one o'clock. They strained ahead watching the western tip of the island slipping into view at last from behind a small point up ahead.

They scanned carefully with the binoculars, their arms aching trying to hold them steady. The noise of the outboard at maximum revs was almost unbearable. Stewart saw the wide fore-shore at the end of the island and the line of the mainland in the distant background. He scanned the foreshore systematically, starting from the area nearest to them as it came into view as they rounded the point. Suddenly Ethne tugged his sleeve.

"Bob!" she shouted, pointing towards the bow.

David was waving at him, telling him to look at the end of the island. He saw something! Stewart swept to the point and quickly re-focused the glasses. There! He saw it too! A man, a single figure sat unmoving at the edge of the water, far out on the mud, almost at the extreme end of the island. He pointed and the helmsman nodded as he began curving their course towards the point. Stewart scanned the entire area but could see no other signs of life. He studied the figure again. It was a white man, almost certainly Roomer or Moriarty. The heat haze made it impossible to make out which.

Time stood still but eventually they closed in on Roomer. They saw him clearly now and approached him slowly, coming in at right angles to the water's edge. They expected the boat to ground some way off but there was a deep channel running straight in towards him.

They slid gently onto mud a few feet from him and at last he lifted his head to acknowledge their presence. Stewart would never forget the look of shocked despair on his face.

"Joe? Joe, what's happened? Where's Paul?"

Roomer began to sob, great involuntary moaning sobs. Stewart's blood ran cold as Ethne wailed behind him. His heart beat rapidly as he stepped out of the boat and went to lift Roomer to his feet. Never before in his life had he felt so inadequate, so overwhelmed, so frightened by events around him. Some spark, some deeply buried instinct seized his consciousness. It told him to hang on to himself, to hang on for grim death. He knew if he did not obey they would all be lost.

It took some doing but, with Ethne's help, they managed to bundle him into the boat. Stewart gently tugged off the soaked and muddy day bag which Roomer still had on his back. They gave him water and made him as comfortable as possible.

"What happened Joe? Where's Paul?" Ethne asked shrilly, close to hysterics.

Stewart tried a calmer approach.

"Come on Joe... You must tell us what happened. We must know. Where on earth is he?"

Roomer gathered himself, nodding, trying to tell them he was rational.

"In a minute... In a minute." he whispered hoarsely.

Stewart caught Ethne's eye over his head and signalled for her to give him space for a moment. She shuffled backwards and sat on a seat. For something to do, he checked Roomer's possessions. His bag was aboard and he was clutching his floppy hat.

The guns! Where were the guns!

He was about to quiz him when he caught sight of the rifle lying on the mud. He stepped out of the boat to get it. It was plastered in mud and needed a thorough cleaning. He checked around but there was no sign of any other gear.

He sat beside him again and Roomer began to speak in a low voice.

"Paul's dead Bob. A crocodile got him."

Stewart's head went light. He began to shake.

"What? A crocodile?"

"Yes. It dragged him under. One second he was there, then he was gone..."

Ethne screamed. She could not have heard Roomer from where she sat but Stewart's horrified reaction told her what she dreaded to hear.

"Oh Joe! Oh Joe!"

It was all he could say. Numb with shock, he had enough sense to stumble back to Ethne who was beside herself. He hugged her tight as David approached, eyes wide with fear.

"What happened Doctor?"

Stewart could only nod towards the forlorn Roomer so he blundered over to question him.

Ethne wrenched free to be violently sick over the side.

It was a very bad half-hour. The worst so far. Coming on top of yesterday's terror, the primeval horror of what Roomer recounted questioned their sanity. Gradually, in fits and starts, he pieced it together for them. They found it almost impossible to accept. Even the locals who must have had some experience of such horrors seemed stunned by the news. David just sat staring out across the lake, this beautiful location so steeped with violence and nightmare.

Stewart cast around for something practical to do. Roomer needed some hot food. He sent two of the men across the mud to gather sticks for a fire. They lit it beside the boat and everyone eventually forced down some hot fish. There was little point in moving. After all the racket they had made it would have become apparent before now if there was anyone else on the island. Stewart decided they would try for the mainland at dusk, in a few hours time. They could hardly stay in their present situation indefinitely. One last check of the mainland before they left, then straight across as fast as they could to find out what the hell was going on and how they were going to reach safety.

So much horror removed any lingering doubts. This was no time for patience and careful planning. To hell with it! Short of being totally foolhardy they would cross this evening. He was decided.

Chapter 11

DEFRA Headquarters, London

0745 hrs, 17 February

Sir John Simpson, Permanent Secretary, forced his way through a noisy throng of pressmen and TV crews gathered at the main entrance to the Ministry of Agriculture, Fisheries and Food. It was early morning on a bright winter day and, other than this jostling mass, there were few people in the quiet London street.

"Sir John! Sir John! Have you any comment?"

"What's the latest Sir?"

"Can you give us a statement Sir John?"

The barrage was shouted from all sides.

He turned at the doorway as security staff struggled to hold the pack at bay. An old hand at this sort of thing, Sir John waited until the heaving mass sorted itself out, pushing cameras and microphones into place, jostling for a good position. Some semblance of order installed, he looked into the nearest lens.

"You will realise that I am not in a position to give a definitive statement at present." He spoke in a rich, slightly raised voice. "Information is still coming in and I am on my way to a briefing just now. I may be able to make a fuller statement later today."

The barrage resumed immediately.

"Are you in contact with the expedition?"

"Any word on casualties?"

"Is a rescue mission being planned?"

"I'm sorry I am unable to add to what was known yesterday evening. I will do so as soon as I can."

With that he rushed inside and security staff protected the door behind him.

Bloody hell….. how in blazes did the press know I'd be arriving this early? Then he realised they must have rung his security staff to ask when he was due. He promised himself he would have a word with those idiots later today. Security in this place is a joke! Struggling to regain his composure, he strode to the lifts. When that lunatic Bamford gets back I'll crucify him, he promised himself.

Safe in the temporary haven of the lift he went over a mental check list of questions he needed answered at the meeting.

Two men were waiting for him in the Private Office on the tenth floor. Peter Smith, Departmental Press Officer, paced up and down in the outer office, flipping through papers in a bulky file. A red-faced and balding fifty-year-old, his obesity was a particular disadvantage for a small man. Smith's expression was grave as he studied the papers. His usual day was a relaxed round of gathering material from across the Department, issuing press releases, or perhaps organising a Ministerial engagement. He maintained good relations with the agricultural press, the main 'buyer' of his wares. Until yesterday, a press problem for the Department might have consisted of defending staff cuts, a plant disease outbreak or some similar trivia.

Still, he thought, I'll soon be out of it. The Foreign Office and MOD boys will take this one over very promptly!

Michael Turner, Under Secretary responsible for Agri-Environmental policy, seemed relaxed as he sat, navy-suited and crossed-legged. Usually unflappable, his supercilious appearance belied a warm-hearted, if ambitious character. He was a tall man with steel-grey hair and a slight tan which showed off his blue eyes to perfection. He had experienced many crises over the years, with very few as catastrophic as this nightmare, but he remained confident of being able to steer Sir John and the Department through safely.

"Right Michael, Peter, let's go through." said Sir John, as he swept past en route to the privacy of his inner office. "Sorry to drag you both in at this hour of the morning, but I'm sure you understand the seriousness."

"Of course... "

"Be seated. Be seated gentlemen."

Sir John sat at one end of his conference table. Red-faced and heavy-jowled, his dark, thinning hair gave him an unwarranted 'flash Harry' look. He was well-built and still in good shape for a man nearing retirement, and he had worked his way up through the ranks to become a skilled administrator in all areas of Departmental business. As Permanent Secretary he was Head of the Agriculture Ministry known as MAFF, answerable only to his political master the Minister and to the Head of the Civil Service.

He leaned forward and informed his two colleagues. "I've just come from the Minister who you can imagine is getting very twitchy about this. I've told him all I can but I must brief him again within the hour. He has a meeting with the PM at ten o'clock. Which reminds me, I trust I hardly need stress the necessity for strict confidentiality in all of this?"

"Understood. Where is he now?" Turner asked.

"The Minister?"

"Yes."

"He's in his Kensington flat. There'll be no time for a typed brief to be prepared. When you've updated me I'll have to go round and give him an oral briefing, unless you have any papers which would assist?"

"Well, we'll see what we have on file John. Peter's been searching the press files." He turned to Smith.

"I've been able to turn up relatively little Secretary." Smith began. "My people are still searching but I have a gut feeling we don't have much of this on paper."

Turner interrupted. "The problem is John, Hugo must have nearly all the material in his office. Some of his staff are on their way in now and we might be able to unearth something useful."

"What about Eaves, or some of Hugo's other deputies? Don't they have anything?"

"I'm afraid not John. It seems Hugo kept all this pretty much to himself. They're even more in the dark than we are."

"Hell's teeth! That's absolutely unacceptable!" he seethed.

"Bloody typical of Hugo! I've let that buffoon run on too loose a rein for far too long. I should have trimmed his wings long ago! Should've rung his neck! Believe me he'll find a different scenario when he gets back… if he gets back, and those poor blighters with him. That's if any of us still have jobs when this is over!"

He calmed himself with an effort.

"Sorry gentlemen. Start at the beginning and take it step by step."

Turner marshalled his thoughts and began in his usual pedantic manner.

"You'll understand if I preface everything I'm about to say by explaining that my knowledge is all indirect. I have not been privy to any meetings or papers, let alone decision-making on this project from conception to initiation. All I know about it is what I can remember from casual conversations over the last few months. I took only a general, overview interest, and only in aspects that Hugo volunteered. I did not actively seek information."

"Right Michael, I know you're not responsible."

"Oh it's not that. Although that's true of course, that I'm not responsible, but I'm not stressing that *per se*. I just want you to realise that I cannot give you a definitive briefing at this stage."

"Understood. Fire ahead."

"Well, it seems the project was first mooted about eighteen months ago, largely through Hugo's personal contacts with individuals in Dublin and Brussels. You'll recall that about two and a half years ago he was the driving force behind a joint industry/public sector project in Poland - basically providing scientific and commercial expertise to a Polish agricultural cooperative. Hugo and his team went out there and told them how to organise and improve their entire enterprise. It was all done under the European Union Foreign Development Programme, an aid programme ear-marked for projects in former eastern bloc countries."

"Michael... " Sir John prompted gently.

"Yes, well it appears this African venture was a similar job. Hugo obtained EU funding in a tripartite collaboration between ourselves, the Irish Agriculture Department, and the Ugandan Agricultural Research Institute. Of course we also had to provide funding. The EU only part-fund this kind of project."

"What?" Sir John sat upright in his chair. "You mean we're funding this? You're joking! Tell me you are joking!"

"Afraid not John. Our Department has expended over 400,000 on this to date, although Finance Division is still checking figures."

"Nearly half a million? I don't believe this! Why wasn't I told? Was my approval ever sought - let alone the Minister's?"

"I'm afraid I can't answer that at present. I can only assume Hugo acted under his delegated authority as a budget-holder."

"We must clarify this as soon as possible. You realise what this means? Up to now I thought some of our people were out on contract to the Ugandan Government and that they were the customers, under EU funding. The fact that we are also part-funding means that our Minister carries responsibility for agreeing to the whole enterprise. If it had just been Brussels money we might have distanced ourselves and the Minister from it by taking the line that we were participating in a purely EU/Uganda-led project, on contract - at their request, which is what I thought was the situation. The Minister will now have to explain why his Department was one of the initiators, and why British taxpayers' money was expended! He'll throw a real wobbly when he hears this. Bloody hell!"

Turner continued, unfazed by the interruption.

"I should add that Dublin has also committed significant sums on this, but of course most of their money for this sort of thing comes from Brussels in the first place."

"At this point in time Dublin can cook its own goose!" Sir John interjected.

"It seems that, in essence, the project team was to spend three months in a Ugandan village on Lake Albert. It's a joint DEFRA/Irish team, four scientists from each department, I think. Personnel are checking, but I believe Bob Stewart is out there too."

"Stewart? Oh dear, oh dear. It gets worse!"

"The plan was to investigate and advise on how to improve the village's crop and fish yields and also the marketing of these products. Experimental work was planned on arable crops and the fish stocks in Lake Albert. The whole effort was to be facilitated by technicians from the Ugandan National Institute for Agriculture in Kampala."

"How do you mean facilitated?"

"They were to organise transport in and out, supplies and technicians to support the field and laboratory work, sampling and data recording, that sort of thing. So far as we can tell, there was a total complement of around twelve in the expedition based in the village since... the third of February to be precise - some two weeks ago today."

"What on earth sort of facilities are there? In fact where exactly is this village, have we got a map?"

"I haven't had a chance to check on Google maps just yet. As you know, Uganda is in east Africa, west of Kenya. Lake Albert is a big lake, hundreds of miles long. At this point I'm really not sure if this village is on the north, south, east or western shore of the lake."

Turning to Smith, Sir John said. "I'll need a decent map for the Minister. If nothing else I at least want to be able to show him where the village is! Peter, could you possibly nip out while Michael continues, and go on line? It shouldn't be too difficult to locate the area and get a printout of it."

"Certainly Secretary." Smith rose quickly. "I'll be as quick as I can."

Giving him a moment to depart, Turner continued. "As regards facilities, I understand they were living in mud huts..."

"Surely not?"

"Oh it's not as bad as one might suppose. I remember Hugo telling me something about this a while ago. They were to have proper beds, mosquito netting and a field kitchen, gas fridges and so on. This was all to be airlifted in by the Ugandan Army."

"Does that mean there's an airfield nearby?"

"No, airlifted by helicopter I think, so I don't think there is an airstrip but I'm really not sure about that. Two laboratory tents were airlifted in as well. I assume that's where much of the cost was, with air-conditioning, electrical generators and so forth. I remember Hugo trying to explain some complicated system for their water supply."

"Michael what about communications? Can't we just ring them up? Surely in this day and age they would have cell phones or even a satellite phone?"

"Again John, I simply don't know. All I can tell you is what I can remember from conversations with Hugo a couple of months ago. I have none of this on paper - and we won't have until Hugo's staff arrive and start digging through files."

"I do realise that, but go on."

"My recollection is that they are out of normal communication lines. It's a very remote area, no land-line phones and no cell net coverage. However, I know Hugo was concerned about the two halves of the team keeping in touch with each other, and ..."

"Two halves?"

"Well, there was a briefing session here on the scientific aspects of the expedition. Two of Hugo's scientists gave it. From what I remember there was to be a shore-based crops group and a fisheries group working on the lake. Each group was to have two-way radios and could keep in touch with each other. Hugo mentioned some sort of regular call in schedule to keep tabs on each other's status."

"But how are they supposed to keep in touch with the outside world?"

"Oh they have a powerful radio at HQ and they're able to contact virtually anyone world wide with this. I remember Hugo telling me how good this radio was. You know how gadget-orientated he is? Well he was playing with this thing and boring the pants off me one lunchtime about it. I'm afraid I switched off, excuse the pun, but that's how I know about it. We'll get on to Brussels and our Irish colleagues to see if they can shed further light on all this."

"Has there been no communication from the expedition since the first report?"

"Not as far as I know. The Ugandans have been trying constantly to raise them ever since, but can't."

For the first time a cloak of foreboding settled over Sir John.

"I don't like the sound of that. You'd think that between the lot of them - twelve people you say? - at least one intelligent adult could have radioed their status."

"You would think so."

"Okay let's leave that for the moment. The next thing I need to know is why on earth Hugo was caught up in this. Surely he wasn't supposed to be there, at least not for the entire three months?"

"No, you're right. It was just bad luck he was there when the attack took place. It seems he flew in for a quick status visit. You know how he's always jet-setting about."

"He should try working for a change! But how could he jet out there without us knowing it?"

"It seems you gave him approval to attend a conference in the Seychelles and he organised the Ugandan stopover en route."

"That's right, I seem to recall something about the Seychelles." Sir John said distractedly.

"Look Michael, the other crucially important thing here is to... is for the Department to inform the relatives of our staff involved. Make sure you get Welfare Branch on to it right away. I want every family to have a personal visit by the Branch before the day is out - and to continue daily thereafter. At least we might avoid criticism on that front. They'll probably hear it on the news first but I want them to get constant updates from us. I'll go and see Hugo's wife myself, at least today, but make sure Welfare Branch look after her as well."

"I'll see that's done." Turner said, scribbling a note to himself.

"Now take me over what we know of the incident itself."

"Well, this is according to a Foreign Office official I spoke to last night. At about four o'clock yesterday afternoon, Uganda time, one of their helicopters was approaching the village on a routine supply mission from its base in Kampala. It sighted smoke and flames the length of the village which was under attack. The crew saw armed terrorists on the ground and people running around everywhere. The attack was still going on. They saw bodies lying too."

"African or European?"

"Apparently it was hard to see through the smoke. I've no real answer on that."

"See if we can follow up on that."

"How?"

"Ask the Foreign Office to arrange for the helicopter crew to be properly debriefed by our Embassy staff in Kampala."

"I'll see what I can do," he said uncertainly, writing a further note.

"What else?"

"After a couple of low-level passes, which attracted automatic weapons fire, the pilot decided it was too dangerous to land and headed back to base."

"Didn't he radio for help?"

"Apparently he did but no rescue force could be scrambled, for two reasons. Firstly, the terrorist incursion was over a wide front and most Ugandan army units were already engaged or were being deployed to counter trouble elsewhere across the country."

"And the second reason?"

"Oh... because it's Uganda." He said grimly.

He went on. "The aircrew tried to raise Hugo's team by radio and indeed were trying for a while during their approach, even before they realised the village was under attack. There was no answer from our people then or since."

"When was the last time they *were* heard?"

"Someone on the team, I'm not sure who it was yet, made a routine radio call to Kampala at nine o'clock that morning, yesterday - presumably from their main long range radio - to log in and check if the supply helicopter would be arriving on schedule. Apart from that, Kampala base heard nothing since."

"Couldn't he have foreseen that?" Sir John snapped, his irritation with Hugo surfacing once more.

"Oh he did. He had a very powerful radio at village HQ and, as I say, one of the team used it that morning to report and inquire about the helicopter flight. The smaller hand held radios were quite adequate to maintain contact between those on shore and the fishing group. I assume the main radio wasn't in use all the time. Kampala would not be able to pick up signals from the handhelds and are admitting they maintained only a casual listening role. There was no real requirement for them to do otherwise. So far as they can tell the last radio signal of any description was heard at nine o'clock in the morning - just a routine call, no hint of any problem. After that, nothing more was heard and that remains the case so far as I know."

"Couldn't the helicopter have made some sort of effort to land? I mean after all he knew there were Europeans down there!"

"It seems we must give him the benefit of the doubt. There's no point in doing otherwise is there? In any event I believe the helicopter suffered some damage from the automatic fire."

"Why didn't they send a fleet of helicopters back out immediately with armed troops aboard?"

"Well, there are only two helicopters in the entire area and the one that was hit is now grounded for repairs. Troops too are thin on the ground. If I was the Ugandan Government it wouldn't be my top priority to commit limited resources in a probably vain attempt to rescue a few Europeans in a remote non-strategic area. They'd be better employed attacking the insurgents which are threatening to overthrow the regime."

"I see that." Sir John said sombrely.

"Michael, do I gather from all this that you suspect Hugo and his party are... dead?"

Turner paused for a moment. "I would be very surprised to discover otherwise."

"I see. What do we do now? How do we find out if they are alive or dead?"

"That John, is the sixty-four dollar question." He said, as Smith returned clutching a computer print out.

Chapter 12

The Island

1430 hrs, 17 February.

Stewart was reluctant to leave Roomer in his present state, but there was no choice. Ethne would have to manage - and the village men were there if she needed them. He and David were going the few hundred yards across the mud to the island. It would be dark in a couple of hours and they must make a reconnaissance of the mainland from the far side of the island, while the light held. He doubted they would be able to see much, to be certain there were no terrorists on the mainland shore, but it was worth having a look before attempting the crossing. It was hardly worth moving the boat from where it was beached. It would be quicker to jog over to the island, have a quick look and then come back to launch the boat. If they left now, they should be back in plenty of time before dusk.

"Don't do a thing Ethne. Just wait here until we get back." he said.

"Joe... Joe!" raising his voice, "Are you okay? We won't be long. Hang in there mate."

Roomer slowly raised his head and stared at him. He seemed not to have understood, but eventually he nodded firmly.

The four locals were huddled in the bow, muttering. They irritated him - quite irrationally, Stewart realised.

'Poor bastards! It was hardly their fault.'

He knew there was nothing they could do to help. It was their withdrawal into a morose group that was the source of his annoyance. He nearly barked at David, to tell him to get the men doing something, anything, but there was nothing useful for them to do. There was no point in them tidying up the boat. Such a meaningless waste of time would only antagonise them unnecessarily, pandering to his need for activity, any sort of activity. He gathered himself. Looking at David who waited patiently for orders, he realised he too must be in a dreadful state.

He asked himself, why do I assume that violence is somehow less shocking to Africans than it is to 'civilised' Europeans? He was beginning to appreciate the extent of a deep-rooted bigotry which, unconsciously, had co-existed with his professed cocktail party liberalism. A part of him registered the fact that if he survived this nightmare he would be a changed individual from the superficial cynic who had jetted in a few short days ago.

He thought again of Sheila and his chest heaved. Dear God in heaven, he pleaded, keep her safe! He could not, did not want to accept they had met only to be separated forever. He could not bear it. He felt such passion for her, such protectiveness. She was all he had ever wanted in a woman - a glorious, tender, kind, loving friend to adore for the rest of his days. Where was she? What was happening to her?

He blotted it out immediately, slammed down the shutters. It was the only way to handle it if he was to continue to function and to survive.

They jogged towards the island. It was very hot and sticky but they had only a short distance to go. He stared ahead at the low spit of grass-covered land that marked the western end of the island. He gestured to David to head for an isolated tree standing proudly some forty yards from the point. As they approached, blue-green trees on the mainland edged slowly into view from behind the low-lying island in front of them. They lay down at the base of the tree and, recovering his breath, Stewart wrestled the binoculars into position. He made a quick scan of the area. Nothing moving. He scanned to his right, to the north, and froze!

Was that smoke?

He realised that the 'smoke' was a dark, brooding cloud-mass gathering in the distance above the lake.

Rain clouds?

He swung back to concentrate on the two-mile stretch of water between the island and the mainland, squinting westwards into the sinking sun's glare on the water. It was difficult to make much out at that distance but a careful sweep of the area detected no signs of any activity on the far shore. It looked deserted. He checked eastwards... only water and trees. They were too far west to see the village.

"Okay, let's get back. I can't see any sign of trouble. It seems to be deserted over there."

As they were getting up David grabbed his arm and pointed northwards up the vastness of the lake. "Doctor, look... "

He nodded. "I see it David. A thunderstorm?"

"Yes, a bad one I think, and it comes quickly."

He stood for a moment studying the great dark mass of cloud that had swollen quickly. It was eerie. The mass now extended right across the northern horizon and was rising perceptibly higher and higher, an immense black curtain being drawn over an azure blue sky. It was dead calm, hot and sticky. The lake lay smooth before them, like stainless steel. There was no sound except their breathing. David pointed again, low and insistent, at the far northern horizon. He focused the glasses on a navy blue line visible low on the water, many miles distant. He could not quite make it out but knew instinctively what it was.

"Come on!" he shouted, running for the boat.

The navy blue line marked the edge of a storm rushing towards them. He had no idea when it would be on top of them but it could only be a matter of minutes.

The storm was a Godsend! If they timed it right they could run through it to the mainland. It would cover their engine noise and if there were still terrorists in the vicinity there might be a chance of landing unheard and unseen.

The locals had seen the clouds for themselves and had made the boat ready to shove off when they arrived back, sweating and breathless.

"Bob... " Ethne greeted him uncertainly.

"We're going now Ethne, to the mainland. There's a storm coming that'll cover us. It's our best chance to sneak across."

Then, seeing her expression, he added. "Don't worry, we'll make it." Please let it be so, he prayed. "Is all the gear stowed?" he asked David.

"Yes, I think so Doctor. Make sure your sat-nav is put away properly - in case it gets wet."

He fumbled hurriedly to seal the instrument in its waterproof envelope and buttoned it in his breast pocket.

They pushed off easily with everyone on board. Roomer and a villager poled into deeper water using an oar on either side. The helmsman whipped the outboard into life. It roared, then cut out immediately. Apprehension flickered through Stewart. The man stood and tried again. This time it didn't fire at all. He pulled it a third time.... still dead. As Roomer moved to help, the man gave a cry of frustration and bent to the fuel line. They saw immediately... out of fuel. Two fishermen quickly changed the fuel line from the empty tank to a smaller, reserve one stored between the seats amidships. As they fiddled with the black rubber hose Stewart looked north towards the approaching thunderstorm. His heart leapt when he saw how close it was! It must be travelling at a phenomenal rate! This was more than a thunderstorm, much more!

The darkness on the water was only two or three miles away and bearing down on them. He knew they must get out round and clear of the point before the storm hit or they would have to drive directly into the teeth of it to clear the island. The man pumped fuel into the carburettor by squeezing the rubber bubble in his fist. The engine fired first pull and they fell into their seats as he slammed it into gear and set off at full speed for the point. They ploughed through glassy calm water watching, spellbound, as the storm swept down from starboard. The air temperature dropped markedly with the arrival of the first of the wind and rain. It charged down the lake so swiftly that no swell, no advance sign preceded it on the surface of the water. The darkness was on top of them. In an instant the lake turned from silver glass to wind-blown blackness and they were engulfed by the dark stain of the storm. The roar of the wind and rain almost drowned the noise of the high-revving engine. They saw frantic waves rushing towards them, racing through dense splashes of torrential rain. Stewart glanced behind him.

Thank God! They were almost clear of the point. A few more seconds!

The full fury struck like a banshee. Howling wind tore through them, stinging rain pummelled them and steep, spume-blown waves crashed upon them. The noise was deafening. They saw it coming but the speed of the transition took their breath away. How could they be in this cataclysm so quickly?

Ethne saw Stewart shouting but could not hear him. She clung to Roomer who clung grimly to his seat. Stewart sensed rather than heard a change in the engine as the man eased back in the face of the storm. He turned hard to starboard to put her head into the oncoming waves, leaving it as late as possible to get maximum clearance away from the point. There was no way to survive this assault broadside on. She would have to be kept bow into it or be swamped. Stewart realised they were lucky in one respect. There was no chance of changing fuel tanks in this maelstrom. They would be swamped in the time it would take to change over, wallowing broadside without power. At least they had changed tanks in time to fight the storm.

They were clear of the point, just. The man tried to ride the waves as best he could, gunning and cutting the engine as the waves dictated. He tried to angle north-west to get well clear of the island but it was impossible to let the boat's head drop off more than a point or two or risk being broached. Slowly they crept away from the island but were being driven southwards all the time. Stewart had never seen such vicious water. He tried to estimate how far it was to the southern mainland shore.

Would they be able to land or would the storm hurl them ashore in pieces? He pushed the thought away. There was enough happening in front of him in the meantime. Worry about beaching later!

In the violently pitching boat the four locals worked their way aft to sit near the stern. Stewart realised this was to raise the bow higher in the water and make the boat better able to meet the crashing waves. The men began bailing with a variety of tins and containers. The old wooden hull had leaked slightly the whole time they were out in it but, until now, it took only a few minutes bailing every half hour to keep bilge water to a minimum. Now they were taking water over the bow when a particularly vicious wave hit and the continued, torrential rain added to the problem. The helmsman was doing well. He kept them angled slightly to port, easing and cork-screwing them up and over the steep-sided waves, gunning the engine as soon as they crested one wave, trying to make some headway before easing back for the next wave. It required intense concentration. The waves were not coming regularly and he had to judge his approach to each one. Every so often a wave broke on top just as they were cresting it, hurling itself against the bow, to be whipped over them, stinging their faces and cascading into the boat. Roomer, David and Ethne sat along the aft cross seat with their backs to the storm, facing astern, shielding their eyes from the rain and spray. Stewart was at the stern, facing forward, to port of the engine. The helmsman sat on the other side staring into the teeth of the storm attacking their starboard bow. They pitched viciously, up steeply as they climbed a wave, then falling sickeningly to crash on the back of the wave and begin the race to meet the next wall of water. They were thrown around like puppets. Stewart's arm muscles were cramping as he tried to hold himself in place in the seat. The wind howled in the near-darkness and the noise level made speech impossible. He began to worry about the light. The storm blotted out the last of the afternoon and it was almost dark. What would happen when they could no longer see the oncoming waves?

The first ferocity of the storm was frightening - beyond anything they had experienced. Now, after nearly an hour battling into it, their initial fear subsided to a unending torture. Soaked, battered, bruised and cold, they were caught in a time-warp of abuse. Stewart watched Ethne hunched against the elements, upper body being jerked back and forward as they rode the waves, arm muscles tightened as she clung to the seat on either side. Her eyes were closed and she endured the situation on a minute by minute basis with no thought as to when it might end. On either side, Roomer and David were much the same, although Roomer looked up regularly to squint astern through the grey wall of spray and rain at the heavy darkness of the approaching mainland. Stewart too peered astern through the gloom. He realised with a shock that the shore was suddenly very close - too close! They would beach at any moment and be smashed to pieces! He grabbed the helmsman's arm.

The man shook him off angrily with a gesture which clearly meant 'I see it you idiot'.

He shouted something at David who didn't hear him. He shouted again and waved frantically. One of his companions stopped bailing and grabbed David's knee to get his attention. The helmsman gestured impatiently to him and he clambered aft. Stewart saw him shout instructions into David's ear and looked astern again. They would beach any minute now!

David translated rapidly, yelling into his ear.

"He'll turn the boat and run ahead of the waves to the beach! We must all jump out as soon as she grounds and try to drag her ashore! Do you understand?"

He nodded.

"Tell the others!" he yelled, and David hauled himself forward once more.

How on earth were they going to turn in these waves? Surely they would be swamped as soon as they turned broadside on?

If anything the waves were getting steeper, more vicious. It must be the effect of the approaching shore, he realised. He realised too that they had no other option. They must attempt a turn or they would be driven stern first to disaster. The men must have experienced this before, he told himself.

A calmness came over him as he recognised the inevitability of their situation. It was one of those rare times in his life when he had virtually no control over events. The realisation calmed him, made him almost eager to see what would happen, how they would fare. He caught Roomer's eye and was surprised to see a broad smile on his face. He too had worked out the situation and had come to the same conclusion - and in doing so was now galvanised out of despondency over Moriarty's death. Stewart nodded encouragement at Ethne as Roomer leant over to shout something in her ear. She looked up at him and flashed a tentative smile.

The helmsman was more and more agitated, looking ahead and astern, searching for a favourable pattern in the waves to attempt the turn. There was no favourable pattern. The best that could be hoped for was a slightly less dangerous wave configuration that offered some hope of a successful manoeuvre. Stewart too swept around, searching for a slight break in the cascade of waves.

What was that? Could that be...

He turned to yell but the man had already seen the break. He opened up the engine and heeled round hard to port. We're not going to make it! Stewart screamed silently.

They wallowed broadside to a huge black wall of water that swelled rapidly above them. Turn! Turn you old bucket!

He willed the boat round. They were caught in the trough between two waves, that dead area where boats wallow, unable to make headway in the transition between one wave discarding them and the next greedily sucking them in. The engine raced flat out. They sat rigid, unable to do anything except watch the dimly-seen elements around them. Stewart thought he saw the bow creep round further to port, just as they started to rise up the face of the oncoming wave.

Don't let it break! Dear God, don't let it break, he prayed. But it must break!

It was too steep not to break, to engulf them. Ethne screamed as the combination of flailing propeller and heaving water slewed them round enough that they rode up the wave backwards. They crested the unbroken top and fell out over the edge, engine racing, propeller clear of the water, to crash down stern first into the following trough. The man got her lined up, stern first to the next wave, bow on to the beach ahead. Surely it would be impossible to ride up and over another wave.

Now every wave was breaking as it reached for the shore. They must surf in on the next one or go under. The trick would be to catch it just right, just as it started to break, but not after it broke or it would toss them ashore like a smashed doll. They had little power to play with. It would be largely chance how the wave picked them up on its rush to the beach. Somehow they all seemed to realise this in the few seconds before the next wave arrived. The four villagers moved quickly forwards trying to lift the stern higher in the water, to give them a slim chance that the wave would not swamp in over the stern as it struck. But it didn't hit. It seemed to swell up around them, one second it was astern, the next, white boiling water surrounded them. The power of it lifted them, soaring, gut-wrenching, sending them flying on a roller-coaster ride to disaster on the beach.

Stewart's arms were sore but he hung on for grim death. Ethne twisted round trying to see ahead as she and Roomer sat facing aft. The four fishermen moved swiftly, two to either side of the boat, crouching, holding tight to the gunnel. For a split second he wondered what they were about, terrified their movements would cause a capsize and they would be lost in the boiling powerhouse of the storm. Then he realised and clambered forward to yell in Roomer's ear.

"Get ready Joe! She'll beach any second!" He yelled at Ethne. "Sit tight!"

Roomer and he went to opposite sides as the boat surged on, driven by the great mass of water around it, the helmsman fighting, uselessly, to steer a straight course for shore.

She stopped dead, for an instant, and the force of it nearly threw them into the water. For a second she surged forward again to come to a shuddering stop almost immediately. The stern lifted high in the air as the wave swept shore-wards, tearing through them as it disengaged and raced on without them. As the stern lifted all six men vaulted into the foaming water, holding tightly to the gunnel, three on either side. They knew instinctively when to jump in the now or never situation. Fear gave them strength and as their feet hit bottom they pumped legs and drove for the beach, hauling the heavy boat through the surf.

Stewart knew they would not make it. The mud underwater was too soft and sucked around their ankles. It was forty yards to the water's edge and there was no way they could reach it before another wave hit. Ethne screamed and he looked back. A monster wall of boiling water was almost on top of them.

He just had time to yell, "Hang on!" before it crashed on top of them.

Everyone had to look out for themselves. Stewart held on as tightly as he could, as the wave battered over and around him. He felt the boat lift off the mud and slew sideways. Suddenly the wave was past. There was no more time. The boat was swamped, full of water. Ethne and the helmsman struggled to get over the side. The boat rolled away from him and he stretched to link arms with Ethne and drag her out of the boat. They tried for shore, hanging on to each other for grim death. Communication was impossible in the noise and darkness. There was no way to check the others.

This was every man for himself. Twice they were knocked down as waves hit them from behind. Both times they managed to stay together and regain their feet. The waves shone with an eerie whiteness and he was dimly aware of clearer skies and a full moon overhead.

A few more steps and they were safe. They slouched clear of the water and on up the beach to the tree line. Roomer and David were there too and each had a bag, salvaged at the last minute. The four men made it too.

Four! Where was the fifth?

"David! Where's the other man?" Stewart yelled.

It was only then the others realised he was missing. They swept around frantically, in case he had come ashore further along the beach. There was no sign of him.

"Where's the boat? Do you see it?" Roomer shouted in the wind. Stewart pointed at the upturned hull, engine dead, wallowing in the waves, crashing over it thirty yards from shore. They studied it carefully but there was no sign of anyone out there.

Ethne sobbed quietly as acceptance came that the man had drowned. He certainly had not made it to shore. Stewart thought he must have been hit by the boat when it was flipped over. The poor bloke probably never knew what hit him. He had another thought. Perhaps he was trapped under the boat!

Then he realised that the chances of that were very slim. It made no difference anyway. It would be impossible for them to wade out into that surf to try to right the boat. Even if they did manage to batter their way out there it would be impossible to turn it over. She was far too heavy for them. If he was under it he was drowned by now. It was a good twenty minutes since they waded ashore.

Another life snuffed out, Stewart thought... obliterated, as if it had never been.

He was too far through to feel much emotion. They were all

exhausted and, while the locals were visibly upset, they too had few reserves left for mourning. Perhaps they would later.

The storm raged on, sweeping down with unabated fury from the north. It moaned through the trees as they trudged inland for shelter. They gave little thought to their surroundings, whether they harboured terrorists or anyone else. They were past caring.

 They found a hollow and collapsed into it to get shelter from the gale. They were wet and very cold, shivering in the darkness, stressed almost to breaking point, each one struggling to hold themselves together, to summon reserves from somewhere to get them through the night.

Chapter 13

The trees

0010 hrs, 17 February.

In the trees the night was absolute, the blackness of the blind. A noise wakened Hugo after midnight.

"Hugo?" Nottes whispered softly. "Are you awake?"

"Yes. Is that you Tom?"

"Yes. I think the others are asleep."

"What time is it?"

"Ten past twelve."

"Everything okay?"

"Seems to be… "

They huddled together in the darkness to continue their whispered dialogue.

An amazing variety of sounds continued in the surrounding blackness. Insects stridulated, (there seemed to be several different species), and strange rustling noises perturbed them from time to time. In the blackness it was hard to tell if the rustling was close or not. They could only guess at what animals were moving around and if there was any risk of attack. Occasionally a lion roared further afield and a hyena barked. At one point Nottes was sure he heard a leopard cough. Neither man was a coward but it took a great effort of will to keep calm as they sat helpless and exposed in the darkness. At least the temperature was bearable, a pleasant warmness. Swarms of tiny flies attacked them, unseen and unheard, but making their presence felt. They worried vaguely about tsetse flies and mosquitoes. They knew trypanosomiasis, 'sleeping sickness', required complex treatment and that many of the malarial strains were virtually resistant to medication. Malaria was no joke at all.

They were concerned about the situation and agreed that, come hell or high water, they must make a move that coming day. Matters were fast becoming intolerable. Nottes was very worried about their ability to endure another night in the open without food and proper rest. Doyle was a major concern. Why on earth had a man in his condition come on an expedition? Even before the attack it was obvious he was suffering badly from the sun and heat. His mood and general behaviour since then was disturbing. Was he in shock, or what? Nottes hoped he would not fall apart on them. Everyone would have to pull together if they were to make it to safety.

Then there was Sheila. He was surprised at her resilience. Like the rest of them, she was terrified when the bullets were flying, but she was holding together well and he doubted she would let them down. She was so vulnerable. The thought of what would happen if they caught her nearly made him sick. He made a pact with himself not to let her be captured, not at any price - whatever it took.

He thought about Rent, and wondered if he would have had the guts to do what Peter had done. Maybe for once his temper had served him well, charged him up enough to kill that terrorist bastard. Shame about the woman. He assumed all the village women were brutalised, probably the children too... He pushed the thought out of his head and decided to keep an eye on Rent to make sure he calmed down. He hoped a few hours sleep would help him rationalise the killing. The way Rent told it, there was no choice. It was kill or be killed. No doubt of that. He would reassure him of that at the first opportunity.

Hugo discussed and analysed every aspect of their situation. Listening to him, Nottes detected a note of uncertainty in his usually arrogant tone. Perhaps even Hugo's towering ego was dented by the brutality of events? Time would tell if this was to be a temporary slip into decency, or if his bullish personality would reassert itself later. Both agreed that, in the morning, they should try to move north towards the lake. Eventually, deep in the night and in spite of their discomfort, they slipped into an exhausted sleep.

Sheila slept fitfully, dozing, drifting in and out. She heard Hugo and Nottes whispering. The night's noises frightened her at first but eventually she became too tired to care. Dirty and sticky, she longed for a bath, a big, bubbly tub to soak in, to draw out her aches and pains, to comfort her. The strong smell of Africa enveloped her, the dusty smell of soil and the steamy odour of vegetation. She tried to remember the last time she slept outdoors, before the expedition. She must have been nine or ten years old, in a tent in their back garden in Ireland. Her older sisters were with her on sufferance, at Dad's insistence, to look after the baby of the family. She smiled at the thought of him. What would he think now about his little girl lying out in the African bush, hiding from terrorist butchers? Life isn't fair, she thought. Why did he have to die when he did? Who was he harming, who were our family harming, as we lived our quiet happy lives in the west of Ireland. We were so happy, Mum and Dad and their little girls.

She longed to feel their arms around her now. If you were here now Dad, I would... Her eyes filled with tears. Why oh why? Is happiness so short-lived? Bob, Bob, where are you? Are you safe? Will you come for me? Will you look after me, for the rest of our lives? Will we have little girls of our own? Dear Lord protect me, protect us all...

In a while she wakened again. Doyle bumped her, unwittingly, wrestling in sleep. Had he cried out? She wasn't sure. He seemed peaceful now. Hugo and Nottes had stopped talking. In a little while she drifted off once more.

***

Dawn comes quickly at low latitudes. This one stole in like water soaking blotting paper, suffusing their environment with a pale, grey-whiteness. Foliage stood stiffly, glossy in its British racing green. Silence was overpowering. The air was gelled, fixed like in a photograph. They lay comatose, together but not touching. In exhausted sleep the vulnerability of their position registered in their subconscious and four of them lay curled in the foetal position. The fifth, Doyle, lay on his back with his mouth open. A large black beetle, antennae waving, was deciding whether or not to crawl down his throat. Its companion sampled the fluid in the corner of his left eye which stared, unseeing, at infinity.

Sheila stirred, slowly and stiffly, trying to make sense of her surroundings. She felt dreadful. Her mouth was parched and she struggled to sit up, carefully looking about for a water bottle, trying not to wake the others. She glanced around, checking their surroundings. It was the same as yesterday - trees, undergrowth and dusty red soil, no sign of immediate danger. Yesterday... It was hard to believe yesterday had happened. Was it real?

One by one she looked at her companions. Hugo, Nottes, Rent and... Self-preservation stifled her scream of horror! She flung sideways, grabbing at Hugo, heaving and retching. Her heart pounded like it would burst.

"What... What is it? What's wrong?" he gasped, coming awake in near panic.

The other two were wakening slowly. She clung tighter to him nodding, dumbstruck, at Doyle's overweight body lying a few feet away.

"My God!" he said in shock. "Tom! Tom! It's Doyle. Look!"

Nottes had seen it for himself. He crawled the few feet to the body and waited, gasping, for his heartbeat to settle. Angrily he flicked the beetles off Doyle's turgid face and forced himself to close the staring eyes, only partially succeeding. He was dead too long - probably since the early hours. Hugo could only stare as Sheila sobbed despairingly at his shoulder. Rent stood over the body as Nottes went through the formality of checking for a non-existent pulse.

"Is he cold?"

"Well, yes... not exactly cold but... "

"Dead meat." Rent finished it for him, his brutality sending another thrill of shock through them.

"What happened? Was he attacked? Has something attacked him during the night? Tom?" asked Hugo. They heard the shock in his voice.

 "I'm not sure. He has no obvious injuries. My guess is either stroke or heart attack." Then, a further thought, "Perhaps snakebite."

"But wouldn't we have heard something?" Sheila asked, then realised that perhaps she had. She remembered Doyle bumping her as he wrestled around. She half-imagined he had cried out. Oh why didn't I do something? she moaned to herself. I might have been able to save him.

"My guess is natural causes." said Rent. "He was overweight and badly shocked. Health wise he was a walking disaster waiting to happen. He's had a heart attack or stroke in his sleep - and a massive one at that. He probably never knew a thing about it."

His detached analysis helped her realise that, whatever happened during the night, nothing she could have done would have made much difference.

"Couldn't it have been a snakebite?" asked Hugo.

"I doubt it." said Nottes, supporting Rent's theory. "If he was bitten by a snake the pain would have wakened him. Death by snakebite isn't instantaneous, no matter what snake it is. He would have wakened one of us surely? Besides, I doubt a snake would strike a sleeping man in the middle of the night. Well, unless he rolled over... "

"It doesn't matter anyway." Rent interrupted. "Heart attack, brain haemorrhage or snakebite, especially snakebite, what were we gonna do to help him. We've no medicine or equipment - to say nothing about our rudimentary medical knowledge. Even if we'd all sat round him in a circle in broad daylight and watched it happen he'd still be lying there like dead meat."

They found his continued crudeness very distasteful but Sheila was almost grateful for his analysis. He was right. What could they have done if she had wakened them in the middle of the night? Oh please God let it be true.

"What are we going to do with him?" Hugo asked.

"Do with him? What do you mean?" Rent replied, knowing full well what Hugo was leading up to.

"I mean we'll have to bury him." Hugo glowered at him.

"Bury him? You must be joking!" he spat.

"Oh Peter... " Sheila groaned.

None of this had occurred to her yet - what they would do with the body. Carry it with them? She dismissed that idea immediately.

Rent rounded on her.

"I most certainly am not joking." he snapped, turning his attention in mid-sentence away from her vulnerability, back to Hugo.

"Look it's time you all faced facts. We're up the creek without a paddle. This is Africa, not Essex! Don't you realise we could be dead ourselves, butchered in a second. What do you think this is? A bloody game?" He was starting to get worked up.

"I killed a man yesterday - stuck a knife in his chest, again and again until he died and his bladder emptied into the soil. Doyle's dead and there's nothing we can do about it. We need all the strength we've got left to try and get ourselves out of this. I for one am not gonna waste my energy digging a grave."

Hugo argued back. "If we don't bury him wild animals will get the body..."

Sheila was appalled at the image.

"In case you haven't noticed Hugo, all the animals round here are wild." Rent's anger vented itself in useless sarcasm.

"Besides, they'll get the body whether we bury it or not. What are we gonna use to dig a grave? Where are the shovels. Are you gonna use your penknife or what?"

Nottes broke in. "Peter!" he snapped, and Rent stopped in full flow, surprised at his vehemence.

"Logic or common sense have nothing to do with this. We're civilised beings and Brendan is... was our colleague. Hugo and I will do him the service of at least trying to cover him up. It's simply not decent to walk away and leave him as he is - in Africa or Essex. I for one want to be able to look his wife in the eye, if I ever get the opportunity. You do what you like. Hugo and I... "

With that he sank to his knees and began digging in the loose soil with his hands. No one spoke. Hugo and Sheila quickly joined him. In a few seconds Rent too began to dig. They worked steadily in silence, not looking at each other or at what remained of Doyle.

***

Sweat dripped off her chin as she checked her watch. It was after one pm.

"Hold it for a moment please." she hissed at the others who laboured on ahead of her.

Hugo took a hard look at her and signalled Nottes and Rent to take a rest. Breathing heavily, they all sank to the ground. No-one spoke as they recovered. They had trudged north for an hour or so. It was hot and humid and the going was proving to be much harder than they expected.

We must be in poor shape, Nottes thought. This is the journey I made only yesterday! I reckon it took me about an hour and a half to get to the lake. He was worried that they were finding it so much more arduous today.

They'd had nothing to eat since finishing the sandwiches yesterday. Water was the main concern. Little remained of what they'd rescued from the Landrover. Before setting out a while ago, they drank a generous ration from the water bottles, to prepare them for the hike and to reduce the weight they would carry. They had not budgeted on sweating quite as much as this. Nottes was sure there was a change in the weather. Today was much hotter and more humid than since the start of the expedition. He estimated they would have some water left when they reached the lake, but not much if they were to replenish fluid at the rate they were sweating it off. He prayed they could find a source of acceptable water near the lake or, if feasible, back at the village. That would depend on the situation there, an unknown quantity at this stage. The two water purification bottles would be of little use in making the strongly concentrated lake water palatable. The rigours of yesterday were taking their toll. They'd had no real rest since the initial attack. Last night's interrupted sleep did little to replenish them, merely staving off extreme exhaustion. It was no preparation for this hike. The stress and strain must be having its effect too, Notte realised. After what we've been through we should be in intensive care for a week!

He thought again of Doyle. He would probably have lived to a ripe old age back in Ireland. All this must have put us under the same stress and strain that killed Doyle, he reasoned. Maybe he would have dropped dead anyway, perhaps sitting at dinner or in his office at home. We'll never know... The poor bugger didn't deserve to die like he did.

He would never forget the sight of Sheila kneeling beside the low mound of red earth, praying, tears coursing down her face as she said goodbye at the unmarked grave. He logged its position carefully in the sat-nav, in case by some miracle they could return soon and bring the remains home for a decent burial. Slim chance of that, he imagined. There was little prospect of the grave remaining undisturbed. Animals would soon dig it up and scatter his bones over a wide area. They were probably digging at it already.

Home. There's a thing! He realised with a jolt he hadn't thought of home for days. He wondered why. Just too much going on, he supposed.

He assessed his own condition and decided he was okay. He was knackered of course, with pains and scratches, but he would make it to the lake without too much trouble. A silly thought hit him. Was he enjoying this? No, not enjoying, that was ridiculous... relishing? Hardly, but the closest he could get to it was that he had a sort of appetite for what lay ahead. He was stressed and worried, sure, but something deep in his psyche that he never knew was there, now surprised him. He wanted to get to the lake. He wanted to find out what was going on. He wanted out of these bloody trees, wanted to take some positive action to shape his own destiny - not have some murdering scum shape it for him. The thought pleased him, gave him a small surge of energy.

It's not death that terrifies me, he thought, but, the old cliché, it's dying. We'll see, but if I get half a chance I'll make damn sure I don't go out like a wimp.

He looked at his companions. Hugo lolled against a tree, red-faced and sweating profusely. He caught his eye and raised an inquiring eyebrow. Hugo signalled peremptorily that he was okay. He was quite certain that he was too, in spite of his superficial appearance. He was a one-off, no doubt about it, a remarkable man. Pity he was such a bastard. It occurred to him that being pleasant and being one of life's kingpins was probably mutually exclusive. They certainly were in Hugo's case. He seemed to be sticking it quite well for an overweight, unfit city-dweller.

Why am I surprised, he asked himself? We're all the same in this situation. We haven't done anything spectacular so far, just scrambled about in the bush - and look at us! Wait to we have to make a run for it, or trek for a long distance. His heart sank at the prospect but he suspected that if they avoided contact with the terrorists, a long overland trek to safety would probably be unavoidable.

He hoped the terrain would improve. They seemed to have taken a slightly different course from what he had yesterday. He didn't remember all these ups and downs. The ground was dotted with humps and hollows, like the area around the Landrover, and it made the going difficult. The loose soil dragged underfoot like sand and, after trying at first to skirt the larger hollows, these were now so widespread that it was no longer worth the energy trying to go round. Struggling around trees and undergrowth as they blundered down into the steep-sided hollows was a great strain on the knees, and the climb up and out the other side left them gasping. They'd staggered into and out of hollow after hollow for over an hour and now badly needed a rest.

The men shared the load between them leaving Sheila, in spite of her protestations, unburdened except for the hand gun still strapped around her waist. Nottes shouldered the heavy Mauser rifle and carried the binoculars and sat-nav. Hugo and Rent each struggled with a water bottle. These were no longer heavy but were awkward to carry, like buckets. They abandoned the empty cool-box, seeing no point in keeping it, yet were inexplicably reluctant to dump this icon of their civilised world.

 "I'm sorry. I'll have to rest... for a moment." Sheila panted.

Rent answered for them. "You're okay... We all need a break... It's tough going..." Turning to Nottes he asked. "Is this the ground you went over yesterday?"

"No. According to the sat-nav we're on course okay, but we must have drifted off onto a slightly different line. I don't think it can last like this for much longer. It's pretty flat nearer the lake."

"How far to the lake?" gasped Hugo.

Nottes checked the instrument.

"Two point four kilometres - about a mile and a half as the crow flies. Another hour or so, depending on our speed and the terrain." He paused for breath. "We should be a bit more circumspect, certainly as we approach the lake. Just because we haven't heard anything since last night - let's not forget those bastards could be up ahead. We'd better move more carefully from now on."

Rent nodded in agreement. He was more even-tempered now. His outburst over burying Doyle, and his capitulation, seemed to have calmed him. The killing must have been shocking for him, Nottes mused. It's hard to accept he killed that man - and the way he did it! In spite of it, he was bearing up particularly well. He was a tough character, yet Nottes somehow distrusted his personality type. He could see his temper flaring again at any time. One day he might crack completely, go overboard beyond recall, might endanger them all. He seemed to have himself under control at the moment, but he resolved to watch him carefully for any signs of instability. Hugo had better watch him too.

He noticed a gradual, but subtle shift in relationships. Hugo still retained the mantle of command, but only just. They all still accepted his leadership but only because it suited them. Decisions were reached by consensus and in truth there had been little choice in practical terms so far. They went along with Hugo, eventually, but only with the force of his logic. The first time there was a fundamental disagreement there was no way they would acquiesce in future. And why should they, he asked himself? Hugo's managerial status had disappeared the instant the first shots rang out, except we didn't realise it then. He wondered if Hugo realised it now.

"I'm okay." Sheila said, struggling to her feet.

They all got up, slowly. Nottes again felt he should give a lead.

"Look, let me go a few yards ahead. I should recognise the area near the lake... when we get there. We might as well try to get back where I was yesterday. At least it was safe then. Okay? Maybe you should follow in single file? No need to advance on a wide front."

"Tom. It should be okay... up ahead I mean?" she asked, hoping for reassurance.

"I hope so Sheila, but we can't be sure. There's been no shooting or anything today - as far as we can tell - so it might well be they've moved on. We'll find out, hopefully. Meantime we'd better play it as safe as we can."

"Yes. Tom's right." said Hugo. "We should tread carefully from now to the lake. Peter, will you bring up the rear? Tom will lead, then Sheila, then me. You don't mind? I think you'll make a much better rearguard than I would," he chuckled, in a surprisingly conciliatory attempt at humour.

"Sure, if you like." Rent replied

They set off once more, trying to move as quietly as possible through the undergrowth. The environment could hardly be described as jungle. The trees were well spaced, and daylight shone down from above. Large clumps of thorn and other bushes grew thickly on the forest floor and grass covered much of the clear areas between. They could walk around the clumps with relative ease, although the sat-nav was an essential check on their overall line of march. Nottes stopped every few minutes to take a reading and to listen to the sounds around them. What they assumed were animal trails ran here and there through the trees, exposing the red-brown earth beneath. They heard bird calls and monkey chatter but saw neither. It was as if they were moving within an invisible, rolling cocoon - like a huge hamster ball - rolling forwards and displacing the wildlife out of sight as they went, leaving it to filter back into place behind, after they passed.

They made slow progress through the afternoon, stopping every quarter hour or so to rest and take rationed drinks of their meagre water supply. The area was quite dry. There were no pools or springs and the soil was dusty underfoot.

Watching him plodding carefully ahead, Sheila was reassured by Notte's steady presence. Not the most exciting man on earth, she smiled to herself, but who needs an exciting man in this situation.

No, Tom Nottes is exactly the type of man I would want with me here - apart from Bob. Where oh where are you Bob? She prayed again that he was safe. Surely they must have seen trouble from the boat before they came ashore, and turned away? She tried not to think about the gunfire they heard yesterday, around the time when the fishing party had been due back.

Rent strode along easily, a few yards behind Hugo. He felt fine now. Yesterday's events grew more distant in the memory with every stride. Strange. He expected to feel shock, disgust even, at what he'd done - what he was forced to do - to that drunken animal of a man. He felt at ease with himself, no remorse, no self-loathing. Why the hell should I? That scum certainly murdered innocent women and children, gunned them down without hesitation, just for the fun of it. He and his comrade raped and abused that poor woman and dragged her up the hill like a packed lunch - something to have when he felt like it, to keep him amused while he stood watch. He deserved to die, to be executed. Besides, it was kill or be killed. A knife in the heart was exactly what he deserved. Rent padded along, rationalising and analysing, to the point where, like Nottes, he felt a sense of... excitement - yes, that was it, excitement at what might lie ahead and a curiosity as to how he would react, how he would perform. He almost hummed, meandering through the trees.

Pity about Doyle, he thought, but there was no pity in his heart. He had a low opinion of Doyle as a scientist and a human being. He should never have come. What a useless bugger! His death did not touch him to the slightest degree. He gave no thought to Doyle's family. There were no glimpsed images of crying daughters or a distraught wife. Doyle had crossed his path, now he was dead. That was that. He really did not comprehend why they should waste time and energy burying the man. What was the point? Still he was in no mood to start a major row and had joined in to get it over quickly so they could be on their way.

He watched Hugo lumbering ahead. A phrase 'The Great Satan' unaccountably sprang to mind. It made him chuckle. Look at him.

The Great Satan! Waddling along there like a sumo wrestler. He amused himself for a while by poking mental fun at the labouring figure in front. He paid scant attention to his surroundings, having subconsciously assumed some time ago that any potential danger would lie ahead of them, not behind.

Hugo was rapidly running out of steam. Years of over-indulgence and lack of exercise were finally taking their toll. He swayed from side to side trying to maintain a straight course behind Sheila. He was blown, breathing heavily in long rasping draughts, not caring what noise he made. She could hear him but after a few worried looks, he signalled forcibly for her not to be concerned. Walking was difficult. Sweat-stained shorts had rubbed his fat thighs and were causing increasing discomfort with every step. Next time we rest I must do something to ease this, he thought. Perhaps if I cut the trouser leg? Typically, his major concern was for himself. Let's consider the situation, he mused, walking robotically in the mid-afternoon heat. We should reach the lake soon. Then what? Should we go back to the village? He decided they must reconnoitre carefully and try to find out if the village was still occupied or not. His impression now was that the terrorists had moved on. It certainly sounded like it. Things had been very quiet all day. Or were they out of sound range? He wasn't sure. Perhaps they were still there, lying drunk. Maybe the reason the firing seemed to have ended was that all the villagers were butchered by now. Still, there must be somebody in charge. Someone must have led them across the border in insurrection. Presumably there was some objective, some target they were heading for by a pre-arranged deadline? They could hardly just lie around for a few days when it suited them, could they? Whoever was in charge, their officers, would have got them up and moving on by now, he told himself. The power of his own logic almost convinced him, but not quite. We'll just have to check it out.

He agreed it was safest to return to the same spot at the lake that Nottes reached yesterday. The terrorists almost certainly came over the border from the Congo to the west. There was nowhere else they could have come from surely? No, his bet was that they came west to east and were intent on causing mayhem and destruction to the farms and villages to the south and east of Lake Albert, en route to Kampala. He speculated widely, pseudo-politician that he imagined himself to be and, like all politicians, deluded himself that he could work out the overall picture. He would not have drawn such firm conclusions from guessed data on terrorist movements if this was a scientific analysis. Still, he felt more re-assured once his spurious conclusions were drawn. It was always best to understand the wider picture, he told himself pompously, before drawing up strategy or tactics. So, we must push carefully east along the lake shore, back to the village. If it's safe we can stay there until a rescue comes.

He assumed news of the uprising would have reached London by now. DEFRA would take charge and would insist on an attempt to recover its personnel. Then he went over it again. Perhaps the village is destroyed, stripped so that there is no shelter left. Then what? Could we stay there then? What if communications are out? Maybe DEFRA don't know yet? Maybe nobody knows, after all it only happened yesterday. Did the Ugandan armed forces know? Of course they did, he realised. The helicopter yesterday would have reported back to Kampala - unless it was hit by gunfire and forced down. But it would have radioed in surely? The more he tried to reach firm conclusions the more elusive they became. Supposing the village was still occupied, what would they do? For a brief moment he fantasised that he might step from the trees and identify himself to them. Perhaps when they realised he was a European and a senior scientist of international standing... No. Even Hugo's ego recognised what would happen. He would be butchered like the rest. He might as well announce he was the last living smallpox carrier on the planet. As soon as they saw him he would be dead meat. How the hell was he going to make it? He would just have to hope the gang had moved on. Surely they would leave something of the village intact, even one hut?

He prayed they would leave the well serviceable. They would not survive long without water. He tried to think through the alternative situation - if they found the village still occupied. He reasoned that in those circumstances they would just have to sit it out, stay hidden until the gang did move, and hope the water lasted out. There was simply no alternative. From what he remembered from the maps, the nearest village was many days march away northwards along the lake. That option was untenable, it was much too far. He would talk it through with Nottes when they reached the lake.

Nottes had gone up in his estimation. He was calm under pressure and had come up with several good suggestions since the attack. Yes, old Tom was doing okay. Rent seemed alright too. It was a pity he had such a short fuse. He'd coped well with the incident yesterday, Hugo thought. He had no difficulty in imagining Rent knifing a man to death. Something close to envy passed through him. If they survived, Rent would be lionised for his action. If I lead this group to safety I should be able to sort things out, he thought. I can hardly be blamed for what happened? We sought and were given assurances that the civil unrest was far away from this area. What more could I do to safeguard the expedition? Pity about Doyle. Damn pity. If he hadn't been so overweight it might not have happened. Damn. Apart from Doyle, he had lost no-one else from the team. Well, no European. How could the Irish let a man in Doyle's condition embark on the expedition? He'd make that point when he got back... if he got back. The next few hours were crucial.

Then he remembered the boat party. Had they escaped? He reasoned that either they were ambushed as they came ashore or they saw what was happening soon enough to veer away - in which case they were long gone. Most likely they were in the village to the north. They could even have been airlifted out by now. He hoped so. That would mean the authorities would be aware of what happened and would be planning a rescue.

***

It was nearly four o'clock when Nottes saw the gleam of the lake. It had taken them much longer than he estimated. They were all in, dusty and dehydrated. He led them the last few yards to the lake. They fell to the ground exhausted, still in the trees and hidden from any patrolling eyes. No one spoke. With an enormous effort Nottes made a final check on the sat-nav. It told him they were four point two kilometres west of the village. The area was quiet with no sign of danger. They lay together yet isolated, bruised and damaged, letting unconsciousness overtake them.

***

While they slept they could not see a dark blue line, low on the horizon, far to the north on the lake, rushing towards them. They neither saw nor heard its approach, nor sensed the gathering gloom as the storm burgeoned in its race southwards. They were unaware of the offshore island disappearing in darkness and rain and they missed the phenomenon of the storm curtain racing across the two mile stretch of water in front of them.

The storm struck like a hammer. They woke terror-struck and disorientated, incapable of rationalising what assailed them.

Chapter 14

West of the village

0700 hrs, 18 February

Somehow they survived the night. The storm had passed as quickly as it came, a couple of hours after they staggered ashore. It deluged the area, leaving red mud underfoot and torn foliage littered the ground. Water dripped from above and lay in scattered pools. They drank the rain as it cascaded off trees and filled their water bottles. Cold, wet and exhausted, the hours of darkness had been passed at the limits of their endurance and despair.

Daylight brought little comfort. Looking at his companions, lying sodden and filthy in the early light, it suddenly occurred to Stewart that they were a hair's breadth away from ultimate disaster. They urgently needed warmth and shelter, proper food and above all care and medication. The locals had probably acquired a level of immunity to disease, or at least had grown to adulthood able to cope with it, but he shuddered to think what parasites they had picked up from the lake and whatever insects were around. Malarial mosquitoes were an obvious threat but there were some pretty horrendous water-borne diseases in this part of Africa - Bilharzia for starters! Everyone had cuts and abrasions, probably already infected, that needed dressed. There was every likelihood that serious medical problems would soon develop.

Everyone was awake, lying dejectedly, staring up at him as he reflected on their situation.

"Joe, Ethne... come on everybody, get up. Get up out of that mud! We'll have to move."

"Move where?" Roomer grunted, struggling to his feet on the slippery surface.

Stewart paused for a moment.

"I think there's only one thing we can do. Go back to the village."

"I suppose you're right."

"Well what else can we do?" he snapped. "Any bright suggestions?"

Ethne intervened. "Oh calm down you two. Stop arguing."

"We're not arguing." he sighed. "Okay Joe, okay. One thing's for sure... we can't just lie here forever."

They talked it over. Roomer asked David to bring the men into the discussion. This was their home ground and he was sure their advice would be crucial. With David translating and Roomer speaking directly to them at times, it was agreed that Stewart's idea was best. The men wanted to find out what had happened in the village and, in any case, there was nowhere else to go. They were in no fit state to attempt a trek many miles north along the lake to the next village.

It was impossible to imagine what they would find in the village. The terrorists might have moved on or could still be there. If they were gone, then hopefully the camp was not totally destroyed. He did not voice his fears in front of the men but Stewart hoped there were surviving villagers and that they would be able to help them. If the bastards were still there they could lie up until they moved on, at least for a while. After that... he didn't want to think about it.

Roomer checked his sat-nav. It had survived the beaching in its waterproof pouch and it told them they were just over three kilometres west of the village. The men insisted they would lead and the Europeans should follow close behind. They would have to move very carefully. It would be madness to assume the terrorists were restricted to the village compound. They could stumble across them at any point between here and the village.

They set off almost immediately. The cold, bleak surroundings provided no incentive to stay. The hike might at least ease their aching muscles, might warm their bones.

A kilometre further west, Hugo's group had spent an equally unpleasant night sheltering from the storm. They too struggled to rouse themselves and now, at eight o'clock, were making their way eastward through the trees along the lake shore, towards the village. The storm had replenished their water supply but they were in poor shape. They trudged wearily through glazed mud trying to keep an eye out for dangers ahead. In reality, they had reached a state of total apathy about their fate. Exhaustion overwhelmed them. Listlessness and automation described their progress. They knew only that reaching the village was their last faint hope. Death could well be waiting there but they had to find out. In their present state, death was certain if they attempted any other course of action. They passed their colleagues' abandoned boat without noticing, its blue, upturned hull almost submerged, wallowing gently in calm water a few yards offshore. It made no difference. Had they seen it, they would not have been certain whose boat it was, let alone been able to work out what had happened to its occupants.

Stewart crept cautiously from tree to tree. In his peripheral vision, Roomer was to his left and David to the right. The three surviving villagers were ten yards ahead, strung in line abreast, stalking noiselessly towards their home. He checked that Ethne was following close behind.

It could not be far now. Roomer thought so too and paused to plot their position. He signalled they were almost there. The locals knew exactly where they were and had already stopped, waiting for instructions. Everyone stood still. This was it. Stewart's heart began to pound. He signalled Ethne to come up beside him and they moved cautiously to join the waiting men. Strung out in a line abreast, they advanced step by cautious step. The open ground of the village was clearly visible now through the thinning trees. There was a faint smell of smoke. Stewart assumed this was the remains of the burning huts from two days ago. Then he remembered the storm. He was surprised the rain had not doused the fires completely. They crept slowly on. Gradually the scene unfolded before them. He was worried that they were becoming exposed. The cover was now very thin and if the area was still occupied they could be spotted. It looked deserted though. He saw the burnt out remains of two huts, thirty yards apart in open, red muddy ground, trees and undergrowth off to the right. There was no sign of life, or bodies, only smouldering embers. He reckoned this area must be the extreme western end of the village. To the left, open ground stretched down to the lake. The village clearing extended about a hundred yards in front of him, curving gently off to the right until it disappeared out of sight behind the tree line. He had not been in this corner before but was certain that the main village area would be visible from the bend up ahead.

Should they work their way through the trees? Too late! Roomer and the men stepped from cover and strode quickly across open ground towards the nearest hut. He just managed to stop himself from calling them back. Ethne and David scurried over to him.

"Bob..."

He put a finger to his lips to silence her, shrugged, and staggered after the others. They caught up with them standing in a semi-circle around the ruin of the nearest hut. Humps of blackened, baked mud lay strewn in piles where the walls had collapsed; mounds of smoking wood ash and a few broken pots was all that remained. The men jabbered in undertones to each other. David did not bother to translate. They headed for the next hut. It was just the same.

They moved on towards the bend. As they reached it, the full panorama of the village opened before them. It was a scene of utter desolation. A few damaged huts still stood but the rest were razed to the ground. As they took in the sight, the smell hit them, permeating through the still air. Stewart had never smelt it before but realised instantly what it was - roasted and putrefying human flesh. He started to gag and heard dry-vomiting behind him. He reeled sideways to Ethne who was horror-struck into gasping rictus. The villagers fell to their knees, wailing skywards in dread of the nightmare that was revealed. The stench was almost unbearable, so primeval it terrified to the core.

They had to go on, to see what they did not want to see. They had to find something in this ruined village if they were to survive. Stewart, hand uselessly over his mouth, signalled them to move again. A deathly stillness hung in the air and the faint smoke haze stung his eyes, blurring the view ahead. They staggered on, Stewart supporting Ethne, Roomer trailing behind with David coaxing along three very fearful villagers at the rear. The poor men wanted so desperately to find out, yet dreaded to know what had happened to their families in this butcher's yard that had been their home. Stewart could not conceive how they must feel. The mind-numbing assault on his senses and emotions was surely only a shadow of what they were going through.

He saw movement, and stopped dead. Almost too tired to care, he peered through the haze. Vultures! Hooded vultures were tearing and devouring the remains of a human body lying obscenely in the open, beside a burnt out hut. Some of the birds stopped gorging to look at him, their skinheads bright red with blood. He stood transfixed as a jackal trotted into view from behind the group of birds, making off with a bloody bone in its jaws, glancing guiltily at him as it went. He looked beyond. Thirty yards further on, more vultures were feasting on a second corpse and at the remains of another hut a pack of hyenas were stirring up ash dust, snarling and chewing over a third body, crunching bones.

"Joe... "

"I see Bob. I see. The whole... The whole damn village must be like this. Bastards! Murdering scum bastards... "

"Bastards." he grunted, struggling to hold up Ethne who was close to collapse.

He pointed through the haze to a grove of trees about a hundred yards ahead. "I think that must be our compound ahead there, behind that clump of trees."

The three Europeans and David blundered on through the village, picking their way round burnt out huts and several more partially eaten bodies. Ethne kept her face buried in Stewart's shoulder as he strained to help her along. Both he and Roomer trudged head down, trying not to look at the horrors they passed, each man struggling to keep a grip on his emotions. David shuffled along, staying close to Stewart. The men were now out of sight, slumped on the ground somewhere behind, shocked into catatonic immobility. Stewart and Roomer gave up on them for the present.

'Let them lie there, poor buggers.'

They were close now. A few more yards and they would get a view of their compound, just round these trees...

***

"We're almost there." Nottes hissed, studying the sat-nav. "According to this we're about four hundred metres from our compound."

"How accurate is that?" asked Hugo.

"Should be accurate to within ten to twenty metres."

"So we could be... "

"Yes Hugo!" he snapped. "We're close. We'll have to move very carefully over this last bit."

"Oh bloody hell! Let's go." Rent said, turning purposely towards the village again, crouched forward, rifle loaded and at the ready.

"Peter! Take it easy!" hissed Hugo, rolling his eyes at the others as they set off after him.

Nottes hissed in her ear as they walked.

"Sheila. Give me the Beretta."

She looked at him blankly, then remembered. She had forgotten all about the hand gun. She struggled to unstrap the belt and holster and thrust it at him as they staggered along.

"Ammo?"

She located the spare clip and the loose bullets in her zipped pocket and shoved a handful at him. A heavy thud made her jump. Hugo had fallen, slipping on the wet ground. He struggled up and signalled he was okay. Rent swung around instinctively at the noise but at least had the sense to point the rifle away to safety. The fall stopped their momentum for the moment. Suddenly, Notte pointed insistently through the trees.

"There it is!" he hissed.

Now everyone could see open ground about fifty yards ahead through the trees.

"We've made it!"

They reached the edge of the trees and stopped at the same spot where Stewart's group had their first clear sight of the village. It seemed deserted and they set off nervously across the clearing, heading up to the bend from where the rest of the village would be visible. As they reached the bend a long burst of gunfire ripped through the still air.

***

Ethne screamed as they dived to the ground. The gunfire was from close behind them. Panicking, Stewart struggled round to look. A heavily armed man in combat gear stood over the three fishermen he had just butchered. As he stared in shock, the man slowly turned his head in their direction and strolled arrogantly towards them, Kalashnikov at his hip. They clambered to their feet in blind panic and turned to run. Two more terrorists barred the way, automatic rifles aimed and ready to fire. Ethne collapsed in shock. The others stood frozen, hyperventilating, eyes widened in terror, staring at the black sweating faces of their captors.

Stewart's heart pounded and his mouth was dry with fear. His breath rasped in and out, sweat trickled.

We're dead, after all we've been through, we're dead.

He glanced behind him as the third terrorist walked up. He reached Ethne lying on her side and casually kicked her in the ribs. Stewart and Roomer both jumped involuntarily to protest but froze instantly as the men turned nasty.

"Stand!" one of them hissed.

Ethne moaned and rolled onto her side, regaining consciousness.

The man standing over her said quietly. "Get up."

She lay in shock, staring numbly up at him.

"Get up!" he screamed, so loudly they all jumped.

This made her move. She rolled onto her knees, trying to rise. He kicked her viciously in the side knocking her to the ground again. Stewart went for him. The man expected it and swung the butt of his weapon around lazily, cracking him neatly on the temple as he charged in low. He fell like a sack of potatoes, face down on the muddy red soil.

Behind him, Roomer and David were held in check by a harsh command and stood rigid as before. "Get up! Get up, or I kill you!" the man screamed again.

Dazed but still conscious, Stewart had no doubt he would kill them in an instant. He sounded deranged.

Must get up, he told himself. Must get up quick.

With a great effort he got to his feet dragging the gasping Ethne up with him, supporting her as they cringed, a hand raised, in front of the very agitated African. The man took a deep breath, trying to calm himself, and the tableau stood unmoving for long seconds waiting for his anger to subside to a manageable level.

"Move." he nodded behind them.

They turned nervously. No one spoke as they walked slowly round the edge of the trees towards the expedition compound, the three gunmen fanned out in close proximity behind. Stewart's head was splitting and he was very unsteady on his feet trying to support Ethne who reeled along, close to hysterics.

***

Back at the bend Hugo's group lay prone in the mud. They dived for cover when the gunfire came, its racket so shocking in the still air. At first they thought they were being shot at but after the initial panic realised the shooting was up ahead and not directed at them.

"Are you okay?" Nottes hissed. "Sheila! Are you okay?"

"Yes. Yes." she snapped, irritated at his fussing.

He realised this. "Sorry. It's just that you were… "

"What? I was what?"

"Well, you were whimpering."

"Oh. Was I? I'm sorry Tom… sorry." she muttered, embarrassed by her demonstration of fear.

Rent cut in. "Whatever it is they're not shooting at us. You stay here. I'm going to have a look…"

"No! Peter wait… " Hugo hissed.

"No, you wait Hugo!"

"But the village is still occupied. We'll have to hide again in the trees."

"No way Hugo. You crawl off and hide if you like, but I've had it! This time I'm going to see what's going on!"

"You'll endanger us all! I insist you do what I say!"

So finally, Hugo went too far, beyond the limit of the final shred of his fading authority. Sheila and Nottes knew it instantly but, still in his dream world of personal dominance, Hugo was genuinely shocked by Rent's response.

"You fat bastard! You insist? Who are you to insist? Who do you think you are?"

Rent was developing full flow, relishing this casting aside of Hugo's imagined power.

"I have news for you fatso! What you want doesn't matter any more. You're no longer in charge! Your arrogance and stupidity brought us to this nightmare and I for one will see you indicted for it when - if we ever get back."

"How dare you!" Hugo was appalled.

"Shut up you fat prick!" Rent's temper snapped.

He sat up, swinging the rifle round to point it at Hugo's still ample midriff.

"Just shut your fat face or I'll shut it for you... "

Hugo swivelled to appeal to Nottes. "Tom... "

"Easy Peter." said Nottes, and then to Hugo, "Peter's right Hugo. You no longer give orders around here."

It took Nottes' mild statement to bring it home to him. Hugo was very shocked, deflated like a soft football, and subsided back to the ground as Nottes and Rent quickly agreed what to do, ignoring Hugo's presence as he lay beside them like some discarded plaything. Sheila looked at him but could find no pity for a deposed despot - at least not now. With gunfire in the air he was the least of their worries.

"We're going to see what's happening up ahead." Nottes told her. "Do you want to stay here or... "

"I'll come with you." she said firmly.

No one asked him, but Hugo also got up and they went carefully to get a better view of the village. Rent had the rifle and Nottes carried the hand gun at the ready.

The smell hit them at the bend and they crouched, gagging, behind the broken wall of a destroyed hut. It took a moment to assimilate through the haze the sight of ruined huts, bodies, vultures and other carrion eaters.

"Oh Tom, Tom... " Sheila began.

"What's that? Look! Up ahead there! In line with those trees!"

Nottes spotted them first.

"Can you see Peter?"

"I see them. It looks like... It looks like Bob and... "

Sheila's heart leapt.

"Where? Where are you looking? "

Then she too located the moving figures about a hundred yards away through the haze. She drew breath to scream but Nottes grabbed her just in time.

"No Sheila. No! They're with those gunmen."

Her panic blossomed.

"Peter?" she pleaded.

Rent paused for a second then ducked down with them behind the wall.

"As far as I could see Bob and Ethne are there and either Roomer or Moriarty, I can't make out which. There are four blacks with them and at least three of them are armed. They seemed to be leading them off. They've just gone out of sight behind some trees."

"What's happened? What was the firing?" asked Hugo, shuffling to join them.

"I don't know." Rent replied distractedly, trying to plan their next move.

"Tom, I don't like it. I have this feeling... "

"Yeah, me too Peter. I think we should get up there right away. Something tells me... Sheila, you and Hugo stay here, this time."

They protested but he cut them off.

"No listen! Peter and I have the weapons. There's no point you two coming. Just stay here! We'll see what's going on."

"Please be careful." she pleaded.

"Yes, of course we will. The place looks deserted except for the ones we saw."

He grunted at Rent. "Let's go."

Sheila was desolate. Never in her life had she felt so dreadful, so helpless, so useless, as she crouched with Hugo behind a soot-blackened mud wall. She stared intently after them as they trotted, crouching, through mud and haze, heading for the spot up ahead where their colleagues disappeared. She saw them pause to examine bodies lying in the open. Unthinkingly, in her confusion, she prayed aloud.

"Dear Lord, don't let them be Europeans."

Then realising what she had asked, began to recite, over and over.

"God protect us, keep us safe. God protect us, keep us safe... "

Hugo shuffled closer and put his arm round her shoulder. The two of them lay back against the wall, all reserves of strength and emotion exhausted.

***

Stressed as he was, Stewart saw that the expedition compound was relatively unscathed. There were signs of damage and mayhem but most of the huts remained intact. Surprisingly, the mess tent and laboratory tents had survived. There was no time to survey further.

"Stop!"

He glanced at Roomer and David a few feet away and felt Ethne shaking in terror as she clung to him. The three men stood in front of them, apparently uncertain what to do next. They were stopped outside a hut, near the mess tent.

Their captors were talking Swahili and the topic of conversation soon became obvious. Judging by their leering grins and crude gestures they were trying to decide which one of them would have Ethne first. Stewart's blood ran cold.

We're dead...

He knew with certainty they had only seconds left to live. As soon as the pecking order was decided they would be butchered so that Ethne could receive their undivided attention. He looked wildly at Roomer and saw he too realised what was going to happen. He could not see David's face but he was tensed, ready to flee. Only Ethne was unaware, sobbing in terror, her face buried in his shoulder.

The talking stopped. Two of the terrorists stiffened and stepped to the side, covering the group carefully, weapons at the ready. The third man, the one who butchered the fishermen, walked briskly up to Stewart, hand outstretched. He grunted, gesturing for him to hand Ethne over. He clutched her tightly. The man stepped closer.

"Give!" he screamed.

She realised what was happening and screamed in terror, flinging herself backwards and away from him. Her reaction made Stewart stumble backwards with her. He tripped and fell, loosening his hold on her. The man lunged forward and grabbed her arm, wrenched her away from Stewart and dragged her kicking and screaming towards the hut.

"You bastard!" He yelled, struggling to his feet.

"Bob! Bob!"

Roomer's hoarse shout made him hesitate and in that instant saved his life. A terrorist yelled something, stepped forward and aimed his weapon at his head. Instinctively he put his hands up and froze on the spot. The man did not shoot.

Ethne was putting up quite a fight but she was no match for the thug who had her. He was having difficulty though, with a weapon in one hand and trying to control her with the other. He gripped her by the hair and dragged her backwards towards the dark doorway. She struggled like a demon and managed to twist around to face him. He tried to hold her at arm's length as she clawed at his face, just beyond her reach. She had no more breath to scream and both of them grunted and moaned with the effort of the struggle. She managed to halt progress towards the hut and it took all his strength to hold her. Finally he had enough. He swung the weapon up from his left and across in a vicious haymaker, crashing it into the side of her skull. She went out like a light, flopped like a rag doll as he let her and the weapon drop to the ground. His temper snapped. He gave an insane whine and pulled a heavy machete from his waistband, intent on hacking her to pieces. Everything happened in that instant.

The boom of a high-powered rifle echoed round the clearing and a terrorist pitched forward, his chest exploded by the impact of a high velocity round. In the milliseconds it took for this to register in his brain, Stewart saw David charge past him, and dive on the man with the machete. The third terrorist started to react but a bedraggled figure stepped out from behind the hut and fired four rounds from a hand gun into him. He went down thrashing. The last man wrenched his arm free and swung the machete wildly.

David yelled in agony as it cut deep into his leg above the knee. The brute was yelling in panic as David grappled for control of the machete. Stewart and Roomer threw themselves at the struggling pair. Stewart's dive knocked them all to the ground but the man rolled clear, landing on his back, still grasping the machete. Before he could move, Roomer jumped forward and, two-handed, fired three rapid nine-millimetre rounds into his face.

Time stood still. They stared, panting in the heavy atmosphere, paralysed by what had happened.

Dimly it registered with Stewart that Peter Rent was walking jauntily towards him, coming out of the trees with a wide grin, rifle slung casually over his shoulder. He looked at their other rescuer and saw Tom Nottes coming forward hesitantly, face full of concern, hand gun held distractedly at his thigh. David sat staring at the scene, in shock. Roomer stood, hunched, as Nottes came up to him.

"Well done Joe. Well done." Nottes said tiredly.

"You did okay yourself," he replied with a thin smile, laying a hand on his shoulder. They turned to look at Rent approaching with a swagger, like a Great White Hunter after a kill. Stewart went to Ethne who lay unconscious, the side of her face bloodied and already swollen from the blow to her head. At least she was breathing steadily.

"Joe, help me!"

They carried her into shade beside the hut and laid her out carefully.

"Get some water. Try and sponge her face."

 His heart was pounding but he had to know. He forced himself to his feet and went over to the others. For a moment all they could do was grin at each other. The grins said it all. They were alive when they could, should, have died. Nottes attended to David.

"Tom... Where are the others?" he asked quietly, looking at his feet.

"She and Hugo are hiding back there."

He waved in the general direction. "Sheila's fine Bob. She's safe."

His eyes filled as a wave of emotion surged through him. He started to shake. "Oh Tom, Tom... " He threw his arms round him.

"Go find her Bob, bring her here. We'll look after Ethne for you. They're behind a wall, about halfway between here and the far trees."

As he turned to go, Rent asked. "Where's Moriarty?"

Roomer shook his head, not able to speak.

"Doyle didn't make it either." Nottes said quietly.

***

She saw him coming, reeling through the haze. Her heart jumped as she gave a great sob of relief.

'Oh dear Lord thank you, thank you ...'

"Sheila. Get down." Hugo ordered, still crouched behind the wall.

"Sheila!"

She was off and running, tears flying, chest bursting, running hard and silently towards him. He swept her into his arms, the impact nearly knocking him off his feet. They clung to each other, long after Hugo blundered past on his way to the others.

Chapter 15

The village

1215 hrs, 21 February

Three days had passed since they were re-united, three days they would never forget. The area was quiet and it seemed they were safe from attack. The looters and pillagers had moved on, on to their next destination, to some other innocent hamlet where the inhabitants would soon have more to worry about than subsistence living. They too would die, tortured and in agony, as these butchers swept down upon them like conquering Hittites on a Middle Eastern plain. Eventually, long after the sated mob moved on, that hamlet might re-form - or it might not. It would be an almost random thing, as it was throughout most of Africa where spontaneity prevailed over logic.

With great perception the Victorians had called it the dark continent. The nights and the skins of the tribal peoples were dark. Minds and customs were dark, hidden from the light in obscure labyrinths, inward-looking and unchangeable. Dark barbarism wailed below the surface of what passed as society, ready to break through, eagerly, at the flimsiest excuse. Early missionaries tried to modernise Africa, to teach European standards of faith, dress and behaviour. In later years illogical liberalism dictated that the African way of life should be allowed to develop in its own way, that the Christian faith was quite enough to impose on these poor people, without telling them how to live every detail of their lives. Meanwhile these same poor people became bored from time to time, or got excited, or angry, or whatever - and butchered their neighbours, sometimes at the level of genocide, often using overseas aid income to finance their vicious tribal wars. Would they never learn? The same endless cycle was repeated time after time, primeval fighting across old colonial borders drawn without regard to tribal areas or nomadic ways of life. Could it ever be sorted?

Not in my lifetime, thought Stewart, or in my children's, perhaps never. Then he remembered Ireland - and Bosnia. Surely they were different?

"Bob!" she called. "Food."

He looked across the compound at her, standing under the awning of the mess tent, smiling at him as if nothing had happened, black hair glinting in the speckled light.

She has come through it remarkably well. Indeed most of us have bounced back pretty quickly, except those who died... They were all close to death just a few days ago. He was confused, still stressed, still not quite rational. It would take long months to shake off the surface effects of their experience. It would never go completely of course. They might imagine it would but, like a computer virus waiting patiently to act, the terrors and black memories would flood back when least expected. He sensed this subconsciously, walking towards lunch.

They had been lucky, very lucky. The three terrorists were the last in the area, either posted deliberately as a guard outpost or unwittingly left behind, lying in a drunken stupor in some unnoticed corner. They may even have deserted from the main column. Whatever, it did not matter now. They buried them two days ago in the rapidly drying red earth. They buried a lot of people, or rather the villagers did. About forty survivors appeared, stepping nervously from the trees a couple of hours after the last terrorists were killed. Grieving and traumatised, a handful of children - now mostly orphans - and a few men and women of all ages had survived the massacre. They survived because they were out foraging or managed to escape in the confusion of the first attack. In ones and twos, they stayed hidden around the perimeter of the village, watching as their homes were destroyed, as family and friends were brutalised and killed. They watched the murderers strike camp and move on, leaving three of their number behind. Those who saw the expedition members returning were too frightened to attempt a warning but, when the last terrorists were killed, eventually the survivors showed themselves.

The Europeans were powerless to help. Exhausted and emotionally drained, they stayed in their compound, licking their wounds and telling each other what happened. Tended by Sheila, Ethne soon regained consciousness and apart from a badly bruised temple, suffered no serious physical injury. She and Sheila hugged each other, crying with relief at their survival. It was some time before all the stories were told, each one telling a part, explaining events from the time of the first attack, the deaths of their colleagues, their return to the village and the final episode with the last of the terrorists.

Rent and Nottes had run swiftly up to where they saw the others being led away. Nottes said he just knew they had to move rapidly. Rent had sensed it too, something made him realise there was little time left to save their friends. They saw Stewart's group halted in the compound and Nottes circled round behind the huts trying to get close enough to use his hand gun. Rent tried to find a firing position that would give him a clear shot without endangering the others. Praying that the group would not move again, he lay down at the edge of the trees some seventy yards away and prepared to shoot, holding the stock of the rifle tight into his shoulder, safety off, aiming through the telescopic sights. He targeted the closest of the two men standing with their backs to him but knew he had to co-ordinate with Nottes who was still out of sight. Watching helplessly, he saw Ethne being attacked but it was much too risky to try a shot. He was almost certain to hit her too. In the end they were lucky. The whole scenario unfolded like a well-rehearsed ballet. Just when Rent decided that, if there was to be any chance of saving the girl he would have to shoot, Nottes stepped into view, pointing his pistol at the nearest terrorist. As Ethne was knocked to the ground Rent held his breath, steadied his aim and squeezed the trigger. The recoil thumped him hard in the shoulder as a great boom echoed through the trees. He almost yelled with delight when his target pitched face down, smacked wickedly by the high velocity round, dead before he hit the ground. Before he could fire again Nottes started shooting and the brawl with the last man began. Getting to his feet, he heard the flat cracks as Roomer executed the would-be rapist.

Roomer told them he had forgotten about his hand gun until they were ambushed. He stuffed it into a large pocket of his bush jacket when they stalked into the village, thinking it was deserted. Their ill-disciplined captors saw no sign of any weapons and did not bother to search them. Roomer said he had made his mind up to draw the Beretta before Ethne was dragged inside the hut. There was no way he was just going to stand there and let it happen. The others had all taken the same decision. Each was on the point of action when Rent's shot triggered a domino effect which, by chance rather than planning, turned out to be perfectly coordinated.

David was in agony, feverish and semi-conscious. His leg was a mess and they feared for him. The ugly machete wound was behind the knee, deep and badly infected. It looked like the tendons were cut, perhaps the bone damaged. The women made him as comfortable as possible in one of the huts and cared for him in shifts as best they could.

They waited for rescue. There was nothing else to do. Whatever way they sliced it, logic drove them to the same conclusion. They had checked it immediately of course, but the main radio was smashed to pieces. They were isolated and had no way of finding out about the overall situation. It would be the height of folly to attempt a trek to the nearest habitation. For all they knew they could well blunder into more terrorist activity anywhere in the surrounding area. There was the possibility that the gang would return but it seemed unlikely. The village was badly plundered and little remained to attract a further attack but, thankfully, the some of the crops and the well were undamaged. They decided to be careful however, to stay out of sight within their compound as much as possible - just in case. The surviving villagers, based on some deeply rooted instinct about such things, were certain they would not be attacked again and no amount of persuasion could convince them to post a lookout on the hill.

Word of the uprising would be known internationally by this time. London must know and they assumed would be planning some sort of action to find out what happened to the expedition. If they stayed where they were then any attempted rescue would surely come to the village. Despite some argument they agreed on the 'do nothing' option.

Hugo and Rent made no reference to their heated words of a few days ago. Hugo put it down to strain. Yes, Peter must have been under a great strain, he told himself. It was most unlike him to be so insulting.

He noted that everyone was behaving somewhat out of character. He decided it was only natural, after what they had been through. Examining himself, he decided that he had come through largely unscathed. He was a bit worried about his physical well-being but, really, his fitness must be okay. This pleased him. Many a man younger than me might not have done so well, he thought. Look what happened to Doyle. Yes, I reckon you did well Hugo. You held our group together and provided leadership which got us through. It was no time for indecision of course. It took an experienced man manager to assume command. Delegation was important too. Even though your fitness stood up, you knew when to delegate to the younger men. It would have been quite wrong to insist on leading the final rescue bid. We only had two weapons and Peter and Tom were best fitted for that incident. Sheila was a massive responsibility too. It's more difficult to wait and protect others while the young blades are in action...

So, as always, he gradually re-built a facade of delusion which rose in tandem with his burgeoning ego, retrieved from its temporary storage file in his inner psyche. He sometimes wondered, fleetingly, in the early stages of these occasional re-building episodes, if an element of self-delusion was involved. However, by the time he had the edifice re-built, all such flashes of decency were forgotten.

He began planning ahead. After all, someone must. The day to day details of survival in this ruined village he could leave to the others. More importantly, it was essential to have a good story - no, a coherent account - prepared for the inevitable inquiry which would start after they were back in London. As Hugo saw it there were a number of key points...

***

The village was severely damaged but not entirely destroyed. Nearly all the huts were burnt out but the expedition compound was more or less intact. Judging by the debris and general mess, the terrorists had based themselves in the compound. It took a full day to sort out and burn the soiled bedding left behind. None of them wanted to sleep in a hut until it was sanitised as far as possible - to remove sight and smell of the occupation. The mess and laboratory tents remained intact although the scientific equipment was smashed and knocked about by drunken vandalism.

Surprisingly, some supplies remained. Much was plundered and strewn about but some boxes of tinned food and bottled water remained intact. The terrorists fed well and had taken as much as they could carry but there was enough left to last for several weeks.

The medical supplies were a different matter. These were almost totally destroyed, scattered and soiled, during drunken searches for drugs. Not so much as a bottle of quinine tablets was left. There was no medication of any description to give to David.

All of their personal possessions were ransacked. Their clothes were all stolen, together with cameras, cell phones, toiletries, shoes and anything else of value. They were left with the clothes they stood up in.

Then there were the bodies, lying where they had been butchered, scattered throughout the village and down to the lake shore. Stewart estimated that about a hundred and fifty men, women and children were dead. Many were partially eaten by scavengers which continued to feed on them even now until they were chased off by the pitifully small groups of survivors who struggled to bury them. It would be many days yet before the last remains were interred.

The Europeans tried to help, especially with the bodies nearest their compound. The foul smell faded after the closest corpses were buried. Smell or not, hunger eventually overcame their sensitivities and they cooked rudimentary meals over a gas cooker that Roomer managed to partially restore. As if relenting at their plight, nature permitted a gentle northerly breeze to blow down the lake for several days, taking the smell of putrefaction off into the trees.

Sheila and Stewart stayed very close, frightened to let each other out of their sight. He fussed over her, insisted on bathing her scratches and washing her clothes at the lake, making her rest in their hut. She was appalled to hear how Moriarty had died, as indeed were all of Hugo's group. She told them how Doyle died in the night. Stewart held her tightly as she trembled at the memory.

Roomer and Nottes went looking for the Landrover. It was gone, discovered eventually and driven away by the departing gang. They wondered how far they would get before it broke down or ran out of fuel. It was no loss. There was nowhere safe to drive to.

They found Mwanga's body lying beside a track on the outskirts of the village. Scavengers had eaten most of it but they found his wallet in the remains of his safari suit. There was no way to tell how he'd died. Nottes stood over the body, remembering the African's enthusiasm for the expedition. He had been so proud of his country, so keen for them to see this model village on the peaceful shore of Lake Albert. With the help of the villagers they buried him at a spot overlooking the lake. Nottes made sure the grave was well marked by a cairn of stones, gathered from the dry mud shore.

Rent's disposition remained abnormal. Apart from the brief period when they were all re-united, he was withdrawn again and kept his own company. After a number of unsuccessful attempts to draw him out everyone eventually gave up. He spent most of the time alone, pacing the lake shore or sitting up on the hill. He asked Nottes and Roomer to go up there with him, to bury the man he killed, and the woman. They watched him carefully but he seemed in control of himself. He showed no signs of distress when they came across the fly-blown and partially devoured bodies and laboured with them silently as they dug the graves. Sheila worried about him and made Bob promise to keep an eye on him.

Sheila began to mend, slowly. Ethne and she helped each other enormously and having another woman to confide in made a great difference. Ethne especially needed comforting and the two women quickly established a close bond. They had been friendly enough before but not close, like now. Sheila thrilled to hear how Stewart had looked after Ethne throughout their ordeal. She watched him now as he worked with the food tent awning. They spent long hours together, exhausted at first but gradually recovering, holding hands, talking and comforting each other. She was unsure how he would be, not wanting to assume too much about his feelings for her. She need not have worried. As soon as they were alone he told her he loved her, that he had been frantic with fear about her, that now they were together again he would stay with her forever and that he wanted to make a life with her - if she would have him. She clung to him sobbing, pent up terrors and emotions released in the warmth of his protection. They slept together, lying side by side in the darkness of the hut. He tried to tell her how much he wanted her but in these nightmare circumstances... She put a finger to his lips.

"I know Bob, I know. Don't say any more. I feel the same way. This place... I just can't... Let's wait until we're out of here, away from this hell hole. Do you think we'll be rescued soon?"

"I don't know darling. It depends on what's happening elsewhere. We'll just have to stick it out. It could be tomorrow or it might be a week or two."

"As long as that?" She was appalled.

"It could be."

"Oh Bob, we will be rescued won't we? Tell me - honestly!"

"Yes, yes! We will - of course we will - it's just a matter of time."

What the hell was happening? Where were they?He wanted to reassure her but really they had no idea when a rescue attempt would be made. DEFRA must know about the situation? Surely the British Government would be organising a rescue by now? Dear God! It suddenly struck him. The helicopter! The Ugandan army helicopter that flew over after the attack - what if it didn't made it back to base? No, that wouldn't matter... One way or another this terrorist uprising would be known about by now - and the fact that it was occurring in the expedition area. What if the helicopter made it back? Might it have reported the village completely overrun and ablaze? Even so, he argued, even if they were all feared dead, they would come eventually to confirm it one way or the other. Surely the uprising couldn't have spread throughout the entire country? Could that be delaying a rescue?

***

Two days later, a week after they returned to the village, it came. Around noon, as they lay resting from the midday heat, they heard it. Ethne heard it first - a faint throbbing in the still air. She sat up quickly.

"Listen! Listen everyone!"

She ran out to the middle of the compound yelling. Now they were all outside, straining to hear.

'Whomp! Whomp! Whomp!'

There was no mistaking it - a helicopter - and it was coming their way!

"Get inside! Inside out of sight everyone!" Stewart pushed and shoved them back into the huts.

"But Bob… " Ethne began to argue.

"Just in case Ethne. Just in case." he insisted.

Her eyes widened in sudden fear and before he could reassure her she ran inside after Sheila. Now they were all out of sight and the compound was deserted. The men had discussed this moment. There was a remote possibility that if a helicopter appeared it could be manned by terrorists. It was unlikely, but they couldn't be absolutely sure. They were in no position to defend themselves against a further attack but it would be sheer lunacy to stand out in the open as an unidentified helicopter approached. If they stayed hidden there was always a chance that, if the worst came to the worst, they could run for it again.

It came straight for them, the engine noise louder and louder. It flew at speed, coming in fast from the north-west. Suddenly it burst across the compound in a blast of noise, making a high speed pass several hundred feet up. Squinting up through the doorway Stewart got a glimpse of its khaki colouring as it flashed overhead, banking to run along the length of the village, disappearing out of sight behind the huts.

Clinging to his arm Sheila asked, "Does it look okay?"

"I don't know yet." He shouted at the other huts. "Stay out of sight everyone! It'll be round again."

It was coming back, lower this time and more slowly. Its roar built up to deafen them and dust and straw was blowing across the compound. Suddenly there it was, hovering fifty feet above the compound, a figure clearly visible in its open doorway. The loudspeaker made them jump.

"This is Major Barnes of the British Army. Is there anyone down there?"

They ran stumbling out into the compound, waving joyously into the noise and down draft, tears of relief blowing in the wind. Sheila sank to her knees, hands clenched in prayer.

"Sweet Jesus thank you, thank you!"

Chapter 16

The west of Ireland

1930 hrs, 9 September

"Hello? Hello there! Anybody home?"

Sheila jumped up, knocking her garden chair flying, and ran laughing up the undulating lawn to meet him.

"Joe! Joe! It's so good to see you! We didn't hear you coming."

She kissed him on the cheek as they hugged warmly. He held her at arms length.

"You're looking well Sheila. How's Bob?"

She nodded down the garden.

"We were enjoying the sun. Come and join us. We'll sort out your bags later."

"Isn't that a beautiful evening?" Roomer said as they strolled arm in arm down the sloping garden to where Stewart stood, beaming, to greet them.

"Joe! How are you? Come and sit down. Have a beer."

"Maybe later thanks..."

"Nonsense! You're on your holidays!"

He reached under the table for an ice-cold can of Carlsberg from the cool-box. Sheila winked at Roomer. Stewart had gone specially to the local pub to get a dozen of Roomer's favourite beer.

"Aren't you two drinking?"

"We've just had coffee. Besides, I have to stay sober - I have dinner to cook." she laughed.

"Well, if you insist... "

Stewart cracked open a can for himself and stretched back in his chair.

"Ah... this is the life... "

No-one spoke as they studied the view from the bottom of the garden. A low stone wall separated them from the calm, sparkling waters of Blacksod Bay. On this warm September evening they had an uninterrupted view for some twelve miles south along the length of the bay to Achill Island where the high point of Slievemore thrust above a low-lying haze. They smelt the sea and watched in the calm air as its blue-green swell came ashore in regular waves, noisily spreading and tumbling the shingle as it swept up and down the shore. They watched a white, snub-nosed lobster boat working its way along the coast, hauling and setting pots, the throaty beat of its engine reaching them occasionally above the sound of the sea. Gulls and fulmars wheeled about it and occasional squadrons of low-flying guillemots sped past on straight-line trajectories.

In spite of himself, Roomer could not help comparing the scene with Lake Albert. Deliberately breaking his line of thought he turned to Stewart.

"How far out of Belmullet are you here? Two miles?"

"About that - as the crow flies - about three miles by road." He replied, aware of Roomer's thoughts.

They all experienced it. Each time Roomer visited they were reminded of the horrors of the expedition. They could not help it. In an hour or two they would be able to submerge the memories again but the scars were far from healed yet - for all of them.

It was only natural, Stewart thought. Till the day I die, whenever I first see Joe walking towards me I'll always see him in my mind, sitting in shock, far out on that muddy African shore.

"How was the journey?" he asked.

"Oh fine. The flight was on time yesterday evening and I was in

Kildare by about eight o'clock." There was a moment's silence.

"How are they?" Sheila asked gently.

"Okay... Well, you can imagine. They'll never get over it Sheila, but they're doing the best they can. They're wonderful people. They always make me so welcome. I think it's because I was with him when he died. I really don't know how they'll manage, in the long run. He was their pride and joy you know... " They gave him a moment.

"Did you see Margaret?" she asked.

His face brightened. "Oh yes! In fact we went out to dinner last night." He flushed slightly.

"And?" Stewart prompted impishly.

"And nothing!" he laughed.

"Oh come on Joe!" Sheila teased. "You and Margaret have been an item all summer!"

"An item? That's an outdated expression surely?"

"Now don't try to go off at a tangent Joe Roomer!" She wagged a finger at him in mock severity.

"I want to hear how you two are getting on. Now come clean!"

"Well, as a matter of fact she's coming back to England with me for a week or so, on my way back."

"To Lowestoft?" They both asked.

"Yes."

"Oh Joe, I'm so pleased. She's so right for you." She said seriously, then, bantering again, "Now don't you mess it up you rough big Northerner!"

"Don't get too far ahead of yourself!" he laughed back. "It's early days yet."

"Nonsense! This is the twenty-first century Joe. You just watch you're not too slow. Time you bucked up your ideas!"

"Now Sheila, leave the poor man alone." Stewart tried to rescue the embarrassed Roomer.

"Alright! Alright! I will - but..."

"No buts! He's quite able to look after himself."

"It's not him I'm worried about you idiot!" She laughed, getting to her feet. "But okay, enough! It's time I saw to dinner if we want to eat tonight. You two just relax there and let me do all the work."

"We were going to!" He shouted after her as she jogged up the lawn to the cottage.

They watched her all the way up to the door.

"This is a glorious spot Bob. It gets better and better every time I come. I'm really glad about you and Sheila."

"So am I Joe, so am I. Now how are the Moriartys, really?"

He sighed. "I have to say th,ey're not good Bob. I wouldn't say in front of Sheila but they can hardly accept Paul is dead. If his body had come home and they had a grave to tend... but just to accept he was taken like that... It's so difficult for them."

"Do they ask much?"

"No, thank God. What could I tell them? I've told them all about the expedition, sure, but not a blow by blow account of how he died. It's... It's as if they're frightened – no, that's not right - as if they're frightened for me."

"How do you mean?"

"They don't want to put me through it again. They don't want me to tell them how the crocodile attacked him, how it nearly tore his leg off, how it dragged him kicking and screaming under the water..."

"Joe, Joe. Don't. I'm sorry." He tried frantically to move the conversation.

"How's Margaret?"

Roomer brought himself under control. The thought of Margaret brightened him once more.

"She's fine, just fine. I don't know what she sees in an old goat like me!"

"You're not an old man yet, but if you go on with that attitude you soon will be."

Margaret was Paul Moriarty's older sister. Joe met the family soon after he got back from Uganda. He made a particular point of contacting Mr and Mrs Moriarty as soon as possible. He telephoned them from the hospital. It was the most difficult call he had ever made. They had already heard about their only son. An official from the Irish Foreign Affairs Ministry broke the news to them just before the story of the ill-fated expedition appeared in the national news media. The man was unable to tell them how their son died, just that he was killed as a result of terrorist insurgency. They were told about the rescue of other members of the expedition, but that it was impossible to retrieve Paul's body. So the Moriartys had to bear their grief almost in the abstract, like all those whose loved ones fell in a foreign land.

Lying in hospital in London, Roomer became more and more concerned about the relatives of his dead friend. He imagined what they must be going through, how they must be hoping that, one day, they could have Paul buried in the family plot in Ireland. He was fairly certain the official version of events would not have disclosed exactly how Paul died. He managed to check this out by getting the British Foreign Office official who had de-briefed him to check with his Irish counterpart.

He was two weeks recovering in hospital. Initially they were all checked over and offered a few days supervised recuperation. He was on the point of declining when the malaria hit him. After the delirium passed there was no option but to recuperate in bed. He was far too weak to go home. Malaria was another thing they all had in common. In spite of attempts to prevent it by medication in

Kampala, every one of them went down with it, to varying degrees. They required treatment too for a variety of other parasitic infections.

When he recovered sufficiently he tracked down the Moriartys' phone number. It was Margaret who answered. He introduced himself and offered his condolences. She made it easy for him with her understanding manner and put him at ease very quickly. He found her very easy to talk to and eventually he hinted at the reason for his call. He was struggling for the best way to put things when she cut across him, sensing what he was trying to say. She invited him to visit them, when he was well enough, to meet them face to face. He realised immediately that of course that was what he must do. A few days later he rang her again. She gave him directions to the house in Kildare and he flew over, nervous and apprehensive, the following day. They greeted him warmly and made him feel right at home. After dinner that evening, he sat with Margaret and Paul's parents and told them all that happened. He felt he owed them the truth and described everything as best he could, leaving out the details of the crocodile attack, bursting into sobs as he finished. The parents were obviously shocked and Margaret came to comfort him immediately. She put her arm round him and cradled his head, stroking his hair. Mr and Mrs Moriarty sat clinging to each other. Then Margaret guided him outside to give her parents privacy for their grief.

He had been back three times since. The Moriartys really took to him and he to them. The parents saw him as the last link to their son. He saw their obvious pleasure as he talked about Paul, his work on the expedition and their friendship. Margaret too was an eager listener and he soon realised his feelings for her were growing rapidly. In her mid-thirties she had not married, preferring to concentrate on a career as a Lecturer in Politics at University College Dublin.

As he got to know them and their way of life, Roomer found his ill-informed prejudices melting away. He had never been a dyed-in-the-wool Protestant bigot but his Ulster Unionist upbringing left little room for understanding or sympathy towards Roman Catholicism or Irish nationalism. Now he discovered Margaret and her family had the same general outlook on life as himself, the same moral standards, the same hopes and aspirations for their family and the future. Irish politics, north or south, was an obnoxious irrelevancy to them, tainted forever by the rabid mouthings of extremists of all shades. They opened their hearts and their home to him and he found it very easy to respond. He and Margaret had much in common and the hours flew by in easy conversation. He had little hesitation in inviting her to Lowestoft and she quickly accepted. She had never been to East Anglia and he was looking forward to showing her around. Thank goodness he had tidied up his cottage before he left!

Stewart was talking.

"Sorry Bob. I was miles away."

"I was asking how work was going."

"Fine. It's going quite well actually."

"You must be back in the swing of things by now?"

"Sure. It's as if I'd... we'd never been away. What about yourself?"

"It's good Joe, much better than I'd hoped. I have to admit my pre-conceptions were ill-founded."

Stewart now worked for the Irish Marine Institute. He changed jobs in May. Like Roomer and the others, he was given two months leave of absence from DEFRA. It was the least they deserved and they needed every day of it, to recover their health and to come to terms with what they went through. Handling the media interest was a major difficulty early on. Thinking about it now Stewart smiled at one aspect. In line with latest practice, they were offered counselling to help them come to terms with the experience. He was immensely pleased to learn that all of them refused the offer in no uncertain terms. For his part he had always looked askance at such mumbo-jumbo. Counselling indeed! The poor buggers that came through the Battle of the Somme, and those that survived many other such nightmares, had to survive without counselling. Their own experience was much less extreme. What sort of adults would they be if they could not cope by drawing on their own resources? It pleased him that everyone obviously came to the same conclusion. There was hope for the educated classes yet.

Sheila and he tried to work out how they could be together. Neither contemplated giving up their careers. It was obvious one of them would have to change jobs, either Sheila moved to England or he would have to re-locate to Ireland. In the event it all happened very quickly and painlessly. A vacancy arose at the Irish Marine Institute headquarters in Dublin and he applied. His experience and current work matched the job advertisement exactly and he had high hopes of securing the position. Sheila of course was thrilled when it came through and flung herself into organising his move across the Irish Sea. It was the ideal therapy. They married quietly in a Dublin Registry Office in April and were living temporarily in Sheila's small flat in central Dublin while their new house was being built. Soon after he started the new job an elderly aunt of Sheila's offered them this weekend cottage in Belmullet. They fell in love with the area from the first and now had use of the cottage on more or less permanent loan. It was a glorious summer and they made the four-hour drive from Dublin to Mayo almost every weekend. They kept in close touch with Roomer and this was now his third weekend visit. He brought Margaret to meet them last month. They were perfect for each other. He hoped Joe kept things moving along!

"So you're enjoying it?"

"Yes, very much. They're a fine bunch of people and Dublin is a wonderfully vibrant place to work."

"I'm very pleased for you Bob, for you both. Sheila's a fine woman…"

" …and so is Margaret. I hope you're not going to hang about there Joe."

"Howd'ya mean?"

"Don't dilly-dally I mean. You two are made for each other."

"Do you think so?" He asked uncertainly.

"Of course you plonker! It's obvious to anyone - and obviously Margaret thinks so too."

"Did she say so?"

"Now stop fishing! You'll just have ask her yourself - and don't take forever."

Sheila's shout interrupted them.

"Come on you too, dinner's nearly ready! Bob, will you bring in the cups and things please?"

They folded away the garden furniture and carried the tray of coffee things and the cool-box back up the lawn to the house, stopping halfway to look back at the evening sky. A bronze sun sank slowly to a glinting horizon.

"I have some news about Hugo." Roomer said, still gazing westward at the dying day. "I'll tell you both over dinner."

They stood on, at ease with themselves and each other, listening to the glorious sound of the Intermezzo from Mascagni's 'Cavalleria Rusticana'. Sheila had set the CD-player to keep repeating the track. The music and the sunset held them.

"What's that music Bob?"

Stewart told him.

"Wonderful."

Reluctantly, as the track finished once more, they left the twilight and went inside.

***

They talked casually over dinner, totally relaxed in each other's company. Sheila produced a simple meal of avocado vinaigrette followed by her lasagne, home-made in Dublin and re-heated, with a mozzarella and tomato salad and fresh crusty bread. Fortuitously, Roomer had brought several bottles of a good Chianti. Stewart was struggling to open the second bottle when he remembered Roomer's earlier remark.

"You mentioned Hugo."

He had been dying to tell them all evening but, by a supreme effort restrained himself until the perfect moment. He played it casually.

"Oh yes. There's a bit of news about him."

He paused for a sip of wine.

Sheila sensed he was stringing them along.

"Joe? What are you up to? What's happened?"

He could restrain himself no longer.

"The fat bastard's been kicked out!" he chortled.

"Kicked out? What do you mean?" they asked.

"Kicked out. Dismisssed. Sacked. Services terminated. Out on the street!"

"You're joking!"

"No! I'm very pleased to tell you that I'm quite serious. As of yesterday Hugo is no longer a Civil Servant."

And so he told them the story. They knew a lot of it of course - they had seen it for themselves. Hugo was hospitalised too, with fever and a mild case of blood poisoning - a scratch on his arm became infected. He bounced back well though, quicker than the rest of them, and began communicating from the hospital. The Permanent Secretary and senior colleagues came to see him in the beginning, often arriving after the evening meal, on their way home from work. The media showed a lot of early interest but, in spite of Hugo's willingness to give interviews and write articles, this waned surprisingly quickly. London and Dublin closed ranks of course. They had no other option. The entire affair was portrayed as a tragic accident - the expedition found itself in the wrong place at the wrong time. No one questioned why it was there in the first place. There was no debate about its rationale, about its objectives, personnel or cost. Ministers in London and Dublin were well briefed and press releases carefully phrased to focus media attention on the events rather than the background. The detail of the expedition was obscured within the overall uprising across Uganda. Then when the Al Shabab terrorists massacred 147 students at Garissa in Northern Kenya it further diverted media attention on both sides of the Irish Sea.

Hugo tried briefly to draw attention to himself but he was firmly sat upon by senior officials and the episode quickly subsided to a side show. They saw little of him, by mutual consent. His concern for their welfare never existed and the charade he maintained on this front soon waned as his interest in his own affairs burgeoned to previous heights. He was the first to leave hospital, declining the two months sick leave on offer, and was at his desk in DEFRA within ten days of arriving back in England.

Roomer returned to work in Lowestoft in mid-April but, as was the norm, was seldom in communication with Hugo. He heard on the grapevine however that he was soon back to his old empire-building style. He tried to give him the benefit of the doubt. Surely, in his quieter moments, even Hugo remembered those who died on the expedition he had planned and brought into being? Unfortunately he heard nothing to convince him that this was the case.

The news had broken yesterday. He heard it from a colleague at Headquarters - the man phoned especially to tell him. Word spread throughout the organisation like wildfire. Hugo was finally nailed, after the dust had settled, after sufficient time had elapsed so that his dismissal would not be linked to the expedition debacle, so that no blame by association could be attached to Ministers. It transpired he was fiddling his travelling claims. It was very difficult to discharge a civil servant, especially a senior one. Incompetence, alcoholism, sexual deviance - none of these was grounds for dismissal. Indeed some said they could be a platform for promotion. The only unforgivable sin, punishable by instant dismissal, was theft - on even the smallest scale. There was no appeal. In fact in many cases there was a very real prospect of criminal proceedings being initiated. Hugo had committed a relatively small-scale theft. He had claimed expenses totalling hundreds of pounds that he had not actually incurred. Roomer's friend told him that the Departmental Accountant, a chap called Bruce, had the evidence for some months but the Department held off acting until now.

They could hardly believe their ears. "Joe! Are you having us on?"

"I promise you."

Suddenly the name 'Bruce' slotted into place in Stewart's brain.

"Wait a minute! I remember... It's coming back to me."

"What?" they laughed.

He told them of the day, way back at the start of the year - when Hugo and he were on their way to a DEFRA briefing about the expedition. In the corridor, Hugo waylaid Tony Jones of Finance Division and at some point in their conversation Bruce's name came up. Stewart remembered vague alarm bells ringing at the time. He couldn't recall precisely what was said - Hugo was telling Jones about some discussion he and Bruce had the previous day - but he clearly remembered thinking that Bruce's behaviour was distinctly odd. He recounted it to them but it sounded a bit daft by the time he finished.

"Oh Bob!" Sheila laughed. "That's stretching things a bit!"

"No." Roomer interrupted. "From what I've heard there may well be something in what you say Bob. It seems Bruce stumbled across Hugo's little indiscretion quite by accident. Apparently he was visiting his brother over Christmas when he caught Hugo out. So the timing would be about right."

"His brother?"

"Bruce's brother lives in Dublin and the two of them were out for a drink - in one of those old-style pubs with booths. Apparently Hugo and Brendan Doyle were in the next booth and before Bruce realised who it was, he heard Hugo thanking Brendan for putting him up on all his Dublin trips and how much money he made on his travel claims. It seems they were both well oiled at the time. Bruce and his brother got offside of course before Hugo spotted them. There was never much love lost between them so Bruce made a point of quietly checking Hugo's recent claims. It turns out he made claims for overnights in four and five star Dublin hotels over quite a long period."

"When he was in the throes of planning the expedition?" Sheila said.

"Yes. Well Bruce checked dates with the hotels and was able to establish that he hadn't stayed in one of them - at least on the dates he claimed he had."

"But that's awful!" she said, appalled.

"But why did Bruce wait so long before he did anything about it?"

"I'm not sure about that Bob, but you know how it is - people are very reluctant to be seen to be telling tales on each other - especially at Grade Five level. In any event he decided to bide his time. I suppose he was waiting for the ideal opportunity... "

"...Which the expedition mess provided!"

"Exactly. As soon as it dawned on him that Hugo's expedition was a monumental cock-up and that he was *persona non grata* with the Secretary and the Minister, well, Bruce knew that was the time to make his move. It's obvious now the Secretary was just waiting for the dust to settle before getting rid of him. The dodgey travel claims business provided the ideal excuse, quick and clean and absolutely no possible appeal or delay. He had him cold!"

"I'd have loved to have been a fly on the wall at that interview." said Stewart.

As Sheila continued to quiz Roomer, he tried to imagine how the interview might have gone. He could picture Hugo bustling into the Secretary's office, eager to enter the inner power sanctum once more. He may have been taken slightly aback to find the Principal Finance Officer and the Head of Personnel there too, waiting for him. Perhaps even his rhino-like attitude may have registered a flicker of disquiet at that stage. It couldn't have been long before the blow fell. Stewart wondered how the Secretary had phrased it. Had he approached it carefully, embarrassed? Decidedly not. Sir John was as tough as they come. You didn't get to his position without an inner ruthlessness. No, he would have come straight to the point, professional enough not to let his anger show. Personally he may have been delighted to see the back of such an unbearable incompetent but the dismissal of an Under-secretary - for theft - was a black mark against his Department. He could not recall it ever happening at this level before and he would make damn sure it never happened again.

What a mess! A disastrous cock-up, the expedition, the deaths... what a monumental mess! How had Finance Division allowed this man to run on such a loose rein for so long? Things would have to tighten up in this Department or more heads would roll! As for those idiots in Dublin, they must be as bad as us to have let it happen. The only saving grace was that the Minister was unscathed by it all - somehow. They'd been lucky, very lucky, so far, but there was always the chance that a TV channel might return to it some time when hard news was scarce and do an investigative piece. God forbid!

The architect of it all now stood blustering before him. "Secretary I... "

"There's nothing to discuss I'm afraid Hugo. I take it you don't deny the deception?"

"No..."

"I want you out of here within the hour. Personnel will advise you about the formalities. I strongly advise against discussing this with anyone. No one here will, for quite different reasons."

He glowered at the men at either side who nodded confirmation, but who would find it impossible to resist the temptation to blab it ten minutes after the interview.

Hugo was tempted to begin a monologue in reply. It was a ploy he often used to gather his thoughts. He just started talking, giving his mind time to marshall a response so that, eventually, as the mental processes slotted into place, he would win his point by a combination of filibustering and logic.

"Secretary I must..."

Sir John would have held up a hand to stop him in his tracks.

"There is nothing more to say Hugo. I wish you good day."

Stewart was certain Hugo would have spoken to no-one as he blundered back to his office to clear his desk and depart. He would never know for sure but would bet he left without so much as a goodbye to his Personal Assistant or anyone. He had no doubt that Hugo, at that time above all others, would have thoughts for no-one but himself.

"But what will he do?"

"Who knows Sheila, but you can be quite sure that no-one in DEFRA, from the highest to the lowest, could care less. Everyone's delighted to see the back of him."

"Oh Joe. Surely he wasn't that bad?"

Stewart answered for him. "Sheila, you have no idea what sort of a man he was - is."

"Really..." she trailed off, surprised at his vehemence.

After coffee and biscuits they sat around the fireplace with their drinks, lounging in the comfortable high-back settee and armchairs.

"Should we light the fire?" Stewart asked.

"Not on my account." Roomer said.

"Yes let's. There's a chill in the air now. After all it's autumn. It will brighten up the room." Sheila said, reaching for matches on the mantelpiece and lighting the pre-set fire.

They sipped their wine watching the flames take hold, listening to the crackle of the sticks. When it was well alight Stewart added another shovel of coal.

"Don't you burn peat?"

"Oh yes we do - but we forgot to bring some in and it's too wet to start a fire with. It's stacked up at the back of the house." Stewart explained.

Sheila laughed. "Listen to him! You'd think he was born and raised out here."

He took a playful swipe at her.

"Sheila. What about Ethne?" Roomer inquired.

"She's fine Joe. Well, maybe 'fine' isn't quite the right word. You heard she is back at work?" He nodded.

"I haven't seen that much of her since we got back, but then our paths seldom crossed before. She works at the far end of the building, in a different section. I think actually we tend to avoid each other. It's as if every time we see each other it reminds us of..."

"She had no problems adjusting..."

"Well no, I wouldn't say that. She went through a bad patch for a while after she got home. Some sort of delayed reaction."

"I can understand that. She had a rough time, maybe rougher than the rest of us. She was badly knocked about. It must have been hard for her to handle, for someone so young I mean." They nodded.

"I think she was on medication for a time. She seems through the worst of it now though. Time will tell."

"How is she - in herself?"

"She's seems very quiet, a bit withdrawn. She gets on with her work. I suppose it's a form of therapy. People have learnt not to talk to her about it, or to me either thank goodness! I'm afraid it will take a while yet for Ethne to come out the other end."

"Tell her I was asking about her Sheila, please."

"I will of course Joe."

"You don't mind us talking about it... now?"

"Of course not. This is different. We were there. The ones in the office don't understand. They chatter on as if they'd seen it in the movies. You just get tired listening to them."

Stewart spoke. "I actually think we should make a point of discussing it when we're together. I think it does us good."

"Really?"

"Well I'm sure the converse is true at least, that it isn't healthy to sweep it under the carpet or pretend it never happened. I just have this instinctive feeling that we shouldn't do that. Do you understand Joe?"

"Yes... I do. I understand exactly what you mean. It will fade through time I suppose, but it's only natural for it to loom large for a while. After all it was a terrifying experience..."

They sat quietly for a while, gazing at the flickering fire.

"The light's gone." Sheila said softly, looking out the window. She rose to pull the curtains and turn on a fireside lamp.

"What about Mrs Doyle?" Roomer asked.

"There's not much to report there." Stewart answered. "She was a very private woman it seems, even when Brendan was alive. It seems very few people in his office ever met her. I suppose he was enough of an extrovert for both of them."

"No word I suppose of..."

"Looking for the grave? No I don't think that will ever happen. Uganda's still in uproar. There's no prospect of it. I know Tom marked its position but the chances are everything will be well scattered by now."

Sheila sighed as they stared at the flickering fire.

"Does Peter Rent know about Hugo?" Stewart asked.

"I suppose he must do by now. I didn't see him before I left."

"Is he... has he becomes any less...?"

"No Sheila. He's as twisted as ever."

"And his case?"

"Oh he's still pursuing it - with a vengeance. The Director had him in you know and there was a rumour the even the Secretary wanted to see him in London. It doesn't faze Peter of course. He's got the bit firmly between his teeth now. He'll push on and on until he nails Hugo and no amount of pressure will make him see reason."

"In a way I don't blame him."

"Oh Bob." Sheila frowned.

"No. I'm serious Sheila. He has every right to sue Hugo and the Department. They put us through that, due to their mismanagement, lack of foresight or whatever. Why should any of us give a toss about the good name of the Department? If the shoe... when the shoe was on the other foot what did they care about us? We went out there without proper protection. Somebody somewhere must have known the reality of the situation out there. It was a simmering mess just waiting to boil over. We should never have gone. People are dead that need not have died if that arrogant sod had bothered to check it out. He should be sued for every penny he's got. Make him see what a stupid, detestable slob he really is. Peter's the only one of us who's got the guts to do it!"

All the years of Stewart's pent up frustrations about Hugo were coming out.

"Don't annoy yourself Bob." Roomer said softly. "We'll get compensation in due course. Sorry! I know that's not the point. I just meant there's no need for Rent to push quite so hard."

"Oh I think there is Joe. I think there is. Peter's a wired up character I know, but in this case I believe he's doing what we all should do. It's our outmoded sense of propriety or decency, call it what you will, that stops us. That's the way they get away with it, those pigs that walk all over us, that insult us and persist in thinking they are somehow society's elite, that they were born to be our masters. Rent's action is one way of showing them up, of trying for once to get it through to them that the rest of the world laughs behind their back. This time there's a chance to spit in their faces. You know I should sue the bugger myself!"

"Peter, you don't mean that." Sheila said softly.

"Oh yes I do!" he snapped.

"No darling, you don't, and I am so pleased and proud that you don't mean it."

They both looked at her. She went on.

"Don't you see?" She smiled gently at Joe. "I believe Joe sees. Don't you?"

Roomer stared at her. She sat on her hunkers in front of them, her back to the dying fire.

"Bob. Do you really want to be like them, Hugo and his... his fellow twits. Yes twits Bob. That's the way I see them - stupid people, people lacking in some attribute that distinguishes them from the rest of us. People to be pitied, in passing, as we get on with our own lives. I could never love anyone like that and I believe the women who do must either deeply regret it or must have the equivalent female condition. I want a man who is loving and kind. Someone who cares as much for me as he does for himself. Someone who will love his children more than life itself. A man who hates injustice or cruelty, a man whose passing will be mourned when his time comes. We have a faith Bob, a faith that tells us our time on earth is like the blinking of an eye in the timespan of eternity. We shouldn't waste that time arguing about Hugo and his like. We have good friends..." She reached to hold Roomer's hand, tears welling, and stretched to Stewart, "...and we have each other."

He knelt to hug her, burying his head in her neck. She smiled over her shoulder, through her tears, at Roomer who patted her hand gently, his head bowed trying to hide his own emotion.

"Bob, Joe. Do you know the best of all of us? It was David."

They looked at her and nodded.

"That poor boy was frightened out of his wits for days on end you know." They nodded again. "He was so proud of his country when we first arrived. Do you remember the way he showed us around the area? Can you imagine how he must have felt when his friends were killed in front of him? He stuck with you out on that lake, through it all. What courage it took for him to throw himself in Ethne's defence at the end. Dear Lord he looked dreadful in that hospital. Even then he was proud to stay and be cared for in his own country."

She started to fill up once more.

"You know I sat at his bed just before we left for England, just the two of us. I asked him if there was anything he needed. He smiled at me shyly and asked if I would mind reading a few verses from the Bible. I was so ashamed I hadn't realised until then that he was a Christian. There was a well-thumbed Gideon's Bible beside his bed. I was looking for an appropriate passage when he whispered

'First Corinthians thirteen'. I sat there and read it out. I will never forget it till the day I die. Let me get it now."

She was back in a moment, kneeling in front of them again, wiping away tears with back of her hand. The men sat back as she read from verse one, her voice catching with emotion.

"Though I speak with the tongues of men and of angels, but have not love, I have become sounding brass or a clanging cymbal.

And though I have the gift of prophecy, and understand all mysteries and all knowledge, and though I have all faith, so that I could remove mountains, but have not love, I am nothing."

Her voice became stronger as she came to the end of the passage, verse thirteen.

"And now abide faith, hope, love, these three; but the greatest of these is love."

She closed the Bible gently and looked from one to the other and smiled.

"You see what I'm trying to say, what David reminded me of?"

Once more they nodded. For the first time they really did see. They saw through the evil and despair of human existence in the early years of the twenty first century. They had their first tantalising glimpse of the green fields and warm sunshine of that other world. Stewart's heart pounded. He looked at Sheila and she saw it in his eyes. Tears of joy streamed down her smiling face as she saw the answer to her prayers.

Outside, the last of the western light was gone. A midnight blue sky over-arched, the firmament filled to overflowing with stars, galaxies and other worlds.

THE END